THE GRAND ILLUSION

THE LION'S DEN SERIES
BOOK 4

EOIN DEMPSEY

D1521769

This book is for my father.

1

Wednesday, July 15, 1936, Berlin

S eamus ran his fingers through the pile of bullet cartridges still warm from the press. They fell like candy from his hand into a massive bucket. Huge posters of the Führer urged on the workers from the wall, pinned up there by Gunther Benz, the head of the Trustee Council. These Nazi government representatives were voted in from within every medium- to large-sized company in Germany. They weren't so much a replacement of the now-illegal trade unions, as strikes and lockouts were prohibited, but more of a visible way for the Nazis to present themselves within organizations in the Reich.

If Benz and his cronies had their way, the whole factory would have been wallpapered with Hitler's face, but Seamus had persuaded him to keep it to his own section. The foreign and Jewish workers never came over to this side of the floor. They stayed in their area, making steel pot helmets for the Wehrmacht. Seamus had persuaded Benz, a metal polisher who'd enjoyed little power prior to the Nazis coming to power, that the Führer's image would be sullied by being associated with the Jews and Russians working in the other parts of the factory, and he bought it.

Business was booming, with orders from the burgeoning armed forces flowing in daily. Germany was regaining its place on the international stage and had shown off the first signs of its new military might when Hitler ordered the reoccupation of the Rhineland five months before. In direct contravention of the Treaty of Versailles, the strip of land—which bordered France, Belgium, and the Netherlands—was now crawling with German soldiers once again. People called it Hitler's biggest gamble. Seamus knew that the German Army could have been snuffed out in a few days by the superior forces of the British, French, and the Russians, but the will to do it wasn't there, and the Führer's gamble was an outrageous success. He was more popular than ever. Workers on the factory floor who'd previously been ambivalent to the regime now wore Nazi pins with boasting optimism.

He took a moment to speak to a few of the men churning out the bullets. The pride they took in their work was unmistakable. The ammunition they produced here was in the guns that the 20,000 German soldiers brought with them into the Rhineland that fateful day in March.

Seamus lived with the shame as a matter of course now. What was to be done about it? This was the business he was in, and if he didn't do it, dozens of other factories would line up to take his place. He comforted himself that none of those others would hire his factory manager, Gert Bernheim, or the other Jewish workers. They and the foreigners had nowhere else to go. The perverse irony of the situation had amused him once, but those days were long since past.

Benz was standing in the corner, glaring at him, and Seamus wasn't in the mood to be lectured by the Nazi-enabled idiot installed as head of the workers. He glided away to his office.

Wednesday, July 15, 1936

The sun was sinking behind the grand old architecture of Kurfürstendamm, but Willi Behrens still hadn't sold enough newspapers to buy more than two loaves and maybe some lard, milk, and tea. His heart ached at the thought of his younger brothers and sisters going hungry again tomorrow. Since his father lost his job in the paint shop, the whole family was almost entirely dependent on the money Willi made from his newsstand. Yet it was getting harder and harder to sell enough papers. Copies of the official daily Nazi rag, *Völkischer Beobachter*, piled up at the end of each day. The newsstand was paid off. The money Bruno Kurth gave him back in '33 for his part in blackmailing that businessman and his girlfriend who killed Ernst Milch started him along the road toward buying out his old boss. It was his business now, but profits were waning.

Journalism had changed almost beyond recognition since he'd become a newsie as a young boy, four years ago. Then there were leftist and conservative and middle-of-the-road papers, and people often bought a copy of each. Selling the news had been a thriving business. He'd been delighted with Kurfürstendamm—what a place it was, crammed with cafés, restaurants and bars. Sauntering dandies tossed him coins to impress their beautiful dates, and craning his neck to the left offered him the reward of beholding the majesty of the golden tower clock of the Kaiser Wilhelm Memorial Church. It wasn't hard to be seized by the magic of this place, even if he was experiencing it from behind the counter of a newsstand. The sound of music almost always filled the air, and his family was well fed and happy.

Now the good times were over. Each newspaper was engaged in a relentless race to see who could fawn over Germany's savior, Adolf Hitler, the most. Goebbels, his Minister for Propaganda, met with the editors of the Berlin newspapers every morning to tell them what they could print, and the people were getting sick of reading the same boring things. Customers saw no point in buying more than one paper, and often no point in even buying one—it was just the same so-called news as they heard on the radio. There was only so much unrelenting adoration of the Nazis that the public could take.

At least *Der Stürmer*, which ran the same headline every day —THE JEWS ARE OUR MISFORTUNE—had disappeared of late. Its blatant anti-Semitic fantasies, many of them about hoof-footed Jews attacking German maidens, were too much for the International Olympic Committee, and they'd made a deal with the authorities that it not be sold in the run-up to the games. Thousands of *Stürmer boxes* had been taken down or filled with harmless sports news, but it was only a matter of time before the old order was restored.

While Willi was thinking about closing up, a late customer wearing a fine suit with a matching hat appeared and pointed to one of the Nazi papers. Willi pushed it across to him and held out his hand for payment. The businessman merely dropped a few pfennigs onto the counter, where they bounced and rolled, forcing Willi to grab them before they fell into the gutter.

Another thing that had changed for the worse was that the papers didn't just vilify the Jews. They accused the Roma of being dirty and lazy, referring to them as *gypsy scum* much of the time.

Willi was a Roma with dark-brown eyes and sallow skin, and many of his customers noticed and took care not to touch his hand, presumably in case they caught something from him. But the Roma weren't dirty. Despite the cramped flat his family lived in, his mother always had the children scrubbed and clean. And they weren't lazy, either. His father had lost his job because so many of the paint shop's customers refused to trust a Roma, not because he wasn't a hard worker.

Sick at heart, Willi tied up the remaining papers and carried them to a dumpster in a nearby alley. No doubt some old homeless fellow would use them for blankets or toilet paper, and what better end for the rubbish that passed for journalism these days? With the few last-minute pfennigs in his pocket, he decided to go for a beer in one of the cafés on the boulevard before heading home. He was still only 18. The event of a lifetime was starting in a little over two weeks, and he longed to soak up some of the atmosphere before facing the disappointed eyes of his hungry family. He took off his cap and stuffed it into his pocket. He wished he were wearing better clothes, like the businessman who hadn't even looked Willi in the eye as he bought his paper.

In the boulevard, he took a seat at a table alone. He knew where the other newsies would be at this hour, but preferred something different tonight. He'd catch up with them another time. They were always available—drunk most nights, and hungover most mornings. He wondered how many of them, swept away by the Nazi tide, secretly held his ethnicity against him. Matters such as being a settled Roma were never a big issue growing up in Berlin. Sure, they suffered insults on the streets sometimes, and had angry slogans daubed in sloppy brushstrokes on the apartment building they shared with other Roma families, but the pressure was never like this. It was beginning to worry him.

Willi reached across to the table beside him and asked for a cigarette from a man in his sixties with an impressive twirling mustache. The man didn't flinch from him; instead, he obliged, and provided the matches too. Willi thanked him and sat back in his seat, letting the smoke fill his lungs. The thought of going home with so little money wasn't an enticing one, but he was tired, and his aching limbs longed for the solace of bed. But first, a beer.

A pang of guilt tugged at him, but he banished it. One cheap beer wasn't going to put his family on the street. The waiter came, took his order, and returned with the tall glass as he finished the cigarette. An SS officer was sitting three tables away, laughing out loud with an attractive woman in her early twenties with permed blond hair. The empty chair opposite Willi seemed to taunt him. It was all too easy to tell himself that the woman was being seduced by the soldier's uniform and his status, but he knew a German beauty like that would never look at a newsie—and a Roma. The caress of the beer down his throat eased his worries. He wasn't going to do this for the rest of his life. One day his siblings would be able to stand on their own two feet, and he could pursue something else—perhaps writing the stories that made the papers he sold every day. Proper stories, after everything had gone back to normal. That is, if the Nazis weren't here to stay.

Tiredness drove him out of the café and back to his bike, locked up in a rack by the newsstand. Darkness had fallen in earnest now, but the excitement in the air on Kurfürstendamm had only grown. Leaving wasn't easy. The ride back to the apartment in Kreuzberg would be a long one. He unlocked his bike and set off.

The warm night air was thick around his face as he went, and he was sweating as he pulled up outside the apartment building on Prinzenstrasse he'd lived in all his life. The sour smell of rotting trash filled his nostrils as he got off his bike. Two local drunks called out to him from the step they were sitting on. Each had a bottle in hand. Both were veterans of the Great War.

"Hello, boys," he said. "How are you tonight?"

The men replied, but judging by the level of slurring, would not provide much conversation. Willi continued toward the door of the apartment building and pushed it open. Even in the dark, he knew every crack, every stain, every peeling layer of paint on those stairs. He could walk them with his eyes closed —and with the lack of lighting, it was almost like he was. The noise from his family's apartment bled down the stairs through the open door.

Why is the door always open? Two of his little brothers, Emil and Felix, were on the landing outside the apartment playing with some dice.

"Getting away from the madness inside?" Willi asked.

"Only place to find some peace at this time of day," fifteen-year-old Emil answered.

Willi didn't respond and entered the open door. The radio was on but tuned to one of the government stations that pumped out Beethoven's Fifth. Willi's twin sisters and his twelve-year-old brother, Karl, lay on the carpet reading, fighting for the little space to be had. His father was sitting on the couch.

"You're back?" his father asked with a brief glance.

"Looks like it. Where's everyone else?"

"In bed."

"Mother?"

"Dealing with bedtime. How was work?" his father asked. Willi knew what he wanted to ask.

"I made enough for some breakfast tomorrow."

He handed over the money he made. His father nodded a silent thank-you.

Willi's oldest sisters were married and gone, but as the oldest boy of the remaining eleven children, he was expected to contribute to the household and had done so since he dropped out of school. His brothers Emil and Felix, the dice players outside the door, lost their jobs in a local linen factory a few months before, and his fourteen-year-old twin sisters, Ida and Lena, were once chambermaids in a local hotel before the Nazi-sympathizing manager fired them. But they'd all get jobs again. It seemed the hope was the younger generation could receive an education and support their older siblings one day. If there was any plan to this jumbled mess of humanity, that was it.

"Did you get dinner?" his father asked as he passed through the living room into the kitchen.

"I had a sandwich at work."

That seemed good enough for his father, who went back to the book in his hand.

His mother emerged from the girls' bedroom, her hair strewn about her head like strands from a bird's nest. Her brown eyes were tired and bloodshot. She greeted him with an embrace.

"How was work today?" she asked.

"Fine. I like it there. It's a good spot."

"Where the action is," she said.

"I'm off to bed," he said.

"Good night." She walked past him. "Don't wake the boys. They're asleep."

Willi knew better than that and pushed into the bedroom he shared with his five brothers. Seven-year-old Joseph and five-year-old Klaus were asleep already in the bottom bunk bed they shared. Fitting so many children into a space the size of most kitchens was a miracle of engineering, yet they slept here every night.

Willi changed in seconds and put his clothes among the others strewn on an armchair. He climbed up to his top bunk and thought about the unreachable girl from the café for a few seconds before succumbing to sleep.

～

Thursday, July 16

They came the next morning. Willi was awakened by the sounds of screaming and thumping on doors. The dull light of dawn leaked in through the threadbare curtains as he jumped out of bed. His brothers were up and around him in seconds, all in their thin summer nightclothes. The sound of jackboots on stairs rumbled through the block. The boys huddled together in the middle of the room.

"What's going on?" Emil asked.

They were all looking at Willi as if he'd know.

"I don't have a clue. Stay here." He went to the door.

His father pulled on his pants and pulled the braces over his muscular shoulders. Mother was in the girls' room, trying to calm them. The screaming from the apartments around them intensified.

"What's going on?"

His father stopped to put his hand on Willi's shoulder for a second, but didn't speak. The thumping on their front door cut him off. And then the door was swelling on its hinges.

"They're trying to kick it in." His father ran to grasp the handle.

The door opened to reveal several armed policemen with batons in their hands. They flowed through the gap in the doorway like water, pushing Willi's father, Manfred, back. Several of the children were outside their rooms now, and Willi's mother screamed. His father held his arms aloft, trying to calm things down. All around them, the screaming and thudding continued from the other apartments in the block.

"What's going on?" Willi's father asked.

His question was met with the swing of a baton, but he deflected it with a swift forearm. He repeated the question, but two policemen grabbed him. One older officer with a black beard and matching eyes spoke over the children's screams.

"All occupants are hereby ordered to vacate the premises. We have trucks waiting on the street. Do not take any possessions. This is a temporary measure, and you will be allowed to return to your home soon. Resistance will be met with force."

As if to reinforce the point, one of the officers struck their father across the cheek with the back of a gloved hand.

"What's the meaning of this?" Willi's mother shouted. "This is our home. You can't just come in here and order us out onto the street."

"That's exactly what we're doing," the policeman who spoke said. "Get dressed, but remember, you're coming with us."

Three policemen dragged his father out of the apartment. Willi was shaking as he turned to his mother. "Get the girls dressed. I'll do the same with the boys."

"Yes," she answered with a quaking voice. "What's this about?" she asked the officer.

"All will be revealed in time."

The noise of the other apartments being evacuated was proof that this wasn't about them. The police were rounding up the Roma families clumped together in this apartment block.

Willi herded his five brothers into the bedroom. "Get dressed."

"Where are they taking us?" Karl asked.

"I don't know any more than you do."

He went to the window. He'd contemplated escaping through it many times, but never considered it something he might have to act upon. Could he shin three stories down the drainpipe? Maybe, but what about his family? Best to go down the stairs, play their game for now and wait for the chance for everyone to escape later. Thirty seconds later, the police were bashing on the bedroom door. Willi buttoned up his shirt and pulled on his pants. He helped five-year-old Klaus get dressed, as it was clear they didn't have the time it would take him. The boys trudged out in a line.

"How many of these rats are there?" one of the policemen sneered.

"Why do you think we're here?" another answered. "Vermin breed like you wouldn't believe."

The boys lined up in the living room. Klaus was crying as Willi held him. A few seconds elapsed before their mother and the girls emerged from the other room. Another inquiry from their mother as to what this was about was met with a swift rebuttal. One of the officers shoved her toward the door with the flat end of his baton.

"Be thankful that's all you get," he said.

Willi's mother didn't answer, just put her arms around as many of her children as she was able as the policemen directed them out the door. The other apartments were empty, their doors ajar and the insides ransacked. Willi was at the head of the procession as the police directed them down the stairs. Still holding his youngest brother, Willi emerged into the cool air of the early morning. The trucks were ready. One was already full of their neighbors and started off.

A line of policemen with their batons drawn directed them into the last truck. The six members of the Rosenberg family were already inside, along with Willi's father, who grasped his daughters as they climbed in.

Willi was in last and sat at the end.

"Where are we going?" Klaus asked him with innocent eyes.

He wanted to tell him they were going somewhere the family would be safe, and that they could trust the policemen taking him there, but he couldn't lie to him.

"I don't know, brother," Willi said.

The truck took off, rumbling through the familiar streets of Kreuzberg.

"Have you spoken to the officer in charge, or anyone yet?" Willi shouted over the noise to his father.

"I tried. I got a fist in the face for my troubles."

"Maybe this has something to do with the Olympics?" The decree from Interior Minister Wilhelm Frick came through a month before. It detailed measures to combat the "Gypsy Plague" within the city of Berlin. Willi hadn't thought that tightening police measures and closing down campsites would apply to his family. They had lived in that apartment all his life, with other settled Roma in the building. His parents had settled in Berlin after they married almost 25 years before and didn't move around from one campsite to another. They were ordinary Germans.

The trucks continued northeast through the near-deserted dawn streets. After about thirty minutes they stopped, and the police came around and opened up the backs. The first thing that struck Willi was the stench of raw sewage.

"Welcome to Marzahn," a policeman said with a grin. So they were in northeast Berlin. Willi had never spent much time here because there was little to see, apart from the sewage works where Berlin's wastewater was processed.

"Enjoy Gypsy Manhunt Day," another sneered.

Willi, his family, and his neighbors were herded toward a group of several hundred other Romas. Few spoke as more trucks arrived, spewing more and more Roma onto the fields between the train tracks and the cemetery. Two wooden barracks stood in the field, along with 100 or so caravans propped up on stones.

An hour passed before the captain of the police stood up on the back of a flatbed truck to address them. He was a short, stocky man with a red mustache, and he began by offering a Hitler salute.

"My name is Captain Rudolf Maninger. You are to be detained here until further notice by order of the Minister of the Interior. Over my shoulder are the quarters you will share." He held out a hand to point out the caravans "You will notice no fences, but the local police will be closely monitoring the comings and goings of every person here, and anyone leaving is required to check in and out. Those with jobs are allowed to leave to go to work and to bring back food. If they abandon their family through laziness, then their family will starve."

Willi glanced at his father, who looked shrunken and powerless.

"A nightly curfew of 10 p.m. is in place," the captain continued. "Violation of these rules will be dealt with swiftly and harshly. Find your living quarters. With 600 of you, it should be a tight fit, but you're used to that."

He stepped down off the flatbed. The crowd was divided into smaller groups and funneled toward the caravans.

"It stinks here. I don't like it." Klaus clung to his big brother's hand.

"I know, kid. We'll be out of here before you know it." Willi hoped there was some truth in his words.

A policeman led them to a small caravan. "We'll need another," his mother said. "There are thirteen of us."

"This is it." The policeman walked away.

His father ran after him, but returned a few minutes later. The mark on his face told them everything they needed to know about how the exchange went. The girls started crying. No one had any food or a change of clothes.

"I need to go to the bathroom," sobbed seven-year-old Ellie.

"I'll take you," Willi said. He wanted to check out the outhouses.

Just two were provided, one for men, one for women. Two toilets to service the needs of almost 600 people. And they were only pits in the ground with wooden seats. The site didn't even have running water. In the end he took Ellie into the nearby scrub land instead, nearly getting shot by a policeman who accused them of trying to escape.

"Filthy gypsy," he sneered when Willi explained his little sister had been on the point of wetting her pants because the line for the toilet was so long. "Get back to your caravan and stay there."

"I'm the breadwinner. I have to go to work."

"Not today. Tomorrow you can apply for a permit to leave. Enjoy the day off, you lazy scum."

Used to making the best of constricted spaces, their parents somehow arranged to squeeze them all into the one caravan, which had been made for perhaps six people. Willi's bed was on the floor, and was to be shared with two of his brothers.

His mother was sitting on the step with her head in her hands. "The children have nothing to eat, or even a cup of water to drink."

"What would you have me do?" his father asked. "We'll just have to stay strong until Willi gets back from work. He'll bring whatever we need."

His siblings were whining with thirst. Unable to bear it, Willi walked around the site in the dark. Some of the other families had lit fires using sticks they gathered from the field. With no chairs, each person sat in the dirt, staring into the flames. Willi recognized a friend from the apartment block. He'd known Ivan his entire life. They were the same age and had grown up together.

Willi shook his hand and sat down beside him. "At least the smoke covers the smell of the sewage."

"We'll get used to it in time," Ivan said.

"You think we'll be here long? Surely we'll only be here until the games are over."

Ivan gestured over toward the police left guarding them. "You think they're going to let us go back home after this? We're 'enemies of the race-based state.' That's what Hitler and his cronies called us last year. We're no different than the Jews."

"I'm Catholic."

"You think they care?"

The police on duty were sharing a cigarette, laughing among themselves.

Willi sat in silence, staring into the fire until exhaustion drove him back to the caravan. His father was sitting on the step of the caravan, staring out into the darkness. Willi put his hand on his shoulder and his father looked up at him. Willi felt a horrible rage within him for what the police had done, and he knew his father did too.

"What are we going to do? We can't stay here. This is an outrage."

"It will be all right," said Willi.

"How do you know?"

"I just know."

Klaus and Emil woke as he climbed into their shared bed.

"How long are we going to be here?" the little boy whispered.

"I'm going to get us out," Willi answered.

"How are you going to do that?" Emil asked.

"Go to sleep, little brother."

He lay there, crushed between his restless brothers, listening to his mother trying to soothe his little sisters.

"Everything is going to be ok," she was murmuring. "We'll soon be home. They can't keep us here."

After the conversation with Ivan, Willi wasn't so sure she was right. He was beginning to think they would need help from someone with power. It was just as well he knew someone with that kind of power—someone he had been harboring a secret about for three years.

2

Friday, July 17

Seamus Ritter adjusted his bow tie in the mirror and smiled at his wife, Lisa. She was radiant in her red sequinned evening dress. She seemed to be enjoying applying makeup, something she seldom wore on the street these days due to the National Socialist distaste for such things. It wasn't that she was willingly submitting to their prejudices; it was just that life was easier if you played by their rules in public. The Brownshirts infected the city like a plague, and were always ready to greet a woman they considered a harlot with a scornful word, or worse. With no recourse, they operated above the law.

"Are you ready for a fabulous night?" he asked her in English. They had been speaking in his native tongue more and more around the house to prepare her and her daughter Hannah for a move to America, should it ever come to that. Lisa's mother had been Jewish, so it was something they had to be ready for. Lisa's Nazi father had been ready to murder his own daughter rather than admit he had fathered a Jew. Luckily,

Seamus had been there to defend Lisa, and now Dr. Walz was dead. In a world without rules, one had to kill—and then lie about it—to survive.

"Yes, I am." Then she stopped and started laughing. "I can understand you, but finding the words is a whole different animal," she said in German.

"Well, are you ready?" He smiled.

"Yes, I am," she said again, switching back to English.

Downstairs, Michael was reading a book about running his coach gave him. Maureen and her boyfriend, Thomas, were playing poker with fourteen-year-old Fiona and twelve-year-old Conor. Hannah, Lisa's daughter, was asleep upstairs, as all seven-year-olds should be at eight thirty. The radio was tuned to a foreign station, and loud jazz was filling the air.

"Turn that down, please," Lisa said. "Your little sister's in bed, and what if the neighbors hear and report you?"

"That's what I keep saying,' said Fiona. "We shouldn't be playing banned music. It's disrespectful to the Führer."

"Old Herr Nussbaum isn't going to call the Gestapo on us over some music," Michael said, ignoring his younger sister. "He's almost deaf."

"You want to take that chance with the Olympics in two weeks?" Seamus asked. "You've been training for this for over two years. You need to be more careful now than ever."

Michael threw down his book and went to the radio. He lowered the volume and returned to his position on the couch without saying anything.

Lisa was at the dining room table with her arms around Conor from behind.

"I'm trying to concentrate on my cards," the boy said in faux annoyance.

"I'm just giving you a hug."

"You look beautiful." Fiona suddenly smiled, the sternness gone. She looked so like her mother that Seamus sometimes had to stop and take pause. This was one of those moments. It was like Marie was here, sitting in front of him as a young girl.

"How is Fiona doing, Thomas?" he asked Maureen's boyfriend.

"Let's just say I'm glad we're not playing for real money."

"Are you leaving now?" Maureen asked. "In that case, I fold. Thomas, I'll be back in less than an hour. I have to drop my parents off to get dinner and go drinking—that sounds so wrong. Don't let Conor bluff you."

"Just as well you folded. You never had a chance against the hand I have," Conor said.

Seamus could see he had nothing and patted his son on the head before hugging Fiona goodbye. She responded like a limp fish—nothing he wasn't used to these days.

His older daughter had the car keys in her hands already and led them out. "You two get in the back," she said. "I'll be the taxi driver for your date. You can pretend you're still courting instead of being a boring married couple."

"In my car?" Seamus asked.

"I'm doing my best."

They were a few minutes closer to town when she asked, "Have you been thinking about your father much?"

"I don't think I'd be human if I wasn't." Lisa said and Seamus clutched her hand. "I try not to, but it seems to pop up when I least expect it. I'm just glad you were there, and you too, my love." She kissed Seamus on the cheek. "You both saved my life, and Hannah's."

"Michael too," Seamus said.

"I haven't forgotten."

"I can't believe what that fiend was prepared to do to appease the will of the Führer."

"I can't believe what the German people are willing to do to appease him," Maureen said.

"It's been a crazy time," Lisa said. "And what about you? Do

I hear the chime of wedding bells in your future? I do like Thomas so much. He's a wonderful young man. You do too, don't you, Seamus?"

"He's been dating you for three years and I haven't wanted to beat him up once," he replied. "But you're too young to get married."

Maureen pulled out into the light traffic. "I'm older than you were when you married Mother."

"That was a different time. I had to get married before I joined the army, but you have your career to think about. If you're going to be a doctor—"

"I don't know what I'm going to be, but I do know I want to be with Thomas."

Seamus kept his mouth shut. His daughter was right—she was older than he was when he married her mother, so who was he to say she couldn't? It didn't make any difference anyway. She was going to do as she pleased. This was an argument he would never win—like most with his eldest daughter.

The city was festooned with flags, but not just the usual Nazi ones. The flags of the upcoming Olympics were now represented too.

Twenty minutes later, his daughter dropped them outside the Taverne, an Italian restaurant on Kurfürstenstrasse. Seamus got out first and walked around the car to get the door for his wife. She stepped out like she was in a dream. Her beauty still stunned him.

He took her arm and they strolled inside as his daughter drove away. "She's going to marry him, you know," Lisa said as he held the door for her.

"I know."

The hostess greeted them and led them through the packed dining room to a candlelit table in the corner. The diners on either side weren't much more than arm's length away. Seamus made a mental note not to mention anything to do with politics. A pianist sat tinkling away at a grand piano in the corner, but they couldn't make out much of what he was playing over the din of conversation.

"This is one of Clayton's favorite haunts these days. He and his fellow journalists often come here on weekend nights."

"Is this a setup?" Lisa asked.

"Not at all. But perhaps if they come in—" He realized Lisa was rolling her eyes. "We don't have to talk to them. I know this evening is just for the two of us."

"It's fine," she said with a wry smile. "It's always interesting to meet Clayton and his friends. I see far too much of you already."

They ordered a bottle of 1933 Château Cheval Blanc with their baked rigatoni starter and were just moving on to their main courses when Lisa said, "Speak of the devil and he shall appear."

Clayton and another man Seamus had never seen before were edging through the tables, past the pianist. Lisa held up her hand to get their attention.

"We don't have to."

"No, I love Clayton. You know that."

The young American journalist waved back at her and arrived at the table a few seconds later, with his companion. "I didn't expect to see you here."

"We get out once in a while," said Lisa. "Who's your friend?"

"This is Ernest Small, a sportswriter for the Associated Press. I bumped into him on the way here and said I'd show him around."

"Pleasure to meet you," said the man. "Small" was a misnomer. He was well over six feet, with broad shoulders and a square jaw; balding but sporting a brown beard.

"No tables left here," Clayton said. "So I'm taking my new friend down the street to find a traditional German café, then we're thinking about heading to Ciro's. You'll meet us for a drink there after?"

Seamus glanced at Lisa, who was smiling and nodding.

"That would be great."

CIRO'S WAS one of the most fashionable bars in the city, on Rankestrasse. They heard the loud jazz music from inside as soon as they stepped out of the cab.

"Seems like the Nazis' reach doesn't stretch to this place," Lisa said in surprise.

"This place is going to be awash with foreigners in the next few weeks," Seamus said. "The Nazis are on their best behavior. I'd say there are tourists here already. This is the best bar in the city for spotting movie stars."

"How about failed movie actresses who get fired for being too Jewish?"

He winced. "I'm sorry..."

Lisa rallied instantly with a bright smile. "No, I'm sorry, sweetheart. Bad joke."

He took her arm. "Anyway, you're not a failed actress. As soon as the Nazis lose power, you'll be back on the screen. Come on—we're going to have a great time."

The bar consisted of two rooms. The main bar, where Lisa and Seamus found a table and ordered two martinis, was decorated in a fashionable arabesque style, with Egyptian hiero-glyphics on the wall and a dome in the shape of a pyramid over their heads.

"I heard the owner of the place is Egyptian." Lisa pointed out a small man with a deep tan in a smart silk suit laughing with some patrons at the bar.

"A slice of home for him." Seamus wondered if Egyptians were among the races the National Socialists disapproved of.

"I'm surprised the Nazis allow this place to remain as it is," she said, echoing his thoughts.

"What better place to show to the throng of tourists how cosmopolitan the Reich is? Let's enjoy it while we can. I'm not sure the powers that be are going to tolerate it too much longer." The relaxed atmosphere in the bar and the martini had loosened his tongue. He felt safe here, among the artists and showgirls. The band on stage was belting out Benny Goodman with breakneck energy. He could have been in any bar in New York—or New Orleans, for that matter. The outside world seemed to melt away.

Clayton and his new friend, Ernest Small, walked in. Lisa stood up and waved them over. The two men pulled up chairs and ordered whiskey on the rocks, which arrived a few minutes later in glasses that looked like they'd been sheared from the side of a glacier.

Ernest turned out to be from Boston, though he didn't have the accent Seamus usually associated with the place. He was covering the Olympics, like half the writers in town.

"Clayton tells me your son is competing in the games!" he exclaimed to Seamus over the din of the music.

"Yeah, in the 100 meters and the 4 X 100 meters relay. We're excited."

"That's incredible. I'd love to meet him. He's running for Germany even though he was born in New Jersey?"

"He only discovered his talent after we moved over here. The training facilities have been excellent—run by the Nazis, of course."

"They seem to be very organized," Ernest said.

The sparkle of a flashbulb exploding behind them caught their attention. Petra Wagner, star of the silver screen, was at the door, dressed in a black dress with a feather boa coiled around her shoulder. An SS officer came to take her arm and they turned to saunter into the crowded bar. Seamus's wife turned white and stared into her drink.

Petra was coming straight toward them. Ciro, the owner, came over to kiss her hand. She stopped for a moment to talk to him, pearly white teeth flashing. Ernest was still speaking, but none of them were listening to him. Seamus wanted to get his wife out of there, but the only way was past where Petra was standing. The SS officer with her was in his early thirties, handsome, with a smug grin.

"Goebbels must have finished with her," Lisa said.

It was rare Seamus heard this level of unvarnished bitterness in her voice.

"Do you know her?" Ernest asked.

"We worked together on a film last year. It came out a few months ago. The Brownshirts and SS packed out the movie houses. Petra Wagner—the new darling of the National Socialists—is honoring us with her presence."

Petra finished her conversation with Ciro and he left her with the SS man, who led her toward their table. The Führer's new favorite movie star was almost on top of Lisa when she noticed her.

"Lisa?" she asked with a smile that seemed genuine.

"You remember me?"

"Lisa, are you sure—"

"It's fine," his wife answered.

"A friend of yours, Petra?" the SS officer asked.

Germany's newest movie star was silent for a second before she answered. "Someone I used to know. Good to see you again, Lisa. How have you been?"

"I was thrown out of the Reich Chamber of Film last year. I'll never work on another set again."

Petra's face dropped. "Oh, no! I'm so sorry to hear that."

"Your acting skills have improved."

"I don't know what you're talking about. I am so sorry—"

"How is your new life? Was it worth it?"

"Was what worth it?"

"Denouncing me to the Gestapo?"

The SS officer grimaced. "I think we've had quite enough of this."

"I don't know what you're talking about." Petra's voice was shaking, and people in the bar were staring now.

"I know you did it." Her former colleague didn't answer. "I told you in confidence. How could you do that?" Lisa was crying now.

"I think it's best you move on," Seamus said to Petra.

"You sold your soul to the National Socialists," Lisa said. "I just hope it was worth it."

Seamus put his arms around his wife to calm her before the bouncers arrived.

"We're leaving," the SS officer said. Petra was staring in silence. It was impossible to know if the look of concerned bemusement on her face was authentic or not. She dropped her head, and the SS man appeared to be trying to comfort her as they walked away.

The owner arrived with a concerned look, but Seamus held his hand up to signify that whatever happened was over.

Ciro showed Petra and her date to a table with a small reserved sign on it and held out her chair for her. The SS man sat down opposite, and they turned to watch the band.

"Let's get out of here," Seamus said.

"No. She's not going to ruin our night out."

"We could go somewhere else. There are plenty—"

"No, I like it here. How about another drink?"

Lisa got up to walk to the bar, even though they'd been getting table service all night.

"This is the first time Lisa's seen her since everything that happened last year."

"What happened between them?" Ernest asked.

"You never know when to stop asking questions, do you?" Clayton said.

"No, it's ok," Seamus answered. "One handy way of getting ahead in Germany these days, Ernest, is to denounce anyone who stands in your way to the Gestapo. We never did find out for sure, but the secret police came for my wife on set of the movie she was making last year, and suddenly Petra found herself propelled to stardom in place of Lisa, who was kicked out of the actors' guild, never to work again."

Ernest drank his whiskey in silence. Several people were at Petra's table, and the young actress was luminescent as she signed autographs for them. Each fan left smiling, clutching the napkins she'd signed like an Olympic medal.

Lisa returned with a tray of drinks, took a deep breath, and sat down. Seamus clutched her hand beneath the table. She seemed determined to stay and he wasn't going to argue.

"Why are you here two weeks ahead of time?" Lisa asked Ernest.

"To inhale some of the atmosphere of the place. We hear so much about Germany and Hitler and all his merry men back home. I asked if I could come early to see it all for myself. Even sportswriters like me need to know where they're writing from."

"What do you think so far?" Seamus asked.

"I've been here five days, and I can't say anything bad about the place. Seems like a well-run, lively city to me. I was antici- pating some kind of outdoor prison camp from what people told me, but it's nothing like that at all."

"I was just telling him that if you read the papers and listen to the radio, everything seems hunky-dory," Clayton said. "Because that's what the Nazis want you to believe."

"We don't possess the rights you do in the US," Lisa said. "We don't have free speech or freedom of the press or the right to congregate and protest."

"Freedom of the press would be nice, wouldn't it, Clayton?" The sportswriter grinned. "If our editors don't want to print our stories, then the world doesn't see them. More for you in the news division than the likes of us sports hacks."

"But the government controls the news here. The Ministry for Propaganda decides what gets put in front of the editors, and if you step out of line, you disappear," Clayton said.

Ernest didn't seem to hear; he just continued on his train of thought.

"Everybody says that in America, people can think and write and say whatever they please, and in Germany they can't, but that's not true. Some things are easier said here than back home."

"Like what?" Seamus asked.

"In Germany you can say you don't like Jews, and say they're bad, corrupt people. You can't say it in America, even if thousands might think it."

Struck dumb, Clayton looked at his new friend in horror, while Seamus put his hand on Lisa's thigh under the table. She was quivering, as if she were about to spring up and assault this man. Yet her eyes were calm and she spoke in slow, measured tones across the table. "You need to be careful, Herr Small. Not all Germans are Nazis. Saying things like that in front of a group of Brownshirts will earn you pats on the back and free beer, but not here."

He looked surprised. "I didn't mean any offense. I was just expressing an opinion—"

"Do you know much about the treatment of the Jews in Germany?" She didn't wait for him to answer. "It started with an organized government boycott of Jewish businesses, just a few weeks after Hitler came to power. Can you imagine Roosevelt doing that, or any politician in America deliberately singling out one minority group on a national basis?"

"Blacks are singled out in dozens of states in America, and

excluded from daily life. How different is Germany from America?" he answered.

"As a national policy? As a recent policy to shun them from society?" She took a cigarette from her case and lit it. "I'm not condoning the policies of certain American states toward black people, and I know Jews are also discriminated against in the States, but last year, the Nuremberg Laws stripped Jews of German citizenship, and of their right to marry and even court Germans."

"Marriage between the races is illegal in America too," Ernest said. "How is it so different?"

"As terrible as that is, it's an old law. These are new restrictions, from last year. Plenty of people in your country speak out against those injustices. Doing so here would land you in a prison."

Lisa was showing signs of agitation now, but Seamus knew better than to try to stop her.

"I wasn't fully aware of that," Ernest replied.

"Have you seen the signs that read, JEWS NOT WELCOME, in shopfronts all over the city? Have you heard of the newspaper *Der Stürmer*, which has drawings of Jews with horns and tails raping innocent German maidens on the cover most weeks, and that more than 400,000 Germans read it every week?"

Ernest looked like he wanted to be somewhere else now, but neither man was about to step in to rescue him. "And it's not just the Jews, either. Have you ever heard of the term *concentration camp*?"

"I can't say I have."

"They're prison camps where the National Socialists send anyone who opposes them or who they simply don't like— Jews, Social Democrats, Communists, homosexuals. Anyone who thinks differently than they do."

Ernest was struggling to make eye contact with her now.

"I went to visit my six-year-old daughter in her kindergarten class last year. We read a book called *Trust no Fox on his Green Heath and No Jew on his Oath* that said Jews were children of the devil. The kids in the class were all staring up at me, listening in fascination as I read that trash."

"I've never had to take a political stand. I'm here to cover the games."

"When you have two Jewish grandparents, like I do, you don't get to make choices like that. We've had politics thrust upon us."

"I'm sorry, I had no idea you were a Jew."

"I don't know what I am. The government defined people like me as a *Mischling*, with just enough German blood in me to avoid the worst pitfalls that would have befallen my grandparents if they were still alive. My daughter is a *Mischling* of the second degree. She won't have to deal with the restrictions set upon my life, and will be free to marry a German if she ever wanted to do so. Not me, however. I still have my husband because we married before the laws were written." She put her hand on Seamus's shoulder. "I was thrown out of the actors' guild and I'm barred from ever working in education or health or the civil service—all because my mother was born a Jew. The fact that I never knew about her heritage and was raised Lutheran is immaterial. Blood is all that matters. It's all written down in the Nuremberg Laws, passed last September."

The man was visibly shocked. He tried to say something, but it came as an inaudible mumble. Seamus almost felt sorry for him. Almost.

His wife continued. "The laws set out last year changed everything for Jews, and even *Mischling* like me. Jews are no longer afforded any protection by the state. They've been rejected as un-German. We're not even aliens—they have far more rights. We're completely at the mercy of the secret police.

Jews don't have access to the law or the court system—that's for citizens, or even aliens. The Jews are neither."

"There's more," said Clayton, now eager to put in a word of his own. "Nuremberg defined *Reich citizens* as those willing and able to serve the German people and the Reich. So even Aryan Germans who don't, or can't, ably serve the Reich as the Nazis want are rejected as noncitizens and stripped of their rights. The Nazis declared the Reich citizen as the sole bearer of full political rights, but what rights are there in a country that offers no elections, no freedoms, and no protection under the law? The only right a Reich citizen has is to consent to the rule of the Nazis, whether by joining the armed forces or shouting themselves hoarse at political rallies."

"Everything here is political now," Lisa said. "It's inescapable. Hitler's changed our entire society. Remember what I'm telling you when you see the crowds lining the streets for a glimpse at their beloved Führer. Remember that his entire regime is built on suppression and lies."

Ernest sat back in his seat and cracked a wan smile like a schoolboy who'd just been corrected by a stern teacher. "Ok. I get it. I guess this is what I'm here to learn. There's more to this place than hot nightclubs and good beer."

"I'm glad you're here and asking questions," Lisa said. "Just make sure you're asking the right ones and you keep your eyes open to what's really happening beneath the façade the Nazis are trying to present to the world. Because we need everyone else to know."

"Who wants more drinks?" Clayton asked, louder than he needed to.

Lisa excused herself to go to the bathroom. Seamus stood up and caught her a few feet from the ladies' room door.

"Are you ok?" he asked. "I'm sorry, I had no idea. And I'm sure Clayton didn't either, he only just met him."

"He knows now. Go back to the table, Seamus. I'm fine." She kissed him on the mouth and disappeared into the bathroom.

Ernest was on his feet when Seamus returned to the table. "I hope I didn't insult your wife."

"Maybe take your foot out of your mouth before you speak next time."

Lisa arrived back at the table. Ernest apologized to her. "I needed that."

"It's all right," she replied, but didn't sit down. "Come on, Seamus, let's go dance."

"Doesn't seem like I've much choice," he said to the other men at the table and stood up. Having a wife who used to be a professional dancer tended to show his lack of rhythm up in seconds, but that didn't stop her from dragging him out to dance every time she got the chance.

The dance floor was packed with men in sharp suits with smartly coiffed hair and beautiful ladies in tight dresses. Lisa blended in like a tributary into a pond. Seamus followed her, trying to mimic her perfect rhythm and smooth moves, but couldn't help feeling like a buffalo with a broken ankle dancing with a swan. Lisa didn't seem to care. The band finished the song to a round of applause from the audience, but Seamus had little respite. They started up again and Lisa grabbed his hand to stop him from leaving. He was stuck here with this beautiful woman and the music pulsing through the air like lightning.

Fifteen minutes passed before Lisa took pity on him and they went back to the table to join the other two men.

"So, what do you do, Seamus?" Ernest asked.

"I manufacture arms for the German Army." He hadn't found a way to sugarcoat what he did. The best way was to come straight out and say it. "Business is booming. I never know if that's a good thing or not."

"If you don't make them, someone else will," Clayton said.

"No shortage of people vying for those government contracts now," Seamus said.

"You lectured me on the ills of the Nazi government earlier. And I concede the points you made," Ernest said to Lisa, "but your husband sells arms to the government you despise so much. Something doesn't add up here." He stood up. "I'll get back to my hotel now. It was a pleasure to meet you all, and the best of luck to your son in the games."

Ernest threw down some money and walked out of the bar. Seamus slumped back in his seat. Clayton made a joke about Petra and Ernest getting together, but no one laughed. "I'm sorry I brought him along."

"It's ok," Lisa said.

The touch of her hand was some comfort to Seamus. He glanced over at Petra and downed his drink.

3

Saturday, August 1

What greater honor could a young person have than to perform in front of the Führer himself? Fiona was near the back, but if she arched her head to the left, she could make out the figure of Adolf Hitler himself on the podium. A sea of young patriots swirled all around. Some said 29,000 would be here, and it looked like that many, at least. Members of the foreign press were milling around the steps of the Old Museum, behind the stage where the Führer and the head of the International Olympic Committee were standing with other dignitaries. All came to witness the rally on the lawn of the Lustgarten between the Old Museum, Berlin Cathedral, and the palace itself. The mass of German youth all offered the Hitler salute as one. The triumph of unity in motion. Fiona shouted the words, tempted to smile at the other members of her League of German Girls troop standing around her in perfect formation. So many young people and not one out of line. No drooping neckties, or even a hair out of place. It was all perfect, and it was all for him, the savior of Germany.

A tinge of regret stabbed at Fiona's heart as she let her arm fall back into place in synchronicity with the others around her. None of her family were here to see this. Not even Michael, who would soon represent the Reich in the games. The sad truth was they didn't understand what was happening in Germany today, or the immense stroke of luck they'd enjoyed in moving here just in time to witness Hitler's ascent to power. She wondered how many others had not told their families they were coming here to rally in front of the Führer today. The shame was that many of her fellow young patriots were likely in the same position as she was.

Her teachers warned her for years that her parents might not understand the revolution. Older people, like her father, were too stuck in their ways. It was up to the youth of Germany to drive the change the country needed to retake its place among the great nations of the world. Her father and his wife thought they were protecting her, but they were holding her back. As her teachers told her, rebelling against the archaic ways and visions of the older generation was not only justified, but necessary.

This immense and wonderful rally was the beginning of the opening ceremony of the Olympics. It was a statement of the belief in, and devotion to, the Führer, that every young person in that enormous mass of humanity felt. It was a demonstration to the foreign press of what Germany had become, and as one of her troop leaders asserted, it was also a warning. The crowd burst into song, Fiona among them. Every voice was loud and true, and each knew all the words of every verse and chorus of "The Freedom Song of the Youth."

Once they were finished, the dignitaries made their way to the platform to begin their speeches. The national leader of the Hitler Youth, Baldur von Schirach, was first, followed by the

Reich Minister for Sport, and then of Education. Joseph Goebbels, Minister for Propaganda, was last. The only disappointment was the Führer himself didn't speak, but he was such a busy man and doubtless had other speeches to prepare for that day and was saving his voice. Just having him there to witness the spectacle was more than enough.

A drizzle began as the speeches ended, but it didn't dampen the enthusiasm of the crowd. The next item on the agenda was something they'd all been told about by their youth leaders in advance, a new tradition devised by the Germans for their games—the Olympic torch. The Lustgarten was the penultimate stop on a journey devised by the Secretary-General of the Olympic Organizing Committee, Carl Diem. Some took it as an ancient Greek ceremony, but they were wrong. Diem's idea was to connect the modern games with antiquity, so the 1,800-mile journey, which began in Athens, was almost at an end. The fact that there was no torch ceremony at the original games was immaterial.

Fiona was only a stone's throw away from where the sea of Hitler Youth parted to let the athlete through. The young man held the torch in his left hand as he ran through the crowd toward the Old Museum at the other end. He wore the full running gear her brother sported so often. The thought that Michael could have been the one to do this entered her mind. What an honor that would have been for the family! But her father and Lisa wouldn't have appreciated it. Better that it went to another athlete—perhaps one whose ancestry was a little purer.

The runner emerged from the crowd and ran up the stairs of the Old Museum to light an altar of fire. He then turned to the sea of youth and offered the Hitler salute. It was hard to keep tears from her eyes as Fiona saluted back. Many of the girls around her weren't able to control their emotions as well as she had. Many were red-faced, with tears rolling down their cheeks. Just being in the presence of the Führer was enough to do that to some of the girls, but Fiona steeled herself for what she knew was meant to be a solemn occasion.

The dignitaries launched a round of applause. Soon they were all cheering and clapping for the games that would bring the glory of the new Reich to the world. The runner saluted the crowd one last time before continuing toward the palace. A fleet of limousines pulled up alongside the podium. Fiona got on her tiptoes to try to catch one last glimpse of the Führer as he left, but the view was obscured by the hundreds of flags in the air, and she soon gave up.

Her friends, Inge and Amalia, came to her with bright smiles painted across their faces. Where better could they have been? Everyone was here.

"That was incredible," Amalia said.

The other two girls agreed. The troop leaders shouted out instructions, and the Hitler Youth lined up.

"Where shall we go next?" Fiona asked. "I can't go home now."

"No one's going home," Inge answered. "We'd never forgive ourselves."

"Let's go to Unter den Linden to catch a glimpse of the Führer as he makes his way over to the Olympiastadion," Inge said.

The three girls listened to their instructions and joined a line of girls shuffling toward the exit.

"Along with everyone else in Berlin?" Fiona said. "They won't be leaving for two hours, too."

"I know where Harald and Georg and some of the other boys are going after this," Amalia said.

"Where?"

"Oh, Fiona, interested in where Harald's going to be, are we?" Inge asked.

"No more than anyone else."

"Pull the other leg," Inge said. "It's got bells on. It's ok to admit you love him and want to produce many sons for the Führer with him."

The other girls seemed to find this hilarious, and it took them a few seconds to regain themselves.

"Where are they going to be?" Fiona asked.

"Over at the Jewish department store on Wilhelmstrasse, helping out with the boycott—or whatever it is now."

"Were they not here?" Fiona asked.

"Yeah, but they wanted to do something to help the cause after the rally. They're nothing if not dedicated." Amalia grinned.

"They're not going to rest until the Jewish menace is eliminated from the Reich," Inge said.

"Nor should they," said a girl who'd apparently been listening in on their conversation.

Fiona stayed silent. It was hard to know what to say in these situations. Lisa's heritage muddied her thoughts on the Jewish problem. And her father's friend, Gert Bernheim, and his family seemed like good people, yet the Führer and all the other people she admired so much railed against them in almost every speech. Perhaps they saw something ordinary people like her couldn't. Did she need to place her trust in them the way her teachers and troop leaders told her to? Lisa was a kind, loving person. Her father was a good man. It was tragic what happened to him—killed by an intruder. But through him, Lisa had enough Aryan blood to counter that of her Jewish mother. Hannah was a sister to Fiona, but the Nuremberg Laws had defined her as *Mischling* of the second degree, with enough German blood to be a citizen. Her mother was not so lucky.

Fiona wondered if the girls, or their friends, like Harald and Georg, knew any Jewish people. It was all so confusing, but it was vital to remember that the older generation didn't understand the revolution. Her troop leaders and teachers reminded them all the time that they were the only ones they could genuinely trust. Perhaps they were right.

The drizzle faded away, but the day was still overcast and dull. Fiona was almost thankful for that. Being in the city with hundreds of thousands of others with the sun beating down would have been miserable. The crowds dissipated and the girls left. The route to the Olympiastadion was already blanketed with people desperate to set eyes on the Führer, even though his car wouldn't pass by for hours yet. The seven-mile thoroughfare of Unter den Linden had been renamed Via Triumphalis for the duration of the games, in homage to the road in ancient Rome where victorious generals would reenter the city to the acclaim of the masses. It was lined with swastikas and Olympic flags, and one couldn't fall without landing on an SA man. It was said over 40,000 of them were guarding the route.

It was a 25-minute walk from the Lustgarten to the department store on Wilhelmstrasse. Fiona saw Harald standing outside, his arms linked with six other Hitler Youth to prevent people from walking in and out of the store.

"I'm surprised it's open on a day like today," Fiona said.

"The Jews never miss out on an opportunity to make money," Inge said. "It's all they care about."

Once more, Fiona stayed silent. Harald Schmidt smiled at her as she approached. The sight of him almost knocked the breath out of her lungs. She tried to keep cool, but his face was too much. He was seventeen, with short blond hair and dark-blue eyes that seemed to dance as he spoke. His broad shoulders rippled under his Hitler Youth uniform. None of the other boys were as tall or muscular as he was. Georg, his best friend, was Inge's cousin, and had introduced them at a rally a few months before.

The boys were arguing with a customer trying to enter the

store when the girls arrived. The patron, a woman in her thirties, pushed past their linked arms. They decided to let her go
inside and turned to the girls to offer the Hitler salute. The girls
reciprocated.

"What an event!" Harald seemed only to be looking at
Fiona as he spoke.

"Incredible," she answered. "I've never seen the city like
this."

"What are you doing here?" Georg asked. He was several
inches smaller than his friend, with sandy-brown hair and
freckles.

"We wanted to get away from the crowds before the Führer
came. No need to be up there yet," Amalia said.

"No one can help themselves. That's the effect the Führer
has on the people," Harald said with a smile that almost
stopped Fiona's heart.

"How long are you planning on staying here?" Inge asked.

"We didn't want the Jews to have their way today, of all
days," Georg answered.

The boys were still standing with their arms linked, a
phalanx of eight Hitler Youth protecting the front door.

"Have the owners been out yet?" Inge asked.

"They know better than to mess with us," Harald said.
"Although we're to play nicely for the duration of the games. No
rough stuff."

"I can wait sixteen days," one of the other boys with his
arms linked said, and they all laughed.

Fiona and the other girls waited on the corner, watching the
boys arguing with the few customers who tried to bustle past
them, until they decided enough was enough. They broke off
and left to see Hitler once more as he drove down to the
Olympiastadion for the opening ceremony.

Harald walked beside Fiona. At one stage, she thought he

would take her hand, but he didn't. She was almost glad—that would have been too much.

"How is your brother?" he asked.

"Ready. He's going to be in the stadium with the rest of the German team tonight, and then they're off to Herr Goebbels' house for a reception."

"Incredible. He might meet the Führer himself. Your parents must be beside themselves with pride. Are they going to the party too?"

"No." Fiona thought it best not to mention that they weren't going because her stepmother had been marked a half-Jew, or *Mischling*, and Herr Goebbels wouldn't appreciate her presence. Few knew why she had quit acting. Thankfully no one in her troop, anyway.

"Why aren't you at the opening ceremony? Did your family go?"

"I'm following soon, meeting them outside."

Their conversation was interrupted as Georg and several of the other boys caught up to them.

They walked together until the swell of the crowd on Unter den Linden came into view. They managed to push up near the front, with the help of the Brownshirts on duty, and were able to see Hitler's car as it passed. The crowd roared as he glided by, dressed in his familiar brown uniform.

Harald turned to Fiona after the cars disappeared down the road. "What a time to be alive! We truly are the most fortunate generation."

She could only smile by way of reply. They stayed another few minutes before walking farther down the newly christened Via Triumphalis to see what else this wondrous day would bring. Ten minutes later, it was time to leave. Fiona promised to see Harald soon, and the smile he gave her in return lit her heart all the way to the Olympiastadion.

4

Saturday, August 1

Seamus took Fiona's hand and pointed out the
Olympiastadion as the massive structure came into
view. Lisa and Maureen were smiling in anticipation,
and Conor was hopping from foot to foot. The atmosphere
among the crowd was electric. The feeling that they were about
to witness something extraordinary was palpable.

This was it—the culmination of years of hard grind,
running miles every day. Working with weights and countless
hours with Voss, his coach. Michael would be walking out
with the rest of the German team in an hour or two. Seamus
imagined Marie, Michael's mother, and what she would think
if she were here today. She died before any of this even
seemed possible. What did she know of her son's athletic
prowess? It was hard to remember her recognizing his talent.
He heard her soft Irish brogue in his memory and realized
how strange it was to love so completely, not once but twice in
a lifetime.

The gates opened and the fans moved as one.

"I can't believe this is happening. My kid brother!" Maureen said.

None of them answered, but Seamus knew they were all thinking the same thing. He looked at his watch as they entered the arena. It was almost three thirty.

"I heard they modeled the arena on a Roman amphitheater," Lisa said to him.

"Let the circus commence," he replied.

"Look at that!" Fiona said.

A massive zeppelin was circling above the stadium. A show of German technological genius, the Hindenburg was over 800 feet long—one of the biggest airships ever built.

Seamus picked up Hannah, his six-year-old stepdaughter, and held her as they showed their tickets and moved through turnstiles. She gasped as they entered the arena.

"It was impressive before, but now..." Conor said.

The new Olympic Symphony Orchestra was set up on the field to entertain the spectators as they took their seats. The sound of Wagner swelled the air. It was hard to escape Hitler's favorite composer in the Reich these days.

The Ritter family found their place in the stands, about halfway up, opposite the box seats where the dignitaries and one living demigod, in particular, would soon sit. Maureen had the good sense to keep her comments about the Nazis to herself. She seemed to realize that today was about her brother's achievements, not the regime that was using the games to glorify itself in front of the world.

As the massive clock on the stadium's marathon tower struck 3:53, trumpets and trombones positioned high up in the stadium began a loud fanfare. Seamus couldn't help but feel swept up in the moment. He gripped his wife's hand beside him and she smiled back, apparently captured by the same spirit. The sound of the brass instruments continued until exactly 4:00, when Adolf Hitler, along with high-ranking members of

the International Olympic Committee, entered the stadium
and strolled down the massive steps of the Marathon Gate. The
crowd roared its approval and stood as one to offer the salute,
but the despot seemed not to notice, instead bending down to
receive flowers from a little girl. The Ritter family joined with
those around them, putting their arms in the air. Only Fiona
said the words, however—something they'd agreed on before
they arrived.

Hitler and the other men took their box seats and the
orchestra on the field began to play the new double anthem
introduced by the Nazis. Everything had changed under the
National Socialists, so why shouldn't the national anthem?
They amalgamated two original verses of "Deutschlandlied"
with their own "Horst Wessel Song," a ballad to an SA street
thug shot in the head by Communists in 1930.

Around the stadium, the flags of the competing nations
were raised.

"Here they come!" Conor shouted.

The Greek national team emerged from the corner of the
stadium, their flag held aloft, and marched to the adulation of
the crowd. All of the athletes offered the Hitler salute as they
passed the Führer. Not all of the teams did, however. The
contingent from Great Britain drew boos as they marched past
without offering the greeting that had become a daily part of
life in the Reich. The Americans similarly kept their arms at
their sides, but Seamus and the children were on their feet,
cheering the American team as they marched past nonetheless.
He never realized until that moment how much he wanted his
son to be among their number, but this wasn't the time for
regrets.

The French team, who seemed happy to salute the dictator
watching from the stands, received a rousing welcome. Most of
the crowd around them had their arms aloft almost all of the

time, and the screams of "Seig Heil!" were deafening as they rebounded around the stadium.

The loudest cheer of the day was reserved for the German national team, who came out decked head to toe in white suits and matching military-style hats.

"There he is!" Maureen roared as they marched around the track to where the Ritters were sitting. Michael was in the third row of men, marching in perfect time with his arm held aloft. Seamus shouted down through the din, and his son seemed to recognize them. He waved up, the solemn look on his face melting into a smile as he used his arm to wave instead of salute.

"It's Michael!" Hannah roared, and Lisa was crying.

Seamus felt a swell of pride, the likes of which he'd never known before.

The German team was the final nation to emerge. They took their place in the field in the middle of the stadium. The head of the International Olympic Committee got up to make a speech that went on for far too long. Hitler spoke next. The crowd fell into a hush, as if they expected him to say something brilliant or profound. They were disappointed when he stumbled through the line declaring the games to be open. He stepped back from the microphone as the Olympic flag was raised and thousands of white doves were released. The boom of artillery guns firing a salute reverberated around the stadium.

"Did you make those shells, Father?" Maureen asked.

Not wanting to get into a fight at this of all moments, Seamus kept his mouth shut.

Lisa slapped her stepdaughter on the wrist but smiled as she did it.

"You ganging up on me?" Seamus's words were lost in the din of the stadium.

A few minutes of Richard Strauss' "Olympics Hymn" later,

the final torchbearer ran through the gate below them. He brandished the flaming torch in front of the crowd, who roared their approval with another deafening round of Hitler salutes with accompanying cries. The athlete ran down the steps and onto the track, leaving a trail of wispy smoke in his wake. The pyre was set at the top of the steps at the other end of the Olympiastadion, and the young blond runner presented the torch to the crowd once more before lighting the flame, which would burn for the duration of the games.

One of Michael's German teammates then climbed up onto a pedestal in the middle of the stadium and recited the Olympic Oath while holding a Nazi flag.

"Isn't that supposed to be the Olympic flag?" Lisa asked, but no one answered.

Seamus felt a weight on his shoulders. If the Nazis could organize a gargantuan international event such as this with such dexterity, using the ammunition he provided them to mobilize for war shouldn't present any problem at all. But what was he to do?

Hitler was still in his seat, observing the spectacle he'd gone so far in creating. The musicians performed the "Hallelujah Chorus" as if it were the only fitting way to honor the demigod walking among them, and then he was gone. The ceremony ended, the flame still burning in the pyre at the end of the Olympiastadion.

~

Saturday, August 1

Not all of the athletes were invited to Goebbels' party, but the track and field competitors were thought of as the elite. So while many of the other members of the German team retreated to the Olympic Village in Wustermark, west of the city, Michael and about fifteen others departed to the hottest party in Berlin. The wrestler who gave the Olympic Oath was brought along too. The fact that he'd held the Nazi swastika while reciting it was bound to make him a hero among the party members in attendance. Michael stood with several other athletes on the ferry over to the island of Pfaueninsel on Lake Wannasse, the venue for the party the Minister for Propaganda was throwing on behalf of the Reich government. The ferry was full of guests dressed in tuxedos, and their glamorous wives and mistresses. It was the only place to be on the first night of the games.

A portly older man with a red mustache approached Michael and his teammate, Alfred Dompert, a fancied 3,000-meter steeplechaser.

A beautiful girl in a red dress, only a year or two older than Michael, stood behind the man as he introduced himself.

"Hello, boys. Erich Miner. I'm in hospitality," the man said. He didn't bother to introduce the young lady, though Michael caught eyes with her over the man's shoulder. "Pleasure to meet you. What are you competing in?"

"I'm a sprinter," Michael responded. "In the 100 meters and the relay."

Alfred told him what he was running, but Miner seemed more interested in what Michael had to say.

"What do you think your chances of getting on the podium might be?" Miner asked.

"Albert has got a good shot. I'd be just happy to get into the final. The Americans are fast."

"Ah, yes. I heard about that negro... Owens?"

"Jesse Owens is the favorite."

"Not with our Führer." Miner laughed at his own joke.

The girl over his shoulder didn't raise a smile and was looking out at the dock. The ferry was no longer the only way to get to the island. Partygoers were streaming across a metal bridge.

"Look at that," the girl said. "That wasn't there last week."

"Yes," Miner said. "Goebbels had engineers build a pontoon bridge across the river especially for tonight."

A company of pages, dressed all in white, was waiting at the dock at the end of the new bridge. Miner and his girl accompanied the boys off the ferry among the throng of people in evening wear. A page greeted them with a bow of his head and offered to show them to where the party was taking place.

As they followed the thin young man, the girl in the red dress walked on the other side of Miner, avoiding contact with the two young athletes. The trees around them were decorated with thousands of butterfly-shaped lamps, bathing the branches and trunks in green and yellow light.

"I'm in the hospitality business myself. We didn't get the contract for tonight, unfortunately. Word is that Goebbels spent upwards of 320,000 Reichsmarks on the event tonight," Miner said.

"What?" Albert gasped.

"I know. Isn't it impressive?"

In a country where two-thirds of Germans earned less than 1,500 Reichsmarks a year, Michael wondered if *impressive* was the right word, but he kept his thoughts to himself.

The page led them to a clearing, decorated like a fairy-tale world from one of the books Michael's mother used to read to him when he was young. Dozens of tables with pristine white tablecloths were laid out, and everywhere were guests and waiters delivering them fine wine and champagne—all at the expense of the German taxpayers.

Miner took the girl's arm and bid them farewell. "Must network with the business people. Maybe we'll have a drink later?"

"I hope we do." Michael looked at the girl, but she just

stared past him, a deeply melancholic look on her pretty face. He stood and watched as the pair turned away to mingle with a group of well-dressed revelers. She stood off to the side, only nodding a greeting when Miner introduced her.

"Don't!" Albert said with a chuckle. "That's the last thing you need with the heats around the corner. There'll be plenty of time for girls when the games are done, and won't they be impressed if we have medals hanging around our necks?"

Michael laughed and followed his friend over to a drinks table, covered in wine and beer bottles. Several butlers dressed in tuxedos stood on hand to pour the drinks, of course. If champagne was more to a guest's taste, several fountains of glasses were prepared, and as people took glasses from the top, more were set to replace them.

A massive kitchen tent stood behind the tables, and the menu was steak and chicken, prepared by some of the finest chefs in Berlin.

"I thought the Nazis were the party of the people," Albert muttered as they perused the food on offer.

"Only when they need to be. Marie Antoinette would be embarrassed by the extravagance on view tonight."

But why not enjoy the experience while they were there? It wasn't every day they were invited to the most exclusive party in Berlin. Michael mixed with the other guests, repeating the same lines over and over about how his training for the race was going and how strong he expected the Americans to be. One man in top and tails implored him to win as a "lesson to the lesser races." Michael nodded his head and moved on.

Goebbels made a speech after dinner and introduced the members of the German team in attendance. The joke he made about them not indulging in the free alcohol was greeted with a chorus of laughter from the many people who already had. The athletes all stood up as the crowd of 2,000 or so gave them a stirring round of applause. The speech ended with yet another

Hitler salute, and the German Olympic Team members sat back down. It was strange to be used as a prop, but Michael dismissed it as the price they had to pay to gain admission to parties like this. Everyone was here for a reason. Some, like Miner, to promote business interests or to rub shoulders with the higher-ups in the party. At least Michael and the others knew why they were sitting at that table eating the finest food some of them ever had.

An orchestra played as the patrons ate, and dancers performed on a raised stage, one of several that had been erected for the occasion.

"You think this is all for us?" Albert asked with a smile.

"I think it's for them. We're the equivalent of that pretty girl on Herr Miner's arm—here to make our hosts look good."

"It's a great party, though," Erich Manteuffel, a fellow 100-meter runner, said from across the table. "I'll bet the American team is home in bed right now. Maybe you should be too, being a Yank."

Michael ignored him. He was used to the digs about his nationality and was done defending himself. Did he want to be an American or a German athlete? He'd reevaluate once the games were done. For now, he was representing the Reich.

After dinner, the army of pages and butlers cleared the tables and a swing band set up on one of the stages. The center of the clearing was transformed into a dance floor, and soon hundreds of revelers were pulsing to the music. The mixture of old men and glamorous young showgirls was comical to watch, and Michael stood to the side with several of the athletes making jokes among themselves.

Midnight soon came, and the massive fireworks display began. The athletes, along with the other guests, watched the dash of colors illuminate the night sky above them. When it seemed like the show would end, it continued on and on. Michael had the idea to return to the lake to watch the shimmering reflections of the pyrotechnics on the water. The thundering booms of the fireworks echoed in his ears as he retraced his steps back to the jetty. The crowd grew thinner as he walked, until he was almost alone—apart from a few couples with the same idea as him. He almost reached the new pontoon bridge when he saw her. The girl in the red dress, Miner's date, was standing alone, with her arms on the metal railing of the bridge. A massive explosion over their heads lit the sky and lake blood-red.

"Hello again," Michael said.

The girl turned, her auburn hair loose around her shoulders. Her pale skin shone as the fireworks burst above them once more.

"Hello."

"You mind if I join you?"

"You're the runner Erich was talking to earlier."

"Yeah, here to be presented to the partygoers. One of the many attractions tonight. I'm Michael Ritter."

"Monika Horn." She turned back to face the lake. "You're American?"

"It's that obvious, is it?"

He came closer, waiting for her to tell him how she knew, but she stopped talking.

"Have you known many Americans in the past?" he asked.

"You might be my first," she said. "I've seen a lot of movies, and tried to learn the language from them."

The sky lit up as bright as day for a few seconds. It was difficult not to stare at her.

"What are you doing here? Are you...?"

"A prostitute?"

"No, I wasn't suggesting that at all."

"I have my reasons for being here. I met Miner a few weeks ago at a club in the city." She turned to him. It was hard to tell if she had tears in her eyes or if the reflection of the lake made them look wet. "Are you a Nazi?"

"No. God, no."

"What's America like? Do they have men who parade around in uniforms and lock people up for thinking differently?"

"No, they don't."

"Do they all greet each other using the president's name? Who is it again?"

"Roosevelt. No. Nothing like that. We moved here back in '32, just before the Nazis came to power."

"And now you're running for them?"

"Not for them. For me. For the people in the stands."

"Same difference. You got a cigarette?"

"I don't smoke."

"Of course. What was I thinking?"

A cascade of red and gold lit the darkness above their heads. A loud *bang* followed.

"Sounds like artillery fire, doesn't it?" Michael asked.

"Maybe it's a sign of things to come."

Michael wasn't sure in his mind whether he should ask the question, but what did he really have to lose? "You mentioned you had your reasons for being here?"

She laughed. "It's not working out well so far. It seems the esteemed Reich minister only has eyes for a certain Czech actress."

"You wanted to meet Goebbels?"

She turned to him and hesitated as if evaluating what she was to say next. "Not for... Only for what I can get out of him. That club-footed little troll doesn't exactly set my heart racing."

Michael realized it was time to meet up with the other athletes. "I should get back to my friends."

"You have to leave?"

She wanted him to stay? He decided to ask the next question too. The idea of wasting his night with some Nazi hanger-on didn't appeal to him, no matter how beautiful she was. "What do you want from him?"

"It's not going to happen now."

A tear ran down her cheek. He took one step closer and stopped. The fireworks continued swirling and booming in the night sky above them. He didn't ask again, just waited for her to speak.

"It's for my father." A sob escaped from her mouth. Her face contorted in pain, and the tears came in earnest.

He wanted to step forward, but realized he didn't know this woman at all.

"Your father?"

"He was taken to one of the camps in '33. I just thought if I could meet Goebbels... I heard his reputation, and I'd do what I had to for my father."

Michael looked around to make sure no one was listening. They were still alone.

"Is he...a Jew?"

"No." She shook her head. "He was a trade union leader."

It seemed that after more than 30 minutes of fireworks, the denouement was finally upon them. The banging in the air increased, and he could see Monika as clearly as if it were after-noon now, but neither of them looked up into the sky. Frustra-tion coursed through the young man. He wanted to reach out, to somehow ease the pain he saw in her, but what could he do? He searched his mind for something he could offer.

Albert's voice from behind him interrupted his thoughts, and Monika looked up as though they'd been caught performing some illicit act.

"There you are," the steeplechaser said. "And look who you're talking to. We're heading back to the ferry now."

Michael looked at Monika, knowing he should leave. "Maybe I'll follow you on."

"Are you sure, Ritter? Coach Voss will skin you alive if he finds out you stayed out late."

"Only if he finds out, and I won't be long. I'm just going to see the lady home. Where do you live?"

"Lichtenberg."

"The complete opposite direction from the village," Albert said.

Michael shrugged.

"Ok, your funeral. See you tomorrow. Don't blow this—you've worked too hard." Albert turned and jogged back toward the party.

"Listen to your friend," Monika said after he left. "Miner will be looking for me. I'm not worth it."

"Do you want to leave with him?"

"Not even a little bit."

He went to her and held out his hand. She took it.

"We can leave together, right now. He won't be any the wiser."

"I don't have any money for a taxi. He was my ride back to the hotel."

Michael didn't want to ask what the sleeping arrangements might have amounted to there.

"Is there someone you can call to collect you?"

"No. My mother's dead. I've been alone since my father went to the camp."

"You have no one?"

She shook her head. "But I don't want to go back with that old man. I know what he's expecting. I thought I could do it, but—"

"Ok," Michael said. "I don't have much money on me either, but we'll figure something out."

"You don't even know me."

"Does that matter? Come on."

Still holding hands, they traversed the bridge back toward

Wannsee, far from the Olympic Village and even farther from her home in Lichtenberg. A few people from the party were also walking over to the mainland across the new bridge, and Michael adjusted their conversation to reflect the loss of their privacy.

"You don't have any brothers or sisters?"

"No. Do you?"

He smiled. "Three sisters and a brother. My littlest sister is a step. My mother died, back a couple of years before we moved here, and my father remarried six months after we arrived."

"I'm sorry about your mother."

"How long is yours gone?"

"Since I was ten."

They reached the other side of the bridge. Two dozen cars sat parked on what was usually an isolated back road. Not many people were around, except for a few drivers throwing dice in a small circle.

"Let me try something," Michael said.

The chauffeurs didn't look up as he approached them. "Any of you driving back toward Lichtenberg? The lady needs a ride home."

One of the men peered over at her. "Not going that way. And even if any of us were, how would it look if we just left without our clients?" The driver got back to their game.

One of the other couples from the bridge got into a car together. Michael went to the window, but they were going in the opposite direction. By the time he got back to Monika, all the other people from the bridge were gone too.

She was pacing up and down. "I really don't want to hang around here. Miner's going to come looking for me soon. I don't want to see him."

"What happened tonight?" he asked. "Why can't you bear to see him?"

She looked around, taking a few seconds to answer. "I think I realized who I was, and what I couldn't do."

She began to walk away and he hurried after her. The glare of the party was far behind them now. The only light was the stars, which dotted the sky like diamonds laid out on black velvet.

"We're in the middle of nowhere," she said without the slightest strain of worry in her voice. She seemed happier now than at any point since he'd met her. "I don't care if I have to walk all the way home, but you need to get back to the Olympic Village. Go and find your friends before they leave."

"I have one more idea."

Dr. Walz's summer house was a short walk away. He'd died without a will, so as his nearest relative, Michael's stepmother, Lisa, had automatically inherited the house. But she never wanted to talk about it, let alone bring the family down to visit on warm summer weekends. So it was sitting vacant only fifteen minutes away, and Michael knew where the spare key was hidden.

"I know somewhere we can stay for a few hours, and go home in the morning when the buses start up again. My late grandfather's house by the lake is empty."

"You're luring me back to an empty house? Is this something you do often?"

"Only on the opening night of the Olympics."

"So, only every four years? That's not a lot."

"Yes. I was fourteen last time. What age were you?"

"The same."

They continued in silence for a few moments. The darkness of the trees on either side of the road seemed to envelop them, choking out the light from the moon and stars. They kept the lake on their left as they walked, and soon the glow of several houses came into view.

It was a strange feeling, coming back—almost like returning to the scene of a crime.

"This is it," he whispered as they rounded the corner to the driveway. The house sat still, the lake lapping the shore beyond the now-overgrown lawn.

"You haven't been here in a while, I take it?"

"It's a long story."

"Too many other lakeside mansions to choose from on your weekend jaunts from the confines of the city?"

"Too many ghosts."

"I know that feeling."

The key was under the third flowerpot by the front door. The interior was musty, dark, and absolutely still, and he went upstairs with her by his side. The beds were still made from the previous summer. Untouched since.

An awkward moment standing by the bed was broken when she suggested they go down to the jetty to look out at the lake. He fought back the thoughts of sleep and the heats for the 100 meters in two days and agreed.

He led her to the back door and threw it open. "Your kingdom, M'Lady." She laughed.

They trudged through the knee-high grass until they reached the jetty. The lake shimmered and shone black and silver in front of them.

"So, you wanted to be Goebbels' girlfriend?"

"Sounds pathetic, doesn't it? I miss my father so much. All his colleagues have been released. I just thought if I could get the ear of someone influential..."

"Isn't Goebbels married?"

"Strictly speaking. Rumor is, Hitler is his marriage counselor. It doesn't show well for the regime if the happily married father isn't faithful. But I couldn't even catch his eye tonight. He was all over that Czech actress like a five Reichsmarks suit."

"What are you going to do now?"

"I don't know. I've written letters, talked to the police, judges, and even tried to use the one thing I have left—my body. But it doesn't seem like anything's going to work."

"I don't know what pull I have, but I'm on the Olympic team. I could try to talk to someone. What's your father's name?"

"Casper Horn. He was head of the Bricklayers Union before the Nazis destroyed it. He's in the Sachsenhausen camp, northwest of the city. Just got moved there a couple of weeks ago."

She turned to him. "Why are you doing this? You should be in bed with the rest of the athletes."

"Yes, I should."

"Why then?"

"You needed help. I couldn't just leave you."

She reached over and took his arm. He put his hand against the feather-soft skin on her face and then his lips to hers. The kiss lingered. Time, like everything else in the world, fell away.

"We should probably get to sleep," she said when they finally pulled back from one another.

"You're probably right. My first heat is on Monday."

"You're running on Monday? And you're up at what time? Three in the morning? Are you crazy?"

"Maybe." He took her by the hand and kissed her again. "Will you come to the stadium and watch me run?"

"I don't know...."

"Please? It would mean so much to see you in the stands."

"I'll try my best."

He knew he wasn't going to get better than that and was angry at himself for begging. *I'll get her to agree in the morning. No use in pushing her now,* he thought.

They strolled back to the house. The tension between them was palpable, but he showed her to the bedroom where Maureen used to sleep.

"The bathroom's down the hall. If you need anything, I'll be next door."

"Thank you, Michael," she said, standing beside the bed.

"You're welcome. I'll need to be out of here early so my coach doesn't eviscerate me."

"Ok. See you then."

Michael forced himself to leave and shut the door behind him. He went to bed in the room next door, fighting off sleep, hoping she'd come in, but his door stayed closed. He submitted to the tiredness that overtook his body.

The house was silent as he woke. The sun was streaming in through the crack in the curtains. It was almost eight o'clock, and he'd have to deal with the wrath of his coach if he didn't get back soon. His cover story—that he stayed in his parents' house —would only be believable if he got back before the team meeting at ten. Otherwise, the presumption that he'd stayed up too long, perhaps with a beautiful girl, would take over. He jumped out of bed. *Monika must still be asleep*, he thought, but a part of him knew already.

He got into his suit from the night before, the same one he'd worn to the opening ceremony, and went to get the girl he'd risked getting into so much trouble for.

The room was empty. He rushed downstairs. No note. Nothing.

He locked the house behind him and ran to the bus stop, but Monika Horn was already gone. The bus arrived a few minutes later. He looked around one last time, helpless, as he boarded. The thought of Voss and the trouble he was in barely crossed his mind as he rode back into the city. She was all he could think of.

_____

5

Sunday, August 2

Fiona wore her League of German Girls uniform to lunch, knowing full well the reaction it would provoke. The love within her for the Führer convinced her to do this. It was time to prove her point.

"How many times do I have to ask you not to wear that at the table?" Her father's exasperated tone echoed his words. Lisa and Maureen chewed their bread rolls in silence, aware of what was coming.

Fiona snapped back, "And how many times do I have to explain to you how important representing the Reich is to me?"

She knew her allegiance to the National Socialists was a constant thorn in her father's side, but her troop leaders warned her many times that her parents might not understand the wonderful bloodless revolution occurring in the Reich.

"Get up." He sounded like a cruel brute, and she knew she had little choice. The others didn't stand up for her. "You're getting changed."

He put a hand on her shoulder, but she shrugged it off. She'd do what he said—for now.

Her father stood at the door of her room about to close the door when he seemed to notice her tears.

"I'm sorry—"

"Have you any idea how hard it is for me that my friends refer to you as a Jew-lover?"

He looked shocked, but his reaction turned to anger in seconds. "Lisa is my wife! You will respect her!"

"It's not her," Fiona said, eager to correct him. "She's German enough to overcome the Jewish blood in her."

"So, you and your cohorts approve of her? How sweet."

She ignored his sarcasm. "You support so many Jews in your factory. Perhaps they need to get out of this country. There's no place for them here."

Her father seemed stunned. *Does he really know that little about me, his own daughter?* He had no idea how she felt.

"Who do you think Jews are? They're just trying to live their lives."

"I've heard stories about what they do—raping and killing young girls like me and my friends. The reports are all over the papers, but you won't read them!"

Her father stared at her for a long five seconds. His voice was calm as he spoke.

"I'm bringing you to Herr Bernheim's house this afternoon, Fiona."

She looked up in horror. "Why?"

"I want you to spend some time with him and his family."

"But... But I have a meeting—"

"You can miss this one. The League of German Girls will survive having one less little girl at their meeting."

"But it's about the Olympics! We're planning another march down the Via Triumphalis."

"As I said, you can miss one meeting. Now get changed." He slammed the door.

Fiona tried to calm herself, breathing in through her nose and out the mouth as she got changed. She hung her League of German Girls uniform on the closet door. Was she really going to have to miss the meeting? All her friends would be there, asking where she was, and soon, questions about her loyalty would follow. And for what? If her friends heard she was spending her Saturday with a Jewish family, might she be thrown out of her troop?

Some of them were crazy with hatred of the Jews. It wasn't something she thought about too much. But she knew not to question the wisdom of her troop leaders because, as they said, that would be questioning the Führer himself. She had to trust Hitler's vision for Germany.

Her closet door creaked as she peeked in at the poster of Hitler she'd pinned inside. The one her father had refused to allow her to pin to her wall. The Führer's stern countenance offered comfort when she needed it most. If no one else cared about her, at least she knew he always did. If her father and all her siblings but Conor were blind to the miracles he was working in her adopted homeland on a daily basis, at least she could go to her troop members, or even her leaders, for the acceptance she never received here. The thing her father never understood was that everything in her life was through the League of German Girls or Hitler Youth now. Every single boy and girl in school was a member. Who would she be if she left? The answer was simple: a social pariah. It was a fate too horrible to contemplate. So she'd continue to march and salute as all the other children did. An afternoon with Herr Bernheim and his family wasn't going to change that.

The knock came just before one o'clock. Her father's voice bled through the door.

"Time to go."

"I haven't even eaten yet."

"You can have lunch with Herr Bernheim and his family at their house."

Tears of sheer bloody frustration came when he opened the door. "I can't believe I have to miss the march because of this. Are you trying to ruin my life?"

Her father paused to look at her for a few seconds, and shook his head. "I told them you'd be at the house at one thirty. We have to leave."

She sat in the front seat of the car with her arms folded like steel girders across her chest. Her father spoke about opening up her horizons and all the different types of people in the world wanting the same things, but she didn't really listen.

The ride to the Bernheims' house was all too short. Her father got out first and held the door open for her.

"At least don't embarrass me by acting like a child," he said through gritted teeth. "Do me that one favor."

Herr Bernheim was standing at the door, waiting for them. She got out of the car and let her hands drop by her side. The League of German Girls troop leaders said Jews were sexual degenerates who hunted young girls. She remembered the talks they gave, warning them to never let themselves be alone with a Jew. They were on the same level as animals, they said, and couldn't control their primeval instincts. She remembered the drawings of Jews with horns on their heads and hooked noses and backs bent so far over their arms nearly touched the ground. One leader, a pretty blond girl from Wedding, called them *a disease* and said Hitler was the only cure.

Her father walked her to the door. Herr Bernheim's wife appeared beside him, looking like she was trying to smile.

Her father shook his factory manager's hand and kissed Frau Bernheim on the cheek. "Afternoon, my friends. Thanks so much for having us."

"It's a pleasure," Gert said.

Her father nudged her so they couldn't see. "Yes, thank you for having me at your house."

She made the lines seem practiced and unnatural as possible—anything to hurt her father for not letting her attend the meeting.

"Come inside." Frau Bernheim put a hand on her shoulder.

"You remember Ben and Joel?" Their two sons sat at the dining room table and stood as Fiona came in. Her tall and handsome sons extended hands to shake hers. Her father greeted them first.

"Ben's almost twenty-one now, and Joel is nineteen."

"I'm fourteen." She greeted them with a shaking hand.

"We were just on our way out to listen to the games, but I'm glad we met you," Ben said.

The two young men left and Fiona was alone with his father's friends.

"Take a seat," Frau Bernheim said. "Gert, get us some drinks, would you?"

Her husband scuttled into the kitchen.

"You have such a lovely name. I know it's Irish. What does it mean?"

Her father nudged her when she didn't answer.

"It means *fair and beautiful.*"

"It suits you, then," she answered.

Herr Bernheim came back with four glasses of lemonade. Fiona put the sweet drink to her lips, wondering what her League troop leaders would advise her to do in this situation.

"You can call me Lil."

Herr Bernheim sat down beside his wife. What were they going to talk about for the next two hours?

"Do you remember meeting Ben and Joel before?" Herr Bernheim asked.

"When I was younger. I was probably around eight at the time."

"We were looking forward to Ben's wedding this year." His wife's face dropped. "He was meant to marry a wonderful girl from Tiergarten. They had been together since they were fifteen. But when the government passed the Nuremberg Laws last year, they forbade it. Ben is a Jew and his girlfriend was a Protestant. The new laws forbid any relationships between Jews and what the National Socialists call *full-blooded Germans.*"

"Fiona is aware," her father said.

"Do you consider yourself German?" Fiona asked.

"I was born in Berlin, and I've lived here all my life. I can't conceive of being anything else," Herr Bernheim said.

"I wasn't born here," Lil said. "I'm an immigrant, just like you. My family moved here after the pogrom against the Jews in Kishinev when I was a little girl. Have you heard of that?"

"No."

"Do you know what a pogrom is?"

She shook her head.

"It's an organized period of violence against a particular ethnic group—usually Jews—in Eastern Europe or Russia."

Fiona wanted to ask what the Jews did to encourage the people to rise up against them, but drank from her lemonade glass instead.

"My parents wanted a better life for my sisters and me, so they brought us to Germany. My sisters live in Potsdam now, with seven children between them. Would you like some lunch?"

Fiona stayed seated while Herr Bernheim went to the kitchen for bread and cold meats. She was hungry and started in on the food as soon as he put it down.

"What about Ben's wedding?" Fiona asked.

Herr Bernheim and his wife looked at each other before he began. "His fiancée was upset...and broke up with him soon after. She's with someone else now."

"An SS soldier," Lil said with an acidic tongue.

Fiona didn't know what to say. It was hard to know why people shouldn't be allowed to marry, but the words came from the Führer, so they must be for the benefit of the Reich. Perhaps Ben's fiancée didn't really want to marry him at all.

"Ben's been working in a store these last few years. He and Joel both wanted to go to university, but they couldn't get in because of their religion," Herr Bernheim said. "Ben still wants to be an engineer, and we managed to get him into college in Bern in Switzerland. He's starting in a few weeks." Herr Bernheim squeezed his wife's hand and they both smiled again.

"I'm glad."

The visions her troop leaders and school teachers ingrained in her mind didn't tally with who these people seemed to be. Perhaps some bad Jews brought the image of good ones down, like Herr Bernheim and his family? It was a difficult subject.

"Life has been complicated since the National Socialists came to power," Herr Bernheim said.

All the old arguments about Germany retaking its place among the great nations of the world and rebuilding the economy flashed into Fiona's mind, but it didn't seem right to bring them up here and now.

"The SA was a terrible scourge, but after the Night of the Long Knives, many believed that the government was trying to restore some sort of order to the streets," Herr Bernheim continued.

"We thought Herr Hitler wanted to blunt the power of the SA and let a normalcy to life return, but we were wrong. Last year the bans began in earnest. Jews were banned from cinemas, theaters, swimming pools, and resorts. Jewish-owned businesses were boycotted or attacked."

"The store Ben works in has been hit three times—bricks thrown through the front window and slurs painted on the walls. He's been hit and spat on," Lil said. "I'm just glad my parents aren't alive to see it. This was where they brought us to escape the pogroms in Russia—a modern, civilized country. And it was...for a while. The 20s were a wonderful time for us. We bought this house and raised our family. After Gert came back from the war—"

"Wait! You fought in the war?"

"Yes, on the Eastern Front. I never faced off against your father, I'm glad to say. My brother was killed at France's Somme Battle in '16."

Fiona turned away. *He must be lying. The Jews are cowards who don't care about the Reich. They didn't fight in the war! They stayed home and prospered while the flower of Germany's youth gave their lives for a government that surrendered and stabbed them in the back.*

Her father remained silent. "You were in battle?" she asked.

"Would you like to see my uniform? I still have it in my closet upstairs."

Herr Bernheim disappeared for a couple of minutes before returning with an old gray uniform on a hanger. "I was in the Landwehr Corps of the 8th Army. I met this beauty after I returned home." He put a hand on Lil's shoulder. "Is it shocking to you that Jews served in the war?"

"I didn't know."

"My brother died for a country that wouldn't recognize him as a citizen today."

"Did your teachers tell you the Jews don't have any loyalty to anyone but themselves?" Lil asked.

Fiona nodded her head, not knowing whether to speak or not. She imagined her troop watching her, their eyes at the windows as she sat here with a Jewish couple. "They tell me a lot of things."

"How often do they talk about Jewish people?"

"Most days."

"I've often wondered why they're so threatened by us. Do

you know how many Jews there were in Germany at the last census in 1933?" Lil asked.

"I don't."

"Just over half a million. Out of a population of 67 million. That's less than one percent, yet they still talk about us all the time? Do you ever wonder why? You can speak honestly here."

"The Führer is trying to secure the future of the Reich against its enemies. Can I use the bathroom, please?"

Lil showed her to the bathroom upstairs and closed the door. Fiona stood at the mirror, staring at her reflection.

It was a fine line between insulting these people and parroting back the information they wanted to hear. She wanted to tell them that she didn't adhere to the blind anti-Semitism of the National Socialists. For her, it was something to endure as she marched with her friends and performed for the Führer. The hatred many of her fellow troop members harbored toward the Jews was alien to her, but it was easy to ignore. It was more fun focusing on the activities and hand-some boys in their Hitler Youth uniforms, like Harald. She had to trust in her leaders and the Führer himself. The vibrant social life she led made up for so much, but, she supposed, to people like Herr Bernheim and Lil, the boycotts of Jewish busi-nesses and the bricks thrown through the windows of Jewish homes meant everything.

They were still at the table when Fiona returned. Perhaps her father's scheme was working, as she felt sorrow for these people in her heart. But the words of the Führer came to her as she returned to the table. He'd urged the youth of Germany to be strong as steel and steadfast in their dedica-tion to the Reich. Was it possible to be so and stand for the Jews as well?

"We're not particularly religious people," Lil said as Fiona sat down at the table. "We used to attend synagogue on occa-sion, until the baiting from the SA and the Hitler Youth became too much to bear. Have you ever seen anything like that? I know you're in the League of German Girls."

"I've heard people talking about it before."

"What do you think about Lisa's status as a so-called *Mischling*?"

She looked at her father before continuing. "It's ridiculous. The government shouldn't bother the likes of her. She didn't even know..." Fiona was unsure of how to finish the sentence.

"She didn't even know she had Jewish blood?" Herr Bernheim asked. "So should the government include her in their laws if she did know?"

"No. It's a complicated matter."

"Do you see a huge difference between her and us?" he asked. "Or your family and mine?"

"The government has many policies. I'm sure that once they figure things out, your lives can get back to normal."

Herr Bernheim stood up without answering and carried the empty glasses back into the kitchen.

"It's a fine day today," he said from behind them. "Will you go for a ride with us, Fiona? I understand that you might not want your peers to see you out with us, but I can assure you it's not far."

"Ok."

Her father approved with a nod and they left together. She and her father drove behind the Bernheim's car.

Herr Bernheim was as good as his word. The Jewish cemetery was only a minute's drive away. Lil pushed the black gates open and the others followed her. The place drew her in as soon as she entered. It was as if they'd left the city behind. They walked the paved paths under tree branches, past graves from hundreds of years ago. Fiona stopped to look at the writing on one of the stones.

"Herschel Beer. Died in 1838, aged 12."

"I wonder what kind of life he had," Lil said.

"It's just a little farther," Herr Bernheim said.

Fiona began to notice more and more gravestones defaced with paint, or destroyed, but was shocked as they reached their final destination.

"This is the cemetery for the fallen Jewish soldiers of the Great War," Herr Bernheim said. "My brother's final resting place."

About 100 small gravestones lay on the ground. Many bore signs of attack and had irregular edges jutting out where they'd been desecrated. Almost all were daubed with red paint. Fiona bent down to read the word *traitors* on one grave.

"I used to come here to see my brother all the time. But it doesn't seem the same welcoming place anymore."

He pointed down to a grave about five from the end. It was so severely wrecked that she couldn't make out the name.

"I can't read it."

"His name was Herbert, and he died fighting for the Reich when he was twenty."

They stayed at the graveside for a few silent moments before her father brought her back to their car.

He waved to his friends before they left. "How was your afternoon?"

She shrugged.

At home, she retreated to her room. She opened her closet door to look at her poster of the Führer. He wasn't perfect. She knew that already. But he was what Germany needed, and if she withdrew from the League of German Girls, she'd be the loneliest girl in school. Her uniform fit her perfectly. It felt good. Her father's face dropped when she appeared at the bottom of the stairs wearing it.

"I'm going out to see if I can catch the end of my meeting."

He stared at her for a few seconds before agreeing to give her a ride.

6

Monday, August 3

Willi woke with the dawn. It had been mercifully cool in the caravan the night before, and he'd slept a few hours. Joseph and Klaus were still asleep, and Willi climbed over them and into the chill of the early morning air. The smell of sewage was thick in his nostrils as he stretched out his aching shoulders. His father was sitting outside on an upturned crate with the twins Ida and Lena. The police were sitting together by the half-built fence that snaked around the exterior of the camp. Ida was scratching a lesion on her face as Will sat next to her.

"That still bothering you?" he asked.

"It's getting worse."

They were all filthy. His father's previously clean-shaven face was covered in thick stubble, and the girls' hair was wild and unkempt. Everyone had skin irritations of some sort, and a few of the families were isolated from the rest when someone noticed lice in their hair.

"When are they going to give us running water? The Nazis

aren't building any pipes—just forcing us to construct fences, and barracks," his father said. "It doesn't seem like they have any intention of bringing water here."

"Did you speak to the head of the guards?"

"Herr Spender doesn't know any more than we do." His father threw a stick he was holding into the ashes of last night's fire. "I keep waiting for them to come to speak to us, to tell us what their plans are, or at least how long we'll be here, but nothing."

"We're not going anywhere," Lena announced. "They'll keep us here for the duration of the games and then ship us off to one of the camps."

"Don't talk like that," their mother said as she approached.

"You really think they're going to send us home after this?" Lena asked. "We're vermin to them. They don't want us in their city."

"Or anywhere else," her twin said.

"Get up and make yourselves useful. The buckets are behind the caravan. Maybe we can bring enough water back today to wash that hair of yours."

"Can't the boys do it?" Ida asked.

"It's your turn. Get off your backsides—it's a long walk into town." The girls got up and followed their mother to the caravan.

With no running water in the camp, each family was forced to walk a mile with buckets into Marzahn's town center and fill their buckets there.

"Keep your heads down and talk to no one," their father called after them.

The people from the camp were pariahs. The Roma received the scraps that no one else wanted, and only from one designated butcher and baker in town. Last week, a woman spat at Willi in the butcher's shop.

Willi ran his hand over the rough surface of his chin. They

were all losing weight. His shoulder bones were peeking through his shirt, and his emaciated face seemed more skin and gristle than flesh. The hunger he felt every day was something he'd never known before.

"You'd better get going," his father said. "Don't forget to bring back some sausage as well as bread, and a newspaper too."

A guard shouted an order and his father hurried over to where the other men had gathered. The head of the police guard began addressing them about the work they were to do. Two sets of barracks were already complete. The onus was on the men to complete the rest required to house the prisoners. Willi watched his father pick up a length of wood with another man and then carry it over to nail it into the foundations.

It was time to go. Leaving this place was about the only pleasure he maintained in life now. He lined up with the others who had permission to leave and waited as the policeman on duty signed them out.

"What time will you be returning tonight?" the portly middle-aged policeman asked.

"Ten."

"Be back here by eight."

"My newsstand stays open until nine..."

"Eight o'clock. If you're late, I'll know you've been drinking and you will be punished accordingly."

The officer stamped a pass and handed it to him. Willi walked toward the bus stop, where he waited with several others from the camp. The other commuters stood away from them, but it wasn't bad. No one spat at them or called them names.

Willi got onto the bus and sat alone. No one ever seemed to want to sit beside him. Perhaps because of the smell, or because they knew where he was coming from.

Today is the day.

It had been less than three weeks since his family was taken from their apartment and dumped in that stinking field in Marzahn, but enough was enough. It seemed logical at first to see what would happen. No one knew if they'd be there a night or two before being let go. Then the idea pervaded that they'd be there for the duration of the games, but the police, who didn't seem to know much else, told them they weren't going home after the games. Why were the men working to build barracks to use for two more weeks? It was obvious they were turning it into a permanent settlement. What place was there for them in Germany now? Perhaps his sister was right, and the next *home* for them was to join the others perceived as enemies of the state in the concentration camps.

He had only one card to play, and he had to play it before it was too late. The time to visit Seamus Ritter had arrived. The factory was about 20 minutes on a bike from where he worked on Kurfürstendamm. He would have to take at least an hour away from the stand, even though he couldn't afford to lose a single sale. His heart sank. The thought of not being able to feed his family was enough to make him want to jump off a bridge.

The city was festooned with Olympic and Nazi flags, and the streets were alive with tourists of every nationality. The Peruvian soccer team was strolling along the broad avenue of Kurfürstendamm. Everyone in the city seemed to have a smile on their face. Did anyone know what happened to his family and dozens of others? It hadn't been reported in any of the newspapers he sold. And what if it was? Would anyone care, or would they react like the people in Marzahn—with indifference, or outright malevolence?

It was hard to get caught up in the spirit that seemed to infect everyone who came to the newsstand. The papers were awash with stories of the already successful German athletes, and the Olympic rings were printed above the title of the official Nazi dailies. Willi knew that expressing his genuine emotions to his customers would do little more than get him fired, so he slipped into the role of jolly newsie he had been playing so well for all these years.

During a lull around eleven, he locked up the newsstand and grabbed his bike. Now all he had to do was convince Seamus Ritter to help him, and hope the man had some way of doing that.

~

Sunday, August 2

"There's Michael!" cried Maureen. Even Fiona was on her feet. Seamus picked up Hannah, who called out her stepbrother's name. The feeling of seeing him walk out onto the track was like nothing Seamus had ever known. They roared his name, calling down to him. Michael saw them and waved back. They were directly above him, looking down at the starting line.

"I could die a happy man right now," Seamus said to Lisa.

"Don't do that, please!" She smiled.

The stadium was less than half full for the first day of the 100-meter heats, but the crowd still offered rousing support as Michael and another German athlete were announced.

"Can we go down to him?" Conor asked.

"No!" Seamus responded.

Michael seemed to scan the stands for a few seconds before beginning his warm-up routine. Five other athletes, one from Germany, one from Italy, a Spaniard, and a pair from England, would be vying for the two spots available to advance to the quarterfinals, which were set to take place later that day. The semifinals and the final were scheduled for the following day.

Seamus closed his eyes and took a deep breath. Michael was good enough to make it all the way to the final, but he had to produce to get there. He would be devastated if he went out today.

Coach Voss was on the sideline, the time for instruction over. The starter called time and the runners returned to the starting line. It was up to the athletes now.

"I can hardly breathe," Lisa said.

"Thankfully Michael doesn't seem nearly as nervous as we are!" Maureen said.

She took Fiona and Conor's hand as the starter raised his gun. Seamus held his breath. The gun sounded, and Michael was off like a hare from a trap. His legs propelled him forward at an almost frightening pace, and the entire crowd was on its feet. Seamus could barely hear himself shouting as Michael took the lead at the halfway point. The other German runner was on his shoulder, and the two runners streaked ahead of the rest. Michael let up a few yards from the line, seemingly happy to let the other German win.

"Yes!" Fiona roared, and the entire family was jumping up and down in their seats.

Michael was bent over with his hands on his thighs.

"All he had to do is come in the top two in the second race, and then the next, and he's into the final!" Conor said.

"Oh, is that all?" Fiona said with sarcasm in her voice. "And then all he has to do is run faster than the best sprinters in the world and he'll win the gold."

"Let him have this moment, Fiona." Seamus patted Conor on the head. "Come on, let's go see him."

Seamus got up and shimmied past the people sitting in their row until he reached the stairs. The rest of the family followed, and seconds later they were at the bottom, waving at Michael, who was still at the other end of the track. He saw them and jogged over. Seamus hugged him across the railing. His son had barely raised a sweat.

"That was incredible!" Lisa said.

"I'll need to tighten up if I'm going to get through the next one," Michael answered.

Coach Voss came to the railing. "Great to see you here. I need my athlete back now. We need to prepare for the next race."

"We'll be right here," Seamus said.

Conor was gazing at his brother in wonder. It was as if the young boy hadn't comprehended what qualifying for the Olympics entailed until he saw it with his own eyes.

"Anyone else here for me?" Michael asked.

"No, only us. Were you expecting someone else?" Seamus asked.

"Just wondering." Voss touched him on the shoulder again. "I have to go."

"Good luck later on. What time is the quarterfinal?" Lisa asked.

"Four forty," Voss said.

"I'll see you later," Michael said, and the two men jogged toward the changing rooms together.

The family returned to their seats. "I'll go get us some refreshments," Seamus said. "Maureen, I could use another pair of hands."

"Couldn't we all?" she replied. "Lead on, Father."

They walked out of the stadium to where the food and beer stalls were set up. Neither spoke until they were clear of the crowd.

"Do you ever feel like a hypocrite?" Maureen began.

Seamus was taken aback by the question. He'd been expecting something about the race, but then, with Maureen, the unexpected was standard.

He looked around to make sure no one was within listening distance. When he was satisfied they were alone, he responded, "What do you mean?"

They passed under one more Nazi flag in a line that circled

the stadium. "We're giving our support to the regime when so many people around the country are suffering."

"We're not here for the regime, we're here for Michael."

"I know that, but I can't help thinking about Hitler in that box and the crowds calling out his name. It feels like just being here, we're complicit."

"These flags hanging everywhere and the Führer declaring the games open... Those things don't delegitimize what these athletes have done to get here. The Nazis don't negate the work your brother has put in over the last few years so he could run in that stadium."

"What about the crimes they've committed? No one's talking about them anymore," she said in an angry whisper. "What about what I saw with my own eyes last summer? You think that's over? What about the new camp they're building in Sachsenhausen, only 30 minutes' drive from here?"

They stopped walking and stood near a pillar. "Today isn't about the Nazis—it's about the life we can create without their interference. They can't steal everything from us. You ask me if I feel like a hypocrite, Maureen? Yes. Every day. I know I'm profiting from arming their soldiers, but what other choice did I have?"

"I'm not blaming you."

Her words were like ointment on an open wound. He paused a second to take them in. "I know as well as you do what the Nazis are doing to this country. One of my best friends is a Jew, and my wife is a *Mischling*. A reckoning will come one day. All this will come crashing down, and I just hope I'm not judged for what I've done here."

"You won't be."

"America is there for us. It's a safety net we have that few others do, but I know you don't want to take it."

"Thomas is here. He's enough reason to work harder to make this country better."

"Have you ever talked to him about leaving?"

"He doesn't want to."

"That's not what I asked."

"He wants to leave about as much as Lisa does, but I suppose we'll do what we have to."

His daughter motioned toward the concession stand. "I think I need a beer."

"It's on me," Seamus said with a smile.

She walked past him, but he caught her arm. "Maureen, promise me one thing. Be careful."

"Of course."

"No. I know this seems like a game, and that you want to cure this country of all its ills, but these people don't mess around. If they find out one word, you'll end up in a concentration camp, like Hans Litten."

"Your old friend? You haven't mentioned him in so long. Is he still—"

"He's still alive, but he's been in prison since the Reichstag burned down. I can't let you end up like him. I won't."

"It's ok, Father. I know what kind of people the Nazis are. Better than most. I'm sorry, I shouldn't have started the conversation."

"I'm glad you did. I just wish we could have it with more people."

Two SS men strode past in their black uniforms. *Enough.* He continued to the concession stands and got the food and drinks.

The next race was several hours later, and they stayed in their seats watching the other qualifying rounds. The black American athlete, Jesse Owens, was greeted with an enthusiastic reception from much of the crowd, and he seemed to use it as fuel and blew the other runners away in his heats.

"I wonder what our beloved Führer will make of him if

Owens wins the Olympic blue-ribbon event," Lisa whispered to her husband with a devilish smile.

"If he wasn't running against my own son, I'd be cheering him on," Seamus replied so only she could hear. The words seemed to delight her, and she kissed him on the mouth.

Michael emerged onto the track at four thirty, looking as determined as one human being could be. Seamus couldn't speak as his son began his prerace routine.

"I just hope he isn't as nervous as you are!" Lisa said.

The five minutes before the race began seemed like an eternity, but the now-much-expanded crowd finally fell into a hush. The athletes crouched down, and the starter fired his gun. Seamus needn't have worried. Michael had never run faster. He came in second to a Japanese athlete and the family leaped in the air once more. The relief and joy were palpable among them and they became one, hugging each other with shaking arms as the little kids yelled out. They went down to Michael again, and this time his face was a mirror of what they felt. He was going to the semifinals the next day.

They stayed another hour before deciding to get Hannah home. The little girl was tired. They all were, and nothing could live up to what they'd already seen that day.

They arrived at the house just after six thirty. The euphoria of the stadium had given way to tiredness, and no one spoke as they got out of the car to drag their tired bodies up to the house. The family spilled inside. Conor and Hannah made straight for the kitchen. Seamus was last in, and the phone rang as he walked past it.

It was Gert Bernheim, the factory manager. "We were all listening on the radio. The factory floor erupted when he came in."

"It was an incredible day."

"There's something else," Gert said. "Someone came to see

you this afternoon. Left a note for you. He said to tell you his name was Ernst Milch."

"What?" Images of the man Lisa killed in self-defense flooded his mind. He fought to regain his composure before he spoke. "Wasn't that the same name as Otto Milch's son who disappeared? Surely it wasn't him?"

"I did have that thought myself, but no, a much younger man. Only looked about eighteen, so the name is a coincidence. Dressed in old suit. Scrawny. He said it was urgent."

"You have the note? I'll be over in ten minutes."

Eight minutes later, he was at Bernheim's door and his friend answered. He handed him the note. "He said it was for your eyes only."

"Did Helga—"

"Not a thing."

He thanked his friend and returned to his car. He waited until he was behind the wheel to open it.

Come to the newsstand on Kurfürstendamm by the Kaiser Wilhelm Memorial Church tonight before 7. I know what you did on Würzburger Strasse. We need to talk.

He hearkened back to the night in '32 when Ernst Milch died at Lisa's hand, the woman Seamus asked to marry him six weeks later. The world was a better place without men like Ernst. Son of Otto Milch, one of the richest men in the city and one of Seamus's most bitter rivals, Ernst was a Nazi who met Lisa when she was working as a dancer in the famous Haus Vaterland nightclub. When Lisa's mother took ill, he had the money for the operation she needed. Lisa did what need dictated to save her mother's life, then fell pregnant with Hannah. Though Ernst denied fathering the girl, he insisted their affair continue and gave her money to support their daughter. Lisa's attempts to end the arrangement were met with threats, and eventually violence, and he died on the floor of the apartment they used to meet in after trying to strangle her.

With no one else to turn to, Lisa came to Seamus, and they disposed of his body together. The one witness was a homeless man called Bruno Kurth, who resurfaced in '33 to try his hand at blackmailing Seamus—first for money, then for a job in the factory. Bruno died under suspicious circumstances when Lisa's father took him back to his office after the war veteran showed up drunk to work at Ritter Metalworks and caused a fuss. No one could prove it, but Seamus knew the doctor murdered him. Perhaps to protect his daughter, or maybe just as one of his twisted experiments. They would never know. He'd thought the specter of Ernst Milch had faded from their lives.

Was he about to walk into some kind of a trap? Who wrote this? A young man? It seemed the answers were on Kurfürstendamm. He put the car into gear and drove into the city.

The avenues were alive with tourists, and the café terraces were full of patrons chatting and dancing in the warm summer air. It took a few minutes to find a parking space, and when he did, it was two blocks away from the news kiosk. It seemed a strange place to meet.

Seamus tried to keep the thoughts polluting his mind from overtaking it. Would they have to run? No way were he and Lisa ever seeing the inside of a jail cell. Not for her defending herself. A man in a suit beat him to the newsstand counter and flipped a coin into the newsie's hand in exchange for a paper. The young man grimaced as he saw him. The other customer left, and Seamus put the note up on the counter.

"What is this about?"

"You know exactly what this is about, Herr Ritter. And don't waste my time or yours pretending you don't. I don't have long before I need to get back to my family. I've already wasted enough time trying to find you today."

The young man's eyes were swimming with intensity. He knew. Trying to lie to him was pointless.

"What do you want? Money?"

"I don't want your money. Let me shut the kiosk. We'll find somewhere we can talk before I get back to my family. You have a car?"

"Two blocks away."

"Let's go there, then you can drive me home."

The young man took a moment to deposit the day's takings in a lockbox and pulled down the metal grating to lock the kiosk.

"I'm ready," he said a few seconds later, and they walked together in silence. A cluster of tourists speaking French engulfed them, and they were in the middle of the group for a few seconds.

Every bar and café was packed to the point that people were spilling onto the street. The entire city was bubbling with life. Seamus kept his focus on the sidewalk in front of him, and the newsie was stone-faced as they went. The young man paused at a grocery store to buy a couple of large loaves of bread and a pound of sausage.

"You're hungry," said Seamus.

"It's to feed my whole family. All thirteen of us."

Several awkward minutes later, they arrived at the car and got in. In the privacy of the car, Seamus turned to him. "Who are you? What's your name? It's not Ernst Milch."

"No, it's not. You can call me Willi. Let me tell you what I know first of all. I know you, or your wife, Lisa, killed Ernst Milch. You carried him down the stairs from the apartment on Würzburger Strasse and then got rid of the body."

"You have no proof—"

"Maybe not, but I knew Bruno Kurth. He told me everything."

"Who else knows?"

"No one. I kept my word to him."

"Until now." Seamus didn't disguise the anger and bitterness in his voice.

Willi looked at a battered old wristwatch on his arm. "Only because I need something from you. Start driving."

"How much money do you want? I'm not a bottomless pit."

"I already told you I don't want your money." The earnest look on the boy's face surprised him. "Start the car."

"Where are we going?"

"East. I'll tell you what's going on as we drive."

Still, Seamus didn't start the engine. "If you're taking me somewhere to mug me, you'd better have backup."

Willi shook his head. "I don't want to hurt you. I'm not luring you into some trap. I just want you to drive me home while you listen to me. Please. I don't have much time."

If the newsie was trying to frighten him, he wasn't doing a good job. Maybe he didn't want money? Seamus started the car and pulled out. Willi directed him until they were on the main road to the northeast, then returned to the subject of Bruno.

"Where's Bruno now? Is he still working for you, cranking out guns for Nazis?"

"He's dead." Seamus didn't take his eyes off the road as he spoke. Everything he was doing was deliberate.

The young man didn't speak for a few seconds. "You killed him?"

The temptation to lie to him was difficult to overcome, but he did. "No, not me. It's a long story, and I don't think we're at the sit-around-and-tell-each-other-our-darkest-secrets stage quite yet."

"You don't need to tell me your darkest secrets, Herr Ritter. I know them already."

A rush of fear made Seamus aggressive.

"You want to end up like your friend, kid?"

"Don't threaten me, Herr Ritter. It doesn't suit you. I know you have children, and I have a family too—twelve brothers and sisters. We need help."

"So you try to blackmail me?"

"Take the next right up here." Willi pointed to the turn. "Then just shut up and listen."

"Ok," Seamus said after taking the turn. "You have my attention."

"My two oldest sisters are out of the house, but the rest of us still live with our parents. We used to have an apartment in Kreuzberg until the police came for us. You ever hear of *Gypsy Manhunt Day?*"

"No."

"That's what the police called it. It was a couple of weeks ago. My parents are Roma who settled in an apartment when they married, with all her cousins and other settled Roma living around us. I've never traveled anywhere—never even left Berlin. Until two weeks ago, I'd never even been in a caravan, but then the police came."

"Why? What did you do?"

"Nothing more than be born a Roma and live in an apartment block full of people the Nazis don't consider 'worthy.' Whatever that means. We didn't commit any crimes, Herr Ritter. They took us because they didn't want us in their city during their precious Olympics."

"Until the end of the games? And then they'll release you?"

"They're building a fence around the camp and forcing the men to build barracks. Does that sound like they're planning to let us go in two weeks to you?"

Seamus gripped the wheel with whitened knuckles. A group of Brownshirts strolled by the car, waving a Nazi flag, as they sat at a traffic stop. The SA men passed. Seamus put the vehicle into gear once more and drove on.

"They can't just do that."

"Can't they? Roma are classified the same as Jews—not German citizens."

Seamus gripped the wheel tighter. "I'm sorry for your family, kid, but what does this have to do with me?"

"We need your help."

Seamus shook his head and saw the sign for Marzahn. It was an area of the city he knew nothing about. He couldn't remember ever coming here.

"I've still got a few minutes," Willi said. "Park over here. We'll get a good view of the camp."

When they got out of the car, they were on a hill, and Willi led him across train tracks overlooking a field. Maybe 100 white caravans were laid out in neat rows below. "Welcome to the camp at Marzahn. The kids call it the *Stink Factory*. I haven't thought of a better name."

The stench of raw sewage hit Seamus like a fist, and he had to keep his hand over his mouth and nose.

Several half-built barracks stood in the field behind the caravans. A few men were still working on them as twilight approached. Dozens of people were milling around the site. Scrawny children chased one another, and fires spewed smoke into the sky. A barbed wire fence extended around half of the perimeter. Dozens of men in uniform stood on the periphery, many of them laughing and smoking cigarettes.

"The men are being forced to build the barracks for the police. We have to look after our masters before ourselves. They don't give us food—we have to buy it in town. And water, too."

Seamus looked at the young man again as if to ask him what he was meant to do about this.

"And you have twelve brothers and sisters? You said the oldest two aren't here?"

"My sisters live with their husbands abroad. Agathe is in Sweden. Mildred is in Poland. My father won't allow them to visit. In case—"

"They get thrown in with you."

"Exactly. They can't help us any more than we can help ourselves. We're all sick and dirty. The kids have scabs all over their faces, and rashes on their bodies. I only get out every day to work and to buy food."

"They're building you a prison."

"To hide away the city's dirty secret while the rest of the world revels in the glory of the Nazi regime."

"I still don't know what I can do for you, Willi. This shouldn't be. I wish you and your family were free, but I'm not that powerful."

"You'll think of something."

"I'm sorry, but—"

The boy's face hardened. "Well, you'd better, or else I'll be going straight to Otto Milch."

"You didn't see anything."

"No, but the man who did is dead. If you want to take the chance of Milch and his friends in the police finding out, you go right ahead."

"You could escape when you leave to go to work."

"And abandon my family? I'd rather rot down there. And besides, the police guarding the camp told us that if anyone escapes, their families will suffer. You're a rich man, Herr Ritter. The Reich has been good to you. Time to share some of that good fortune. Come up with a way to help us, and soon. That fence is closing in by the day. It's going to be finished in two weeks. Once it's in place, we'll never get out."

In his desperation, the boy didn't seem to have noticed that he'd just told Seamus exactly how long he would have to wait until he could never trouble him again.

Seamus stared down at the camp, 50 feet below them. He didn't speak for a few seconds. *How many people are down there? At least 500. More.*

"I have to go. They'll start asking questions if I don't show up by eight. Don't forget about Thursday. Come about seven."

"Of course," Seamus said under his breath.

The young newsie left, carrying the bag of food for his

family. Seamus stood by the rail tracks for a few minutes alone, studying the layout of the camp and the movements of the guards. He wondered how many patrolled the perimeter after midnight. The kid was right that once the fence was finished, so was any hope of escape.

The car started and he left the camp at Marzahn behind. The people in the caravans were being starved to death. And for what? Being unacceptable to the Nazis' racial policy? He pulled the car over and put his head on the wheel. Thoughts of Lisa and Hannah and the horror of the unknown flooded his mind.

7

Monday, August 3

Michael was lucky to be in the final. He ran his personal best of 10.7 seconds in the semis and scraped in behind two American runners, Frank Wykoff, and the imperious Jesse Owens, who seemed to glide above the track.

Michael beat the man in fourth by a nose. That was his best. His body couldn't go any faster. Not yet, anyway. Maybe in the next Olympics he'd be able to compete with the Americans. Perhaps he'd be one of them.

Sharing negative emotions out loud wouldn't have been a wise move. Coach Voss would garotte him with cheese wire if he admitted any kind of weakness. Michael kept his mouth shut. He was sitting in the changing rooms before the big race. The clock on the wall was ticking down, and the young man felt a wave of nausea coursing through him.

The Americans—Wykoff, Owens, and Ralph Metcalf—were on the other side of the spacious changing room. Wykoff and Metcalf were pacing up and down, shaking out their legs. Owens was sitting, staring into space as his trainer whispered in his ear. Voss clapped Michael on the shoulder. Erich Borchmeyer, who won silver in the world championships in '34, sat down and laced up his cleats. The great hope of the Nazi establishment, he had a genuine chance of a medal. Michael was here to make up the numbers, but as his father said to him after the semifinal, he was one of the six fastest men in the world now. Nothing could erase that. Anything that happened from here was a bonus.

"This is it," Voss said to them. "It's time."

His two runners nodded their heads. Michael was too nervous to talk.

"Let's go," Voss said.

All six runners and their coaches formed a line at the door. A man in a white bib opened it, and the noise from the stadium poured through like water cascading into a stricken ship.

Michael found himself behind Jesse Owens as they walked down the hallway into the arena.

"You American?" Owens asked Michael in English.

If anyone else heard or understood him, they didn't show it. "Born and raised there."

"Why are you running for Germany?"

Michael wanted to tell him that he wondered why himself sometimes, and that he'd rather have the American singlet on, but the volume of the crowd drowned out his thoughts.

"Good luck," Michael said to Owens. The American returned his gesture with a handshake. Voss stood before them as they emerged into a cauldron of screaming fans.

Michael peered up into the stands to pick out the figures of his family in a sea of faces. They were on their feet, waving down. He drew comfort from seeing them and waved back. Then he ripped his focus from his family and stared down the track. The other athletes were already warming up. He ran down the track, shimmying from side to side.

The Führer was in his box seat beside the head of the IOC. It was no secret that Borchmeyer was his favorite. Michael wondered how the despot would react if he won. The American-born stepson of a half-Jew? He almost laughed as he returned to the starting position.

If the German athlete was Hitler's favorite, Owens was that of the crowd. Hundreds of people were chanting his name as the athletes readied themselves for the beginning of the show-piece event of the games. He didn't seem to notice. His face was pure focus.

The athletes got set. Michael had drawn the lane next to Owens, and he was glad to be able to keep an eye on him. Perhaps if he got a good start and got on the American's shoulder... Anything was possible.

The starter introduced himself and explained the rules.

"A new stop-motion camera system is in place for the games. When the starting gun is fired, it'll send an electrical signal to start the race clock and the camera at the finish line. In the case of a dead heat, the judges will be able to use it to judge the placings."

Michael cleared his head of details and tried to block out the crowd, who had fallen into a hush of anticipation. Ralph Metcalf was on Michael's left side. The American appeared to be praying under his breath.

Michael crouched into starting position. The only sound he could hear now was of his own breath.

The starter broke the silence. "On your marks... Get set..." The gun sounded.

Michael sprang out from the starting blocks, but Owens was already faster. The sound of the crowd filled his ears as Owens sprinted ahead. It was a funny feeling to know you were beaten after 30 meters, but Michael knew that unless Owens and Metcalf both fell, he wasn't catching them. Time slowed to a crawl as he pumped his arms and legs to no avail. The Americans were only extending their lead.

And then he heard a *pop*. It was almost as if someone had shot him from the crowd. An avalanche of pain came from his left hamstring and he felt his body going down. His velocity was too much to stay vertical, and he collapsed to the track. The roar inside the arena didn't fade. He raised his head to see Owens had his arms aloft, but it was impossible to know who came second and third.

Michael raised himself to his feet. His father's words were in his ears—the only thing stopping him from weeping in front of the 80,000 people in the Olympiastadion. He was one of the six fastest men in the world. The sixth fastest, as it turned out. Stabbing pain in his hamstring hobbled him, and the 30 meters to the finish line suddenly seemed a long way away. But he had to finish. After all the hours of training that led him here, he was going to cross that line. He kept on, the pain in his leg restricting him to a snail's pace.

Owens and Metcalf were celebrating at the end of the track. Borchmeyer cut a solitary figure at the side, his face drenched in disappointment. Hitler's seat was empty now. Apparently Jesse Owens' victory hadn't sat well with him.

The sound of the crowd rose again, on their feet. Hundreds started to chant his name, and more and more joined in. Why were they cheering for him? He'd come in last. The determination within him drove him forward, and he noticed even the other athletes had stopped to cheer him on now. He inched closer and could see Jesse Owens' eyes as he encouraged him onward. A white-hot dagger of pain struck, and he collapsed to the track once more. The crowd gasped, and hot tears welled in Michael's eyes. The chant spread through the spectators once more and he heard a voice, saw a figure above him on the track.

"Get up, son," his father said. "You can do this. You can finish."

He held out a hand.

"I don't need it." Michael rose to his feet. The crowd erupted, along with the athletes behind the line. Michael limped onward, the line growing ever closer.

"I'm proud of you," his father said.

He didn't answer. He couldn't focus on anything but getting to the white line. He was out of the relay the week after, and his hope for a medal was gone. All that mattered now was to finish. His father was beside him, but all he offered was moral support. Michael limped on himself.

The crowd's roar came to a crescendo as he collapsed over the line, and Michael was surrounded by the other athletes and trainers. His father helped him to his feet, and between him and Voss, they supported his weight on the way back to the dressing room. Jesse Owens took a break from waving to the adoring crowd to run over. He shook Michael's hand again.

"I'll see you in '40, kid."

"You'd better believe it. I'm coming for you, Jesse," Michael said with a smile.

"You'd make a good relay partner. Just saying," Jesse said and returned to his victory lap.

They were almost at the dressing room when Michael heard a voice calling out to him from the stand by the exit. Monika was standing at the railing, waving down to him. The young athlete tried to shrug off the men supporting his weight, but wasn't sure he could stand.

"Bring me to her," he said.

"A girl," his father said. "I should have known."

"He deserves his fun now," Voss said.

Monika looked luminescent in a white summer dress. Her auburn hair was tied back.

"You came!" Michael shouted up to her.

"I wasn't going to miss this," she answered. "I thought you

were going to win, though. I might ask for my money back."
She smiled.

"You and me both."

"You were incredible," she said over the din of the crowd.
"Just amazing!"

Michael didn't think he'd ever seen anything so beautiful as
her. Even more so in the daylight.

"Where can I find you later?"

"I'll come to the athletes' door. I'll find you."

"I might be an hour or more. I'm going to have to get some
work done on my hamstring."

"Ok."

"We need to get some ice on that leg," Voss said. He kept on
inside, and Monika's face disappeared from Michael's view.

Sitting in a bath of ice water, Michael reflected on the race.
His father was still with him.

"You were an inspiration to thousands today, son."

"I lost."

"You never gave up. You refused to. I'm a happy man, and I
know your mother would be too if she were here."

A slow smile spread across the sprinter's face.

Voss came back to critique the race with him and Borchmeyer a few minutes later, but neither man was listening much.
Borchmeyer was finished. He was thirty-two and would likely
retire after the relay in a few days. Michael's thoughts were in a
far different place. The girl in the stands was all he could see.

Voss left after a while, and the ice began to melt.

"What time is it, Father?"

"Almost six."

"I have to go. That girl will be waiting for me outside."

Despite the protestations of his father, the young man got
out of the ice bath and hurried over to his locker to get dressed.
His leg was sore, and he'd walk with crutches for a week or two,

but he'd be all right to run again in two months. But until then, he had more pressing issues.

He dressed in his suit and was ready to go in a few minutes. His father walked out with him and held the door open. Michael scanned the crowd of two dozen people for the girl in the white dress. She wasn't among them. Several fans asked him for autographs. Perplexed as to why, he signed them anyway.

"She's not here, Father."

"I'm sorry. Maybe she's at the other door?"

The crutches would take a little getting used to and Michael's armpits hurt as he arrived at the other door the athletes used. No one stood there.

Voss's voice came from behind him.

"Michael!" his coach shouted. He caught up. "You've been invited to a reception in the American Embassy tonight. You and your whole family." Michael looked at his father. "You should go," Voss said. "Enjoy the fruits of what you've sown." The coach handed him an invitation in a crisp white envelope. His father took it. "You did well today."

"Thank you."

Michael's father helped him look for Monika for a few more minutes.

"She's not here, son. We need to go home and get ready for this party at the ambassador's house tonight." His father put a hand on the back of his neck. "Don't worry about her. There'll be plenty of young girls at the ambassador's reception tonight, and wherever you go."

Michael tried to raise a smile at his father's words, but couldn't check the sadness in his heart for the girl he hardly knew, but thought about almost all the time.

∼

No one was under any illusions, least of all Michael himself. Going to the American ambassador's reception was a statement, perhaps of loyalty, or intent. Anyone watching would see that. He just wondered if anyone was. He came last—the sixth of six. In the final, all right, but no one would remember him, and he certainly wouldn't have been invited to this reception but for the muscle tear that brought him down at the 50-meter point. The irony that his worst nightmare coming true in the final had brought this measure of fame wasn't lost on him. This wasn't what he'd been dreaming of these last two years, but it was a start.

Jesse Owens would be at the party tonight, and Michael remembered his words about the relay. Perhaps they would be teammates in '40 in Tokyo. Was the race today the culmination of his time here in Germany? He'd hidden behind his training regimen since he was fifteen and turned his head to the abuses of the Nazi government. They'd been a necessary evil until now.

He got off his bed and hopped over to his closet. A row of running singlets were hanging together, each with the swastika emblazoned across the front. He plucked one from its hanger and held it in his hand.

"They're everywhere," he said under his breath, staring at the black swastika on the red background. "I saluted like everyone else—almost everyone else."

What now? The Reich Labor Service would come calling soon. Most of his friends who'd grown up in the Hitler Youth were now in the middle of their six months of service to the Reich. Many of the rest had been drafted into the swelling ranks of the army. Soon, he would be building roads in Bremen or tilling the land in Saxony, all in military formation.

He took a letter from his friend, Artur, from his drawer. His old pal from his troop was in the countryside north of Essen. The letter was likely censored, but Michael read between the lines. It was dripping in sarcasm. Artur wanted to be a lawyer like his father.

MICHAEL,

HERE I AM—WORKING ON A FARM LIKE I ALWAYS WANTED! YOU KNOW ME, MY DREAMS BEGIN AND END TILLING THE FIELDS AND THRESHING HAY! STILL, AT LEAST I'M GETTING A FEW PFENNIGS FOR MY TIME. A HUNDRED OF US ARE HELPING TO RESTORE THE LAND. THIS PLACE IS ENORMOUS. IT NEVER SEEMS TO END. ANOTHER FIVE MONTHS HERE. I'VE NEVER BEEN SO EAGER FOR CHRISTMAS BEFORE. I'LL BE HOME WITH MY FAMILY, AND WE'LL SHARE A BEER WITH THE BOYS TOGETHER. GOOD LUCK WITH THE TRAINING. I'LL TRY AND LISTEN IN, ALTHOUGH THE ELECTRICITY HERE AND RADIO RECEPTION ARE SPOTTY AT BEST. NO DOUBT THEY'LL SET US TO WORK FIXING THAT SOON ENOUGH!

YOUR FRIEND,

ARTUR

Michael replaced the letter in his drawer and put on the suit laid out on his bed. The prospect of a future toiling for the Reich, or even being drafted into the military, wasn't one he relished. But what to do about it? He could ride out six months and then see...or was it time to make a move back to America now and start training for the Tokyo games? Jesse Owens would be twenty-six then, but he'd only be twenty-two and ready to challenge the best in the world. Today was a brave start, but only that. His running journey wasn't ending here, but perhaps his affiliation with the Reich might be.

He buttoned up his best shirt and put on the blue tie Lisa bought him for Christmas the year before. Monika drifted into his mind as he dressed. He imagined seeing her at the party and whisking her off her feet. But he put her out of his mind. He was sick of her letting him down. First leaving without saying goodbye, and then not showing up after the race. But she'd come to see him and made sure to speak to him from the stands. Trying to work out a woman's intentions was like trying to read Chinese writing—impossible and a waste of time. He pretended not to care and reminded himself of all the other pretty girls he'd meet tonight. Lying to himself was easier than he thought it'd be. Believing his own lies... Now that was the trick.

A knock jarred him from his thoughts.

"Are you ready yet?" Maureen asked through the door. "Boys are meant to get dressed quickly. I've been waiting for ten minutes."

"Just a minute." He slipped on his jacket.

It was frustrating not to be able to walk, and he was already getting blisters from the chafing of the crutches under his armpits. He made his way over to the mirror on the wall.

"Forget about her." He turned for the door.

Everyone was ready except Lisa, who insisted on putting Hannah to bed herself despite the babysitter who'd come over at the last minute.

"I still don't see why I can't come," Fiona said with her arms crossed.

"Because people will be drinking and smoking, and it's not for fourteen-year-olds," her father said.

"Yeah, and your Nazi heroes won't be there either, so what's the point?" Michael asked.

"Cut it out," his father snapped.

Michael knew he shouldn't have said that, but didn't apologize. His sister gave him a look that could turn milk sour. She flopped back onto the couch and turned up the radio so loud that no one could talk. Another fight with their father ensued, and Fiona stormed off to her room.

"Have a good time," Conor said.

"We will," Maureen replied.

She was wearing an old evening dress of Lisa's. It fit her well. It was lucky they were both the same size.

"Here she is—the belle of any ball," Michael's father said as Lisa came down the stairs in her red gown.

"She's asleep. Let's get out of here while we still can."

The four of them said their goodbyes, and Lisa went over some last-minute things with the babysitter. Fiona and Conor would both be here, but Michael knew better than to say anything. Why bother?

It was a short drive to Tiergartenstrasse, where the ambassador lived with his wife and grown daughter. The four-story mansion across the street from the park was lit up in white light like a beacon, and they could see it shining from 500 yards away. Michael's father parked the car and presented their invitation to the bouncers at the front gate. The Ritters stepped inside the lavishly furnished house lit up in gold. A butler offered them champagne at the door. Michael picked it up with a smile.

"Here's to the end of training," he said and downed the glass.

Drinking on crutches wasn't easy, but few worthwhile things are.

A young blond woman held her arms out as she saw them. "Maureen, how are you?" The lady hugged Michael's sister and insisted she introduce her.

"This is Martha Dodd, the ambassador's daughter," Maureen said. "We've run in similar social circles before."

Martha shook everyone's hand. "Are you Michael Ritter? From the stadium today?"

"Yes," Michael said with a sheepish grin. This new celebrity status was going to take some getting used to.

"Oh, my goodness, my father is just dying to meet you! Now, where is the old man?" She scanned the crowd for a few seconds before zeroing in on him. "Come with me." She grabbed his arm.

"I'm a little slower on my feet than I was earlier."

Martha laughed. "Of course."

The family followed the ambassador's daughter through the partygoers as fast as Michael could go. William Dodd was smoking a pipe in the corner with some other men in their sixties. The stern look on his face changed as his daughter whispered in his ear.

"Good to meet you, son. That was one incredible thing you did this afternoon."

Michael wanted to remind the man that he lost, but accepted the prevailing optimism on his performance. "Thank you, sir."

"You showed us all the true meaning of guts and determination."

Dodd shook his hand up and down.

"Good to see you again, Mr. Ambassador," Michael's father said.

"Seamus, so good to see you and Lisa again."

Maureen was talking to Martha in the corner, and Dodd waved to her.

Michael stood and talked to the ambassador for a few minutes.

"What now?" Dodd asked. "Are you going to come back and run for America? With them?"

Dodd pointed over toward the US runners who were walking in to the crowd's acclaim. Jesse Owens had his gold medal around his neck and Ralph Metcalf held his silver aloft. It was a strange sight to see the crowd of white people fawning over two black men who wouldn't have been allowed to sit at the same counter as them in many diners back in the States.

Dodd made his excuses. Apparently his time with the sideshow was over, and the real attraction had arrived. Michael understood well enough. It only made him more determined to be the one who walked in with the gold medal around his neck next time.

Michael hopped over to the table laid out with food and did his best to help himself. A few seconds passed before Lisa took pity on him and helped him with his plate. The family sat down together and feasted on the delicious food. His father seemed distracted and wasn't drinking much, but everyone else was having a great time.

After dinner, Michael hobbled into the backyard where a pianist was playing "Clair de Lune" by Debussy. He stood alone. Lisa and his father seemed to be having a fight, though they were trying to hide it. Maureen was off with Martha, who seemed to know everyone his sister wanted to be introduced to. He couldn't stop thinking about Monika and was annoying himself now. The shackles of his training regimen were finally broken, and he was hung up on one girl he'd probably never see again. Michael peered in the window. Jesse Owens was still surrounded by white people in evening dress.

I'll wait.

He knew his fellow athlete would give him time when he had the chance.

Now, go and find a nice girl to talk to.

A pretty brunette was standing 30 feet away—suddenly daunting distance now he was on crutches. He had just started the journey toward her when a large man in a tight-fitting gray suit stepped in front of him. They both apologized, and realization struck Michael.

"Hello," Erich Miner said. The man from Goebbels' party after the opening ceremony smiled and shook his head.

"What are you doing here?"

"My company is catering the event," Miner responded.

Michael hoped this wasn't about to get awkward. The man was standing directly in his way.

"Did you see her?" Miner asked.

"Who?"

"Monika Horn. She came to me yesterday, desperate for a ticket to the final today. Did you at least see her?"

"Yes," Michael said. "She called down to me from the stands."

Miner nodded. "She's something else. I assume you left the party on Saturday with her?"

He didn't know whether to apologize or not. "She wanted to leave."

"It's ok, kid," Miner said. "I understand. She's a beautiful girl. You want a cigarette?"

Michael thought about it for a second before refusing. Drinking was one thing, but he couldn't bring himself to smoke, even when his training was done for the time being.

"She's trouble, though. What did she tell you about me?"

"Just what you expected of her."

"Of course." He shook his head. "Easy to paint me as the villain. Did she tell you she approached me in the club, and not the other way around? Did she tell you she promised herself to me if I'd get her an invite to the Reich minister's party?"

"I'm not judging you," Michael said. "As you said, she's a beautiful girl."

"I'm not sure my kids would agree with you. Their mother's in the grave less than a year, and I'm cavorting with a girl younger than they are. But who was I to resist her?"

The man's face softened, and his mustache was twitching above his lip.

"You want to sit down?" Michael asked and motioned to a couple of free chairs by the musicians.

Miner agreed, and the two men took the seats.

"So, you don't know Monika well?" Michael asked.

"I knew her father a little."

"She told me about him."

"It's such a shame what happened to him. He was a great man."

"Was?"

"Yes. He died a few months ago in a camp—in one of the Reich's new *Konzentrationslagers*."

Michael lost his breath for a moment. A dozen questions came at once like a logjam.

"Why did she want to go to the party? She told me—"

Michael stopped. What had she told him? He realized he'd only assumed her plan to seduce Goebbels was about getting her father out of the camp. If not that, then what?

"Why does any young girl want to go to a party like that? Monika's on her own. She probably wanted to meet a younger, more handsome rich man. It's not hard to see what she saw in yours truly. I'm not about to make my breakthrough as a matinee idol anytime soon."

A passing waiter gave Michael a fresh beer. Miner declined, saying he was working.

"But she came to you again for a ticket?"

"To the bottomless pit of charity that is Erich B. Miner." The man smiled, but it faded almost as soon as it came. "She wanted to see you run. Being the idiot that I am, I gave her a ticket."

"Why?"

"After she left with you the other night? I suppose I realized who I am. I imagined my poor late wife looking down on me. A girl like Monika should be with someone her own age. Her father was a friend once. She deserves better than a fat old fool like me." He took another cigarette from his silver case and lit it up.

"She told me she'd see me after the race today—that she'd wait by the athletes' door, but she wasn't there."

Miner laughed. "Now you're getting to know women, aren't you, boy?"

"But she came to the stadium and then disappeared."

"Certain things in life are indisputable. Water is wet, the sky is blue, and we men have no idea how the female mind works."

"Amen." Michael drank from his beer glass. "I thought you would have been—"

"Angry at you?" Miner stubbed out his cigarette. "No. You woke me up. I should be grateful."

"You think she'll come to you again?"

"When she wants something, maybe, but the charity stops now. It's time she stood on her own."

This man was the only link he had to Monika. It was decision time. If Michael walked away, he'd never see Monika again. He'd never know why she lied about her father and why she went to the party that night. He'd never touch her or make her smile. Someone else would.

"You know where I can find her?"

Miner turned to look at him. "Are you sure? You're an Olympian—a sprinter, no less. You could have any girl here."

Michael shrugged. What did that matter? "Where did you meet her?"

"Are you sure you want to know?"

"Yes. Where?"

"You know the Hotel Adlon?"

"Who doesn't?"

"Of course. She's what's known as a *professional dance partner* there. But only sometimes. She's new. Been there just a few weeks, as far as I know."

Michael wondered what *professional dance partner* meant exactly. How far did her services extend? Did it make any difference?

"When does she work?"

"The weekends mostly, but during the Olympics, she might be there on Thursday. I really don't know, kid. She isn't one to share details."

"Not with me either. She didn't mention any of that."

"I'd better get back to work. Congratulations on what you achieved today, kid."

"What? Nothing?"

"I was in that stadium. You were an inspiration to us all. Good luck with Monika—you're going to need it."

Michael shook the older man's hand again and sat back in the seat after he left. The brunette he was going to talk to earlier was still standing there, alone now. He knew he should hobble over to her. She'd talk to him once she realized who he was, and who knew from there? He closed his eyes, trying to force himself to his feet. The brunette was beautiful, but Monika was all he could see.

"I've never been to the Adlon before," he said to himself and laughed.

THE EXHILARATION of the afternoon had faded, and the problem with Willi and his family reappeared in Seamus's mind once more. He tried to ignore the pressure the young man had tried to exert on him, but even at this glamorous party in the US ambassador's mansion, all he could think about was that field in Marzahn. The stench of that place seemed to hang in his nostrils, and he was only there a few minutes. It was hard to imagine living with it. Those 800 or so people didn't have running water. He picked up a canapé with his free hand.

How viable was the threat from the newsie? Who would listen to him about a missing person's case from 1932? No one. He wasn't a witness and had no evidence. It was difficult to see the police reopening the case without a body, and only he and Lisa knew where Ernst Milch was buried. Seamus wondered if he could find the spot again among the mess of trees in the Grunewald Forest if he tried.

Of course, Otto Milch already had a vendetta against Seamus after he refused to sell him the factory. The opportunity to put Seamus in jail would be like Christmas morning to him. But how would a Roma, locked up in a stinking camp with his family, get to talk to a multimillionaire business magnate? Even if the young man somehow got to Milch, Seamus and Lisa would deny every allegation. Milch's only path in that eventuality would be outside the bounds of the law. Seamus didn't put that past him, particularly to avenge his beloved son against a hated rival. But that seemed like the last of dozens of dominoes that had to fall for that to occur.

Seamus finished the canapé and took a sip of champagne. Lisa was a few feet away, practicing her English with Jesse Owens and Ralph Metcalf. All three were laughing at her thick accent.

The real question was, did Seamus want to walk away and ignore Willi? And if so, would his conscience drive him insane? He knew he could never help all the poor people in that camp, but perhaps just that one family. Would he be able to go back to his privileged life and forget about the children in that camp, snatched from their home and left with no food or running water? And Willi was right: the Nazis had no intention of letting them go free after the games. Things were far more likely to get worse for those people after the international press took their leave.

The things Maureen witnessed in the summer of '35 haunted him. Who was to say the people in that camp wouldn't end up like the patients murdered in the gas vans in Babelsberg? The Nazis' definition of people "unworthy of life" could change to include the Roma they'd hidden away in the camp at Marzahn. Would the Nazis eradicate them? After all, wouldn't that be the easiest way of dealing with them? Trusting the Nazis to do the right thing was like hoping a lion wouldn't close its jaws around you with your head in its mouth. And the Roma in Marzahn were in the lion's den now.

But how? The same question bounced around inside his brain like a rubber ball. The police weren't about to let Willi's family walk out of the camp. They needed permission to go to work, or to the store to get food. It was a prison, and when the fence was finished, it would be nearly impossible to get anyone out. And if he tried, he risked everything... He could imagine Fiona spitting in his face—*You've destroyed us all, you Jew-lover. You Roma-lover.*

Seamus walked over to his wife.

"Excuse me, gentlemen," he said in English.

"You're Michael Ritter's father?" Jesse Owens asked. "That's one courageous kid you raised."

"Crazy, too!" Ralph Metcalf said with a smile.

"I think it's fair to say both of those things," Seamus replied. Pride swelled within him once more. He wished Michael was here at his side to hear this. "And thank you."

Lisa turned to him as the athletes walked away. "Did you hear me practicing my English?"

"I did. Shakespeare made up his own words, so why can't you too?"

His wife punched him in the arm.

"Can we talk outside for a minute? On the street?"

It took them a couple of minutes to slalom through the crowd of partygoers in the mansion and get out onto the street. Seamus led her several paces up the sidewalk before he was sure they could speak with no one else listening in. She seemed able to tell he had something serious on his mind and put down the champagne glass in her hand. The words spilled from his lips like water from a burst pipe. He told her about Willi coming to him and the situation his family faced in Marzahn. She was shocked at first, but he eased her anxiety as he explained how little they had to fear from the young man.

"I don't think we need to be worried. He doesn't mean us any harm," Seamus said. "He's just desperate to help his family."

"You sound like you're feeling sorry for him."

"Don't you?"

"You can't save the world, Seamus." She put a hand on his cheek. "I know you want to help him, but it's too dangerous."

"You didn't see the conditions in the camp. These people were living in their own apartment three weeks ago, minding their own business, until the Nazis came for them."

Lisa seemed to take stock of what he was saying for a few seconds. "We can't help them."

"What if we could?"

"I don't want you ending up in one of those camps yourself."

"I'm not suggesting we go in with guns blazing, but if we put our minds together, we can come up with some way of doing something. I know we can."

"And you'd do that to help someone who helped blackmail you before?"

"If he goes to Milch—"

"You think he'd listen to a newsie? A gypsy?"

"If he heard his son's name he might."

Lisa digested what her husband said for a few seconds. "Then we need to agree with Maureen what to say if the police come to interview us again."

"I'm not getting Maureen involved."

"We have to. If we don't agree in our story, it puts us all at risk. Her too. She was wonderful that night the police came in '32 when she gave us an alibi. She'll do it again. Stay here." A few minutes later, she emerged with Maureen

His daughter stood and listened as he told her someone had appeared from their past—an old friend of Bruno Kurth's, and he meant to blackmail them. Only Maureen's eyes betrayed the shock she felt inside.

When he finished, she merely said, "We have to get them out of the camp!"

He sighed. "I wish we could, but it's not possible. It would endanger our whole family. We just have to be prepared in case Willi goes to Milch. If the police talk to you, just say the same as you said before."

She didn't ask questions about where they were that night in '32, or anything about the blackmail itself. In fact, she barely seemed to be listening anymore.

"I know some people," she said. "Do you know anyone in the embassy who could help? Anyone with some sway who could get visas?"

"To America? For Roma?" Lisa asked in disbelief.

"Or anywhere out of Germany!"

Hearing his daughter talk like this made Seamus feel both guilty at lacking her courage but also annoyed at her for being so naïve. "Let's enjoy the party and talk about this tomorrow. The most important thing is that we don't jeopardize our family. We have to always make sure of that first."

"But Father—"

"Don't make me regret talking to you about this," he snapped at his daughter and went back inside.

He went to the bathroom and stared at his face in the mirror for a few seconds. Could he really do nothing and live with himself? But what choice did he have?

He emerged into the crowd once more and was looking for his son when a voice he thought he'd never hear again called his name.

"Seamus Ritter?"

He swiveled around. "William Hayden?" he asked and shook the man's hand. "I haven't seen you since—"

"We were up to our ears in mud and gore on the Western

Front back in '18?"

They embraced. The shock of seeing his old friend
rendered him dumb for a few seconds. Hayden was around the
same age as Seamus and wore a thin brown beard. He was still
muscular and fit. His thinning hair was the only noticeable way
he'd aged.

"What are you doing here?"

"I work in the embassy. Just arrived a few weeks ago. I heard
about your son. I couldn't believe it at first. I made sure you got
the invitation here tonight."

"Thank you. What do you do for the embassy? Are you a
diplomat?"

"Something like that."

Seeing Hayden brought back an avalanche of memories
he'd tried to repress, and they seemed to choke him from the
inside as they came to the surface of his consciousness.

"You see anyone from the old unit these past few years?"
Hayden asked.

Seamus remembered meeting the most decorated man in
the battalion on his way home from the train station in Newark
when he returned home from Ohio. "I saw Billy Tyler back
in '32."

"How is that old firebrand? What a man he was."

"He was living on the street, sucking out of a bottle, last I
saw of him."

The words seemed to extinguish the flame in Hayden's eyes
and he dropped his head for a moment. "Too many of the old
troop like that. I thought surviving the meat grinder would
have been enough, but coming home was even harder for some
of the guys. You want to get a drink?"

"Yeah."

The two men went into the living room where a bar was set
up below a painting of George Washington crossing the
Delaware River. The bartender was in a tuxedo with a white

jacket and spoke English to the two men. Hayden ordered two whiskeys without asking Seamus what he wanted, then handed the tumbler to him.

"To the fallen," Hayden said.

"To the fallen."

They clinked glasses and took a sip.

"Did you keep in touch with those families you used to write to?"

"I did for a while, but after the war, it fell away."

"You ever think about Captain Bellingham anymore?" Hayden lit up a cigarette.

"Not much. I tried to leave the war behind. It took a while, but I think I got there eventually. You?"

"I see him and the others sometimes."

"You ever settle down, Bill? With one of those French *mademoiselles* you used to talk about?"

"I have an ex-wife and a son in Maryland. I was never much good at being a husband."

"I'm still working at it."

"I was in the stadium today. That was quite the event. You must be proud."

"More than I can say."

"I wasn't surprised to see your son's courage. He obviously takes after his old man."

"I'm still in debt to you for your bravery," Seamus said.

"Everybody owes somebody. None of us would have gotten back without the man on our shoulder watching out for us."

Michael hobbled in. "This is my son," Seamus said.

Hayden shook his hand. "What a day. What did it feel like to have the crowd on their feet, cheering you on like that?"

"For getting injured? Weird, but good."

"More than one way to win over people's hearts, and you certainly did that today."

The three men talked about Michael's training regimen and

the possibility of running for America one day. Lisa and Maureen found them a few minutes later, and Hayden greeted them with the same gusto as Michael did.

"Two beautiful ladies," he said, switching to German for Lisa's benefit. "Maureen, I remember seeing photos of you as a baby when I was hunkered down in the mud in France with your father."

"I've never met any of his old war buddies before," Seamus's daughter said.

"You never had the need to," Seamus said.

"He doesn't talk about what happened over there much," Maureen said.

"It's not a topic easily spoken about. We don't want to sully anyone's ears by what we went through. It was bad enough being in the war. Sometimes it's best to forget."

"Or to talk things through." Lisa put her hand on her husband's shoulder.

Seamus was almost squirming with the mention of the war in front of his family.

"We should get going soon," he said.

"Can I borrow your old man for a few minutes before you go?" Hayden asked. "I won't keep you long."

"Of course," Lisa responded. "I don't want to leave yet, anyway."

"Sounds like my wife," Seamus said with a smile.

She kissed him on the mouth and went to the bar with her stepchildren. Hayden led Seamus through the now-thinning crowd, up the stairs to the second floor. He took a key from his pocket and opened the door. The walls of the room were covered in old books. Seamus picked up a copy of *The Book of Songs* by Heinrich Heine.

"Better be careful who sees you with that one," Hayden said. "Heine was a Jew. His poems are kindling for the Nazis' fires these days."

Seamus replaced the book. "I know. It's a disgrace."

"You know why I invited you and your family here tonight?"

"I'm beginning to have an inkling."

Hayden sat down in a red leather armchair and motioned to Seamus to take the one opposite. The American waited until his old friend was seated before speaking again.

"I know you're no fan of the regime. You make bullets and shells for them, but your factory manager is a Jew, and so are a couple dozen of your workers."

"I made the decisions I needed to so the business survived."

Hayden got up and went to a table in the corner, and picked the top off the crystal decanter sitting on it. "You want another drink?"

"I think I've had enough."

"Wise man." Hayden replaced the top and sat back down. "A man in your line of business could be useful to me, and to your country."

"How?"

"In any way you want. Having someone like you here is priceless."

"And what is it that you do here in Berlin?"

Hayden smiled. "Officially, I'm a diplomat."

"And unofficially?"

"We can get to that later. But are you willing to help me out?"

"Of course." Seamus owed this man his life. Besides, he needed to do something to assuage his endless guilt: guilt about making munitions for the German Army, and now guilt about Willi and his family, doomed to rot in that camp.

It had been some time since dreams of the war invaded his sleep, but he knew they'd return soon. Seeing Hayden again had opened up a Pandora's Box within him, and it would be his job to force it closed once more in the coming weeks and months.

8

August 8, 1918, outside the city of Verdun, France

Seamus sat on his heels, his knees jutting out in front of him. He tried to wipe some of the mud and grime from his fingers before he reached into his pocket to read her letter. He knew every line by heart, but seeing those words she wrote with her own hand swelled his heart. It was comforting to know something beautiful still existed in this world. Colonel Armitage strutted along the length of the trench. Seamus was happy to see him go past. Word was that he was looking for volunteers for a mission. He had no idea what for, and didn't want to find out either. Dozens of soldiers sat around him, basking in the warmth of the afternoon sun. The worst days were when it rained—then the mud sucked the boots off their feet. The ground was still wet from the soaking it took yesterday, and the craters in no-man's-land were knee-deep in mud and filth like he never imagined. If rats and dirt were all you found at the bottom of those holes, you counted yourself lucky. No-man's-land was still littered with bodies from the push over the top the day before. Soon they'd start to decay in the warm summer sun.

The trench was a good one—dry and well tended. The Germans always took better care of their trenches. This one had been theirs the week before. It was heartening to know they were advancing and the Germans were almost done, but home remained an impossible dream in his mind. Maybe he'd never see it again. So many men had died here. What made him special? Not a scratch in three months. He'd seen men fall to his right and left, thrown into the air by artillery shells like rag dolls, but he'd avoided every bullet and piece of shrapnel. Did that mean his time would be up soon? Sometimes it seemed like none of them would make it out of there, and they'd all end up buried in the French dirt. Some of the other men had taken to calling him "Lucky," though he didn't feel it sitting here in the dirt.

He took Marie's letter from his pocket and blew off some dirt that settled on the paper. He thought of her voice as he read.

DEAREST SEAMUS,

I'M HOPING THIS LETTER FINDS YOU SAFE AND WELL. I'M PRAYING FOR YOU AND YOUR FRIENDS EVERY NIGHT. I FEEL LIKE I KNOW THEM FROM HOW MUCH YOU MENTION THEM IN YOUR LETTERS.

WE MISS YOU SO VERY MUCH. MAUREEN IS TODDLING AROUND THE HOUSE CONSTANTLY NOW. IT'S ALL I CAN DO TO KEEP HER OUT OF THE CUPBOARDS! SHE BROKE A CUP THE OTHER DAY AND LAUGHED WHEN I CORRECTED HER. SHE SEEMS TO FIND IT HILARIOUS. I HOPE SHE'S NOT GOING TO BE A TEARAWAY WHEN SHE GROWS UP. I DO WONDER SOMETIMES.

MICHAEL MISSES YOU EVERY DAY. IT BREAKS MY HEART TO THINK THAT YOU'VE NEVER HELD HIM, NEVER FELT HIS BREATH

ON YOUR SKIN. HE'S A WONDERFUL BABY AND SLEEPING THROUGH THE NIGHT NOW.

I STILL HAVEN'T HEARD FROM YOUR FATHER. I'M BEGINNING TO WONDER IF I EVER WILL. INCREDIBLY, HIS LOYALTY TO HIS FORMER COUNTRY IS MORE IMPORTANT TO HIM THAN HIS GRAND- CHILDREN. I'M SURE HE'LL FORGIVE YOU FOR FIGHTING AGAINST GERMANY SOMEDAY, BUT I THINK IT'S GOING TO BE UP TO YOU TO MEND THOSE BONDS.

I LONG FOR US TO BE TOGETHER AGAIN, TO BE A FAMILY ONCE MORE. PLEASE KEEP YOUR HEAD DOWN. DON'T BE A HERO TO ANYONE BUT US. YOU'RE THE TYPE TO RUN TOWARD THE FIRING TO SAVE YOUR FRIENDS, BUT KEEP THE PICTURE OF US—OF THE BABY SON YOU'VE NEVER MET—IN YOUR HEART. COME HOME TO US. ABOVE ALL ELSE, COME HOME. NONE OF THIS WORKS WITHOUT YOU. I DON'T.

ALL MY LOVE,
MARIE

Tears welled in his eyes as he imagined their baby in the crib and his daughter in her arms. No one was afraid to cry here. Before the war, it seemed unmanly or weak. Here it was a way of coping with the intense pain they endured every day. The longing and the agony of loss. He folded the letter as carefully as possible and slipped it into the envelope and back into his side pocket. All he could hope for was another letter, and for this to end soon. That was the most any of them hoped for.

The guns were silent today. The air was clear of bombs and the whooshing of artillery—for now, at least. The hush was almost enough to make one forget that the enemy was only a few hundred yards away, and although they were weakened and retreating, their guns were still trained on anyone sticking his head over the trench lip. Death was everywhere here. He'd lost too many friends to want to make more. What was the point in getting close to other soldiers when they could be wrested from you at any moment? It was better to keep to yourself. At least that way, the death didn't affect you so much. Carrying the weight of grief here could kill you faster than a bullet.

Seamus opened up his rations and stuck a stale biscuit into his mouth, forcing himself to chew and swallow it. Some warm water washed it down, and thankfully, he still had a few squares of chocolate left. He was just finishing his dinner when the figure of Colonel Armitage appeared around the corner again. Armitage was from North Carolina. In his late thirties, pure West Point. He'd probably been waiting for this war his entire life, and it was clear he didn't intend to waste it.

"Ritter. On your feet."

Seamus did as he was ordered.

"Come with me, soldier."

Seamus heard Marie's closing words in her letter as he trudged after the officer. Whatever this was, it wasn't good.

"Am I in trouble, sir?" Seamus asked.

The officer didn't answer, just kept on through the trench. They passed hundreds of men sitting, eating, smoking, and chatting. Why had Armitage chosen him?

Another soldier Seamus had never seen before threw down his rations as Armitage called his name. The man stood to attention.

"Come with me, Hayden."

The other soldier grabbed his rifle and fell in line behind Seamus. They reached a bunker dug into the back of the trench. Armitage continued inside, and the men followed him. They stood to attention as the officer addressed them. He had a thick southern accent, and the mustache above his pink lips twitched as he spoke.

"You're probably wondering why I called you men in here today. I need two volunteers for a mission. Are you prepared to do it?"

"Yes, sir," both men said in almost-perfect unison.

"I chose you because I need someone I can rely on. Good men."

Seamus would rather have been mediocre and back eating his dinner with the other men, but knew he couldn't refuse.

"As you know, the attack yesterday didn't go according to plan." Armitage shifted on his feet, standing two feet from them with his hands behind his back. "Plans are being formulated for the next push as we speak. But we lost something valuable yesterday."

Apart from the dozens of men still lying out there? Seamus wanted to say.

"Due to a mix-up—which you don't need to know about—Captain James Bellingham went over the top yesterday with certain sensitive documents we can't let the Krauts get their hands on. You both knew Captain Bellingham, didn't you?"

"Yes, sir."

"Well, he didn't make it back yesterday, and neither did those documents. I need you two men to go into no-man's-land and find him, and bring the satchel of documents back to me."

"Permission to speak, sir?" Seamus asked.

"Granted."

"Do we know for sure he wasn't captured?"

"I have reliable witness accounts that he was brought down by gunfire."

"Any idea where, sir?"

"We'll get to that, soldier." The officer took them over to a makeshift table in the corner of the bunker. He took a map and rolled it out. "We're here." He pointed. "As far as we know, Bellingham fell somewhere around here."

He indicated an area right in the middle of no-man's-land, about 200 yards from the German guns.

It seemed like suicide.

"We won't send you out in the daylight. Their snipers would

put you down before you took three steps. Take a break. Have a bite to eat—I'll get you some decent chow. We'll be pulling back from the line in a few days, so get this done and then enjoy your time off. You can wait in here until dark. Should be ready to go in about three hours."

The officer walked out. The men waited a few seconds before daring to speak.

"What did we do to deserve this honor?" Seamus asked.

"Hell if I know. Sounds like a one-way trip to me."

The two men sat down on the small wooden chairs by the table. The map was still laid out, and Hayden stared down at it.

"I reckon we make our way from the side. That way, if the body's not where they think it is, we might stumble over it."

"Crawl over it, you mean," Seamus said.

"Yeah."

"Where you from, Hayden?"

"Virginia. A little town called Round Hill. My pop has a dairy farm. What about you?"

"Newark, New Jersey."

Seamus neglected to mention the interesting detail that he'd lived in Germany for years as a kid. The other men wouldn't appreciate that.

"You got a wife and kids?"

"Nah," Hayden answered. "I've enough trouble looking after myself. You?"

"Yeah. A little girl, and a baby boy too."

The men fell silent for a moment. "Be good to get some of that chow the officers get for a change," Hayden said.

They spoke for an hour or so, swapping stories and cigarettes as they sat in the relative comfort of the bunker. Hayden was the oldest of four brothers and had never been out of Virginia before he joined up.

"Can't say I think much of this part of France, but Paris was pretty sweet, and those *mademoiselles*? Whoo-ee!"

"I've heard more than a few tales," Seamus said.

Armitage came in again, and the men stood to attention. "At ease."

Two privates came in behind him carrying trays of food they laid down on the table.

"Enjoy," the officer said. "I'll be back in a couple of hours for your final briefing."

The two men sat and ate the meal of Spam and almost fresh bread. They were nearly finished when Hayden said, "They always give you one last meal right before your execution."

"Seems like a waste of food, doesn't it?"

"Not when you're the one facing the chop."

Seamus reached into his pocket for his photograph of his family. Marie sat with Michael on her lap and Maureen by her side. It was faded and worn, but it was his most precious possession.

"Your family?"

Seamus nodded and handed him the picture.

"Beautiful. Every one of them. Let's make sure they see you again."

"Amen to that."

The fading sun outside signaled that the mission was getting closer, and Seamus found it more and more difficult to stifle his nerves. Neither man had spoken for several minutes and were both smoking when Armitage reappeared.

"On your feet, men."

They threw down the cigarettes and stood up.

"Grab your rifles. Bring weapons only. Anything else is going to slow you down."

The two men left their packs in the corner, but took rifles, sidearms, and bayonets. The moon and stars were covered in a blanket of clouds. *Maybe we might have some chance of getting out of this alive,* Seamus thought.

The ladder over the top was set, and two spotters were on either side, peering out with trench mirrors.

"Go to the left, and then straight for 200 yards or so, and you should find him. Godspeed, men."

The two soldiers nodded, but they already had their own plan. It wasn't Armitage going out into no-man's-land in the middle of the night.

"It's all clear. Nothing moving," one of the spotters said.

"Time to go," Armitage said. The officer stood aside and motioned to the ladder. "Code word for coming back in is *Idaho*."

Seamus looked at Hayden. Going up that ladder was the last thing on earth he wanted to do. He hitched his rifle over his shoulder and climbed up to an eerie, dark, and almost silent landscape. Seamus stayed in the dirt in front of the trench as Hayden climbed up behind him. He waited until the man from Virginia was beside him to move. They crouched down, taking one slow step at a time. Any kind of noise would bring the attention of the German spotters, who would send up flares in seconds and unleash the snipers who were ready with their fingers on the trigger.

Ten minutes passed before Seamus took the time to look back at the trench. It was still only 15 feet away. They had about 10 hours until the sun peeked up over the horizon at six in the morning, and the men intended to use all of that time.

They made it to the line of barbwire that extended along the trench. It had been shredded in preparation for the attack that Bellingham and dozens of others died in, so they had little difficulty crawling through it. The ground was still relatively warm from the day, but Seamus could feel dirt and grime all over him already, like a second skin. He tried to retain the image of his family in his mind as he went. Not at the forefront —he had to concentrate on the task of staying alive—but he kept them like a painting on the wall of his consciousness that he could gaze at when he needed to. It was hard to know whether to be jealous of Hayden or not. Having no family meant fewer lives would be destroyed by your death. Hayden's parents and brothers, though they would mourn him, didn't rely on him. But it also meant he had less to live for, less to survive for. Seamus had no other choice but to live through this. Dying wasn't an option for him.

A raised tree stump provided a place to stop and take stock of the progress they'd made. Seamus reached it first and reached for the water bottle on his hip. He screwed the top back on and replaced it as Hayden arrived. The two men sat with their backs to the tree stump, their entire bodies covered from sight. They'd come about 50 yards in over an hour.

"How are you doing?" Seamus whispered.

"Muddy, but alive. I reckon our friend is somewhere behind us to the left."

"I reckon. You ever talk to him?"

"I saw him around. He was an officer, though. You know?"

"I do."

They took another few seconds before slithering around the tree and out into the open of no-man's-land. Bodies littered the ground. How were they going to find one man among this mess of death? Seamus crawled between two corpses torn apart by machine gunfire. The darkness was a blessing here. This wasn't anything he wanted to see. The worst sight in this parade of horror was the dead brought down by artillery. Their mangled bodies were hardly recognizable as human.

The two men kept crawling through the quagmire of dirt and gore until they came to a large bomb crater. Seamus heard rats scuttling around inside it and tried not to peer down at what they were doing to the bodies down there. The German lines were so close. He could get up and run to them in less than a minute—although he knew if he tried, he wouldn't make it more than five steps.

The two soldiers crawled around the hole, checking each body they happened upon now. The thought occurred to Seamus that Bellingham might have been at the bottom of one of those holes submerged in yesterday's rainwater. They'd stick to the plan for now. According to Armitage, Bellingham was 50 yards or so ahead of them. He just hoped the colonel was correct. If not, they'd be returning empty-handed. *I'm not dying out here tonight.*

What was to stop them from just turning back now? Duty, he supposed. Perhaps this one small act could speed the end of the war and help bring a halt to this misery. They would try to find Bellingham. They weren't giving up yet.

Hayden tapped him on the shoulder and pointed onward. The man from Virginia took the lead now, and Seamus crawled after him. They checked body after body in silence and motioned to each other to move on when it was time. Every corpse was American. The Germans had stayed in their trenches and cut down the onrushing soldiers, just as they always did. When were the generals going to change? The American top brass had three years of this to learn from, yet they adopted the same playbook as the British and French that had wiped out millions. *Lions led by donkeys.*

An hour of crawling and checking corpses later, the two men were beside a large artillery crater, about 200 yards from the German lines. A dead soldier lay face down a few yards ahead of them, a satchel on his back.

"I think we have a winner," Hayden whispered.

Seamus put a hand on his shoulder and crawled forward. It was Bellingham—or what was left of him, at least.

The captain was a tall, muscular man and a serious, committed soldier. Seamus checked him. His face was covered in dried blood, half-submerged in the dirt. This was it. All they had to do now was get the papers and crawl back to the safety of the trench. Armitage said they were leaving the line, and the

Germans had to give up soon. Maybe this was the end of their
war. Seamus signaled to Hayden that they'd found him and
reached up for the satchel on his back. It was untouched by the
gunfire that had ripped through him. The strap was around his
torso. He tugged at the bag, and then thought to reach inside it.
His fingers moved under the flap and a shot of white-hot pain
jolted through his arm. He pulled his hand out and saw a rat
attached to his middle finger. He shook the rodent off. Its body
went flying and landed on something sounding like an old tin
can as Hayden arrived beside him. Seamus clutched his
bleeding finger to his mouth as a flare from the German trench
went up, and suddenly the two men were bathed in white light.
Seamus was on his knees and turned toward the enemy position. Muzzle flashes of German rifles burned in the dark, and
Seamus realized this was the moment of his death.

"Get down!" Hayden said and threw his body over
Seamus's. A bullet zipped past, and Seamus was on the ground,
using the captain's corpse for cover. More bullets flew, and an
explosion thundered a few yards from where they were lying.

"Get the satchel," Hayden said.

Seamus realized he was still alive and grabbed for the bag.
It wouldn't budge. He took a bayonet from his belt and cut the
strap. Bullets thudded into Bellingham's dead flesh, and the
Germans fired another flare.

"They've zeroed in on us," Hayden said. "They must have
heard the rat landing on the ration can."

Seamus had regained himself and swiveled his head
around, searching for cover.

"Come on."

The two men crawled past Bellingham's body. A machine
gun opened fire, chewing up the ground around them. It
seemed to be spraying the area in front and to the left. The only
place with cover was a large bomb crater about six or seven
yards to the right. A hand grenade exploded in front of them

and a bullet struck the mud six inches from Seamus's face. Getting up would mean instant death, but could they crawl to the hole fast enough? They covered the ground in seconds and tumbled into the puddle of muddy water at the bottom of the crater.

Seamus gasped, wiping the filth from his face. Hayden was a few feet away in the crater, which was perhaps five yards wide.

"Watch out for grenades," Hayden said.

The Germans fired another flare, and the full horror of the crater was revealed. Two corpses were floating face down in the water. Seamus turned away. The light faded, but the shooting continued. Neither man spoke as they pressed their bodies against the side of the six-foot-deep crater. Both were up to their knees in muddy water. Seamus cursed the rat and lifted his finger to examine the bite. Blood was coursing down from below his nail, but he didn't have time to dress it now. He took the rifle from his shoulder and readied it.

A hissing sound caught his attention. Hayden reacted instantly and picked up the grenade, sweeping it up and over the edge of the crater. It exploded in the mud as both men took cover. More grenades landed short of their position.

The shooting from the German trenches continued for a few more minutes, and both men hid in the mud as flares went up again.

They waited until silence fell on no-man's-land before daring to whisper.

"You ok?" Seamus whispered.

Hayden patted down his body, checking for wounds. "Somehow."

"Keep your head down. Best thing we can do is wait this out. They're not going to shoot at two men all night long."

"You got it."

"Thanks for saving my hide."

"Don't mention it. You got the satchel?"

Seamus held it up.

"Great. So we stay put a few hours and crawl back the way we came before dawn. Your finger ok?"

"Bleeding a bit, but fine. In the grand scheme of things, I'll take it."

"You weren't expecting that rat, huh?"

Hayden laughed silently, and Seamus couldn't help but join in.

"No. Who would have? If we get out of this alive, I swear..."

"You swear what?"

"I'm never letting my wife and kids go, and I'm having more."

"More wives or more kids?"

"I don't think Marie would approve of the former, so let's go with the kids."

"Seems like the safe option."

They stayed quiet for a few minutes longer, waiting for the gunfire to begin again, but it never did.

"What about you?" Seamus asked. "What are you going to do if we get out of here?"

"I've been thinking that over, way down here in the mud."

"Apart from getting drunk and having some fine *mademoiselle* sit on your lap."

"I'm glad you understand that goes without saying," Hayden said. "It means we're not so far apart. I think I want to serve my country."

"A lifer?"

"Maybe, but not doing this, that's for darn sure. I don't wanna end up like those poor bastards in the water." He motioned to the two bodies floating behind them.

Seamus had done his best not to look at them to that point. It was as if denying their existence could shield him from the terror of this place, but he shouldered his rifle and slid down into the water.

"What are you doing?" Hayden asked.

"These guys were soldiers like us just two days ago." He reached around the first man's neck for a dog tag and ripped it off. He did the same to the other man.

"Who were they?"

Seamus squinted at the writing etched into the metal in the dull light. He used his finger to help him read the letters as if he were blind. "Corporal Leonard Bloom and Private George White. They've got to have families, right?"

"Most of us do."

Seamus slipped the tags into his pocket. "Maybe I'll write 'em a letter. Somehow, I feel I owe them that much."

"For letting us share their hole? I'm sure they'd appreciate that."

The two men slipped into silence once more. The Germans weren't about to charge the bomb crater, as the American snipers would open up just as quickly as theirs had. Once their spotters concluded that the two Americans in no-man's-land were dead, they could crawl back. But who knew when that would be?

Time moved more slowly than Seamus had ever known. Every minute seemed like an hour, every hour seemed like a week. The hands on his wristwatch seemed to grind to a halt, but they both knew that if they were still here once dawn broke, they'd be trapped until the next night. The prospect of spending the entire day among the decaying bodies of no-man's-land made the idea of sprinting back to their own lines a lot more enticing.

Five o'clock struck. The German guns had been silent for more than four hours.

"I think it's time," Seamus said.

Hayden nodded in the darkness, and the two men crept up

the side of the crater. Nothing was moving. The German line was quiet, and Captain Bellingham was still lying on his chest. Seamus felt a tinge of regret at not taking his dog tags. But the captain would have a place in his memory forever now.

Seamus and Hayden crawled back toward their own lines in a race against the sun. They only had just over an hour, so they quickened their pace from earlier. The German spotters were watching, but would only send up a flare if they heard something, and no one could see them on the ground in the darkness among the mess of bodies. The men moved silently, only stopping a few times. It was difficult not to keep going with the American trench, and safety, so close.

They reached it just after six o'clock, with about 20 minutes to spare until the sun came up.

"*Idaho, Idaho,*" Seamus called out.

The American guns stayed silent and the men collapsed into the trench.

"What the hell happened out there?" the sentry asked.

"We need to see Colonel Armitage," Seamus said, clutching the satchel to his chest.

Hayden sat up beside him as the two filthy, exhausted men waited for the officer to wake up.

"We made it," he said.

"Somehow."

A man he'd never met 14 hours before knew him now as well as anyone for thousands of miles in every direction. And even if he never saw him again, the bond they formed this night would remain for the rest of their lives.

9

Wednesday, August 5, 1936

Maureen took her usual place beside Thomas at the meeting. It was the six-month anniversary of his father's death, and her boyfriend was quiet. Maureen got the attention of the group and they raised a toast.

"To Joachim Reus," Herr Schultz, Maureen's old teacher, said. "The finest of all of us."

"How is your mother?" Gilda Stein's husband had been murdered by Stormtroopers.

"Some days are better than others," Thomas said. "It was so sudden. The doctors diagnosed the cancer in January, and a month later..."

Maureen held his hand and kissed him on the lips. "I love you. We all do."

They sat and talked about Thomas's father for ten minutes before the meeting began in earnest. Maureen never let go of his hand.

Herman was more cautious about the music they played these days, so the jazz on the record player came more as a low, steady stream than a gush. Several of his neighbors had remarked on hearing it in passing. None were committed Nazis, but in a country where everyone was a potential informant, the lesson was clear. The meetings continued nonetheless, and Maureen was grateful for that. It was refreshing to escape the cloistered atmosphere of the university, which seemed to grow more fervent in its support for the regime by the week. They were no longer being trained as doctors. They were being trained as Nazi doctors now.

The avalanche of questions about Michael came. She told them every conceivable detail for the first fifteen minutes of the meeting. It wasn't a chore—she was proud of her brother. With the other members' curiosity satiated, they moved back to regular business.

No new members of the Subversives, the group of liberal thinkers Joachim Reus introduced them to, had been admitted since she and Thomas the year before. The way things were going in Berlin, she doubted any more would ever be allowed to join. The weekly opinions expressed around this table were more than enough to land a person in a concentration camp. Stories circulated in the newspapers every day about people sent away for less.

Her old teacher, Herr Schultz, who spent several months in a camp back in '34, was an ever-present warning of what the state was capable of. The meetings were more dangerous than ever, yet here they all sat. This was a special meeting—not on Monday due to the big race, and a little earlier than usual at five o'clock.

"The city is crawling with foreign journalists," Gilda said. "Does anyone think it'll change the world's opinion of what's going on in this country?"

"I'd say yes, but not in the way that we'd like it to," Herr Schultz said. "The games are the biggest media event in the history of the world. Eighteen hundred reporters have descended on our city, but do you think they'll see the new concentration camp the Nazis are building in Sachsenhausen?"

"Where is that?"

"Five miles northwest of the city, in the town of Oranienburg," Schultz answered.

"How did you find out about it?"

"My cousin's friend is an SS guard there. I met with him on Friday night, and a few drinks was all it took to loosen his tongue. The conditions in the camp are inhumane. There's no direct water supply or proper sanitation. The prisoners, who are building the camp themselves, are confined to barracks all night long, and are abused and tortured for the most minor infractions. They're made to stand to attention for hours and beaten with sticks, or hung up like slabs of meat. No, the foreign journalists won't see the real Germany, just the façade the Nazis present to them."

"They're experts at that," Herman said. "It's the same smokescreen they use on the general population of the country every day."

"Exactly," Leon Gellert said. "Hitler has never been more popular than he is today. The tactics used to control the media are working. When lies aren't questioned anymore, the truth ceases to exist."

"I don't see the foreign journalists scraping below the surface to find out what's really going on," said Thomas. "They're all here to enjoy the city and to revel in the atmosphere of the games. They're too busy reporting on the events and attending the lavish parties the regime is throwing for them."

Gilda said, "But who knows if the international community even cares? The German free press abroad publishes stories of Nazi brutality all the time. It doesn't seem to make a difference. I got my hands on this last week." She took a pamphlet from her pocket and held it up so all twelve around the table could see it. "It's published in Prague. This one is especially for the games. The headline reads, 'Get to Know Beautiful Germany in Time for the Olympics.'"

She opened it to reveal a picturesque shot of the German landscape, but on the next page, a map showed the locations of all the known concentration camps, penal facilities, and court prisons. "The footnote at the bottom reminds the reader that 'SA torture facilities' aren't listed, as there are too many of them to show."

She threw the pamphlet down on the table. Being caught possessing it would mean years of detention in one of the camps shown on the map inside. Maureen was almost afraid to touch it, but as Thomas passed it to her, she read through it as everyone else did.

More talk about the games followed and, as sometimes occurred, the other members of the group began to argue amongst themselves. Maureen waited to broach her own concerns.

This was her chance to do something good, and perhaps to assuage the guilt of doing nothing that assailed her on an almost-daily basis. She was sick of just talking. So many people were suffering because of the Nazis. Helping to free the people in Marzahn—however they were going to achieve that—would be doing something. It would also be food to her soul, and perhaps the first step in a new direction in her life. The reasons why didn't matter. The fact that her father and Lisa wanted her to cover for them again didn't matter either. She was confident that whatever they did was just and for the good of the family. She didn't want to know anything more. The important thing now was rescuing that poor family.

"Something's on my mind," Maureen began. "Something I haven't even told you about." She squeezed Thomas's hand.

Each member sat in silence as she told them about the

camp in Marzahn. None seemed surprised. She detailed what her father told her outside the American Embassy.

"You want to get them out of the camp?" Thomas asked.

No one around the table spoke.

"We sit here every week discussing the evils of the regime that's taken over this country, but we haven't turned those words into action."

"We tried last year, at the hospital in Babelsberg," Gilda said. "Your American friend couldn't publish the story."

"This is different. We have an opportunity to help people victimized by the Nazis for their race."

"Why them?" Herman asked.

"Because we can't save everyone. And they asked."

Thomas let go of her hand. Silence filled the room like a balloon.

"My father won't do anything. He says it's 'too dangerous.'"

"Can't say I disagree with that," said Herr Schultz.

"What if it were your family dragged from their apartment and dropped off in some godforsaken hole? What if those who had the opportunity to help you said it was too risky? Who are we?"

She stopped and looked around the table. A torturous five seconds followed until Herman spoke.

"I'll help you. I know the area."

She turned to look at Thomas, whose face softened under her gaze. "Ok, I'm in too. As if I ever had a choice! I know Marzahn a little too—my uncle lives out there."

"I'll help too," Gilda said.

"And me," Herr Schultz added.

Maureen couldn't help the smile that spread across her lips, but knew the others were looking to her to lead.

"We need to see the place first," Maureen said. "We can't formulate a plan until we know what we're working with. When should we go?"

"No time like the present," Thomas said.

"Take my car," Herr Schultz said.

Twenty minutes later, she and Thomas were in the car on the way to the camp at Marzahn. They were halfway across the city when he asked, "Why are you doing this? For someone you've never mentioned? Who is this boy, Willi?"

"A newsie on Kurfürstendamm. His family needs help. He came to my father, and I said yes."

"Why you?"

"Because he knows I'm someone he can trust. Please don't make me regret telling you about this." She hoped her tone was clear: motivations weren't something she was willing to go into. She'd never spoken of covering for her father, and never would.

Thomas clammed up and spoke little until they reached Marzahn. He directed her the last few turns and turned to her as she parked the car. "Promise me you won't do anything stupid."

"I'm not an idiot, and you're going to have to trust me."

They got out of the car and crossed the train tracks. The stench was almost vomit-inducing, and she held her nose as they went.

"What is that smell?"

"The sewage works."

She crossed the tracks over a footbridge and peered down at the camp. Sadness struck her like a fist. A hundred or so caravans sat in the field. Several barracks were under construction behind them, and the sound of hammering and sawing was clearly discernible. The fence, which was also in the process of being built, snaked halfway around the camp. A dozen or so policemen, several with guard dogs on leashes, patrolled the scene.

"They were taken from their homes and dumped here," she said.

The façade of civility the Nazis wore for the Olympic

Games was nowhere to be seen here. These people were nothing more than an embarrassment to the government. Those sitting outside the caravans on this overcast morning, the mothers watching their children playing, were as unworthy of life to the Nazis as those poor men she'd seen murdered in the gas vans the summer before. She had little doubt that these people would end up with the same fate. Perhaps Hitler and his minions hadn't figured out what to do with them yet, and everything about the camp screamed of its temporary nature, but this wasn't going to be forever.

"They've been relegated to the role of animals, but no zoo in the world would treat them like this."

"Do you know who Willi's family is? Or which caravan is theirs?"

She shook her head. "This is so wrong."

They stood in silence, watching for a minute or so. She studied the fence for weak points. One side of the rectangle around the camp was finished, and the others were closing in like a pincer around the people inside. They watched in silence as a truck approached the camp with the words MARZAHN CONSTRUCTION SUPPLY daubed on the side of it. It drove into the camp, scattering children and adults alike in its path. Two men in overalls got out and unloaded several barrels of what she assumed were nails, before loading the used ones back in the truck, along with some broken lumber.

She wished she'd brought a camera, but knew how dangerous it would be to get caught with one. She set about assigning the shape of the camp to memory and would jot it down later when they got home. Then something occurred to her.

"Wait here a minute," she said, knowing he wasn't going to accept that.

"No way. What are you doing?"

"I want to go down and talk to one of the police."

"Are you insane?"

"I'm not going to tell them we're trying to break someone out, but I need to speak to someone. Trust me on this."

"I'm coming too."

"No, you're not." She watched him bristle at the answer.

"Please be careful, Maureen. If anything happens to you, I'd—"

"I'm just going to talk to them. I'll be back in a few minutes." She took his hands in hers. "I'm not going to do anything stupid. Wait here. I need to do this alone."

She left him standing there and took a path that led down a hill thick with shrubbery, toward the camp. "Otto! Otto!" she called out.

A guard in police uniform stood smoking a cigarette near a gap in the fence. He looked up as she approached from around a line of bushes, but seemingly more out of interest than suspicion. He was tall and slim, with a thin mustache. His brown eyes were on her like magnets as she approached.

"I've lost my dog—my little schnauzer. Have you seen him?"

"No."

He was young, perhaps twenty-two or twenty-three, and fresh out of the academy. *Perfect.*

"When did you last see him?"

"I was out walking with my father and Otto got away from us. Perhaps he's found him already."

"I hope so," the young policeman said.

"What's going on here?" she asked with her best Berlin accent.

"The camp? Undesirables. Had to get them off the streets with the games going on and all. Can't have them stealing the tourists' wallets." He spoke with a smile, as if he expected her to understand. Most of the locals seemed to.

"I suppose my father must have found Otto by now. I can't hear him shouting anymore." She made a show of leaving, but then turned back, smiling as if the guard had piqued her interest. "What's your name?"

"Moritz."

"I'm Gisela. How long have you been doing this?"

"Since the middle of July."

"Are these people dangerous?"

"They're not to be trusted."

Several grubby, skinny children were playing about 15 yards from where they were standing. She couldn't help herself. "I suppose the young ones are the worst?"

He failed to pick up the sarcasm in her tone. "You're quite right, fräulein. Very dangerous." This boy in uniform was as stupid as she'd hoped.

She simpered, "I'm so grateful the city has brave men like you willing to protect the people."

"I'm just doing the job I was assigned, fräulein."

Several other policemen were shuffling around, smoking cigarettes and talking among themselves. The group of children started throwing stones, and Moritz turned around to check on them. He shouted at them to stay away from the fence and then turned to Maureen to show off a job well done.

"Little brats," he said with a crooked, yellow-toothed smile.

"They'd have your wallet if you let them out," Maureen answered. "Do you live around here? My friends would be so impressed if they saw me with a man in uniform."

"I live in Kreuzberg. What about you?"

"Not too far from here. Do you ever get off work? All of you must be here day and night."

"I'm off at six tonight. Twelve hours on, twelve hours off."

"You ever go out to celebrate? How many guards are here?"

"Twelve of us right now."

"What if they rush the fence? Don't you ever get scared that might happen?"

"We're prepared for that." He showed her the leather holster on his hip. "These vermin aren't going anywhere."

Said like a true Nazi. "I'm out celebrating most nights with my friends during the games. Where do you boys go for fun around here?"

His face lit up like a firework. "Walter's Bar. Just down the street in Marzahn. Do you know it?"

"I've been there a few times," she lied.

"A few of us are planning on going on Saturday night when we get off our shift."

"At six?" The young policeman nodded. "Well, I might just see you there, Moritz. Make sure you come over and say hello."

"You can be sure I will."

"I'd better get back and see if my father found the dog. I'll see you soon."

"I look forward to it." He was beaming now.

She almost felt sorry for him until she looked back over her shoulder at the camp.

10

Thursday, August 6

This was Michael's first major injury—the first time in his life his body hadn't obeyed his wishes. Pain wasn't new to him, but this was different. Before, he'd always been able to push through it, to master it. Now it was sending him a clear message to slow down, but it was hard to listen.

His stepmother called the family for dinner, and Michael picked up his crutches to make his way downstairs. He took his place at the table beside his father.

"I'm so sorry about the relay," Lisa said as she served sauerbraten with boiled potatoes.

"It's fine. I'm only eighteen, and the next games are just four years away. I ran in front of 80,000 people yesterday."

"And the Führer himself," murmured Fiona.

He glanced at her. "Yes, that's true. I'm experienced now, and I'll be even more prepared next time."

"I told you, you were going to fall," Conor said.

"But he got back up again, didn't he?" their father asked.

"And we'll all be there in Tokyo in four years' time, cheering you on again."

They finished their food. Michael had the privilege of leaving the table straight away after dinner, without helping to clear up—something he'd earned in the 100 meters final, apparently. He wondered how long this special treatment would last.

The exhilaration of the final had faded quickly. All he could think about was Monika Horn. He doubted she was pining for him, but then, why did she go to Miner for tickets to see him run? "Probably to see what rich men she could meet," he said out loud, but didn't believe that either. Miner was a wealthy man and would have punched whatever meal ticket she demanded, but she left him. She left the old man at Goebbels' party and went with him. None of it made any sense. Finding out seemed like enough justification to take a trip to the Hotel Adlon tonight.

He hobbled off toward his room to hunt down his tuxedo. The Adlon was one of the most exclusive hotels in the city—the type of place he'd need to wear white tie to get in the door. The idea to invite one or two of his friends along for moral support crossed his mind, but what if things went wrong? It was best he did this alone. The purpose of tonight was to answer his questions about this girl and free himself or entangle himself further in her web. He wasn't going to be a fool about it—he just wanted to know. If she wasn't worth his time, he'd let her go.

A knock on the door interrupted his thoughts. His father's voice bled through the wood. "What are you doing tonight?"

He called back, "I'm going out in a few minutes. You ever spend any time in the Adlon?"

"On occasion. What's going on there?"

"I'm meeting a friend at the dance."

His father laughed. "I don't mean to burst your bubble, kid, but I don't think you'll be doing much dancing tonight."

"There's more than one way to enjoy a dance."

"How are you getting into town?"

The Adlon was opposite the French Embassy on Unter den Linden, the spacious avenue that formed the city's heart.

The door opened before Michael answered. "A cab, maybe?"

"I'll give you a ride," his father said.

"Thanks." Michael pushed up his tie.

"You missed a button."

Michael made sure to correct the mistake and was ready. He picked up his crutches and raised himself to his feet, refusing his father's help in getting down the stairs. The older man waited at the bottom for a few seconds.

Once in the car, his father started talking as he drove. "You've been training so hard these last two years, haven't you?"

"Don't I know it!"

"So what now, son?"

"I'm going out to meet a friend—"

"I don't mean tonight, Michael. With your life. School always took a back seat to training, and I was fine with that because it was your choice. You've always been smart, but your sole focus was on getting faster. What now?"

"The training won't end. The Olympics isn't the only show in town."

"You're not following me. I mean what are you going to do to make a living? You've never mentioned much about that. I've never pushed you on it, either."

"Until now."

"Is this your definition of pushing?" His father waited for him to answer.

Michael let the words sink in. It was true. That race was all he'd thought about these last two years. While his friends were preparing for university or learning a trade, all he'd done was run. He couldn't make a living from that. Not even Jesse Owens could. Monika jumped into his mind. Perhaps she'd replaced his obsession with running. Probably only temporarily, but she was all he'd thought about since the race. He wished he had some answer for his father, and knew he had to be the one to speak next.

"I've thought about running for America, but I'd have to go back."

"We could look into getting you into college in the States. Is that something you're interested in?"

"I don't know if I want to leave Germany or not." Monika flashed into his mind again. He tried to dismiss her, to wipe her away like chalk off a blackboard, but he couldn't. "We haven't talked about moving back much lately."

"It seemed like the answer to all our problems last year, but with your training, and Maureen being so settled, we stayed. It was hard to say how the Nuremberg Laws would affect Lisa and Hannah, but I suppose you could say that so far, they haven't."

"Hannah won't have to worry, and Lisa might be ok too. I mean, she can't work, but—"

"I don't think she'd get the roles she wants in America, though. It's hard when you don't speak the language. As terrible as it is, she's come to terms with the fact that her career's over."

"And Petra Wagner is a big star."

"Don't mention that name in front of her."

"It's disgusting—the whole situation."

His father changed back to the original subject. "You don't even have to go to college if you don't want to. You could come and work for me."

"In the factory?"

"Yeah. I could teach you how the business works."

Michael had never given any serious thought to becoming his father. Those ideas could wait until tomorrow.

"I don't know. I've never considered getting into the armaments business before."

"Neither did I...until I had to." Seamus glanced at him. "I wasn't expecting answers from you tonight, Michael. Just think about what I said. You're not going to be able to run all your life, but you are going to need to support yourself."

After a short silence, he asked, "So, you're meeting someone in here tonight?"

"I think so."

"That could only mean a girl. Who's the lucky lady?"

"That's what I'm meaning to find out."

"Is it your friend from the stadium?"

"Very astute, Father."

"I didn't come down in the last shower, as my old Irish mother used to say."

"I think *my* Irish mother might have said the same thing."

His father smiled and patted him on the back of the hand. They arrived outside the Adlon two minutes later. The Brandenburg Gate, 200 yards away, was lit up gold in the fading light.

"Good luck, kid," his father said after Michael got out of the car.

"With a face like this, I don't need luck."

His father laughed and drove off.

The doorman looked him up and down as he limped up the steps. "Can I help you, sir?"

"I'm going to the bar," he answered with enough confidence that the man let him by without another word.

The elegant lobby was extravagantly furnished, with chandeliers hanging from the ceiling. In the middle of the room, a fountain dashed with gold spewed water from elephant trunks. People in evening dress stood around, laughing and smoking with drinks in their hands. It was refreshing not to see any Brownshirts or men in uniform. Tuxedos were required for men, and evening gowns for women. Whatever the dress code, money also seemed to be a requirement for anyone coming in the door.

Just yesterday, 80,000 people had cheered for him, but now he felt alone. His celebrity status seemed to have faded already. The ballroom was down a hallway to the right of the check-in desk—the jangling of his nerves grew to a crescendo as he hobbled toward it. The sound of the band flowed through the hallway. The hatcheck girl was about his age and ogled him as he approached the desk to pay the princely sum of five Reichsmarks for entry. It was the most he'd ever paid anywhere.

"She'd better be here," he muttered as she gave him his entry ticket.

She heard him and winked. "If she's not, I am."

The music had stopped, and clapping sounded as he came through the double door into the ballroom. The dance floor was packed, with couples standing to applaud the singer, dressed in red satin, and her band on stage. She thanked the crowd and bowed her head before the band started up again.

Michael scanned the people dancing, but didn't see Monika. The terrible thought that he'd wasted his time coming here—and he'd never see her again—crushed his insides. He moved around to get different views of the people dancing, but couldn't make out any familiar faces. The bar in the corner offered some hope of refuge, and he rested against it as he ordered a beer. The bartender handed him back an ornate glass that looked like someone had blown it minutes before and charged him what he'd pay for three in most other places.

The man beside him looked like he used 20 Reichsmarks notes to blow his nose. The whole room reeked of wealth and privilege. *Sleeping four in a room in Aunt Maeve's house was only four years ago*, he thought. *And look at me now.*

He asked the barman to have a waiter follow him with his beer to a table. Sitting, he studied the crowd. It seemed the role of professional dance partner wasn't exclusive to women. He counted five younger men with older women, and perhaps double that number of younger women with men twice their age or more. But he didn't see Monika.

He sat alone for a few minutes, wondering how he could ever beat Jesse Owens, when, across the dance floor, he saw a spill of auburn hair. Monika was waltzing with a man three times her age and four times her weight. Michael stood up to get closer. The older man seemed transfixed by her.

"Should I just leave her be?" Michael asked out loud.

He was standing about 20 feet from her, and her eyes flitted over to meet his. He thought to raise his hand to greet her, but decided against it.

Monika dropped her hands and stood back from the man she was dancing with. Michael knew this was his chance and haltingly approached them.

"Gerhard, I'd like to introduce you to a friend of mine," she said. "This is Michael Ritter, the Olympic athlete. He ran in the 100 meters yesterday."

Gerhard didn't seem impressed. "Can we finish the dance?"

Michael nodded. "I'd like to speak to you when you're done, Monika."

"Ok," she said in a low voice.

Michael went to the bar once more to order another over-priced drink. The song ended as he sat down and the waiter set his drink before him. Monika stepped back from her dance partner, but he grabbed her by the arm.

Michael stood up, grabbing his crutches and hobbling over. "The lady doesn't want to dance with you anymore."

"Stay out of this," Monika said to him.

"How can I? This slob is mauling my girlfriend."

With a disgusted grunt, the fat man let her go and marched off.

Monika turned on him in fury. "What are you doing here? You can't be here. The men can't think I have someone else."

"That you have someone else? Am I your someone else? Is that why you never came to see me after the race yesterday?"

"You came all the way to ruin my job for me just to ask me that? Go away." As she spoke, she looked over his shoulder and her eyes widened. "Now look what you've done. Gerhard went to Kristof."

He looked around. The man she'd been dancing with was talking to a tall man in a white jacket.

"Who's Kristof?"

"The maître d'. The closest thing I have to a boss. Damn, here he comes."

The man arrived, with Gerhard by his side. "Monika, I've just had a most unpleasant conversation. Herr Riedle is an important customer of this establishment."

"I finished the dance he paid me for," Monika said. The contempt in her voice was unmistakable and seemed to rile the maître d' further.

"Her boyfriend assaulted me," Gerhard said.

"He's not my boyfriend. This is Michael Ritter—the Olympic hero from the 100-meter final on Monday."

"The one who came last to that *Schwarze*?" Gerhard sneered. "Some hero."

Monika bristled. "You slob, you couldn't get your fat ass through the entryway to the track!"

"That's it, Monika. I never want to see you in here again," Kristof snarled. Dozens of people were staring at them now.

"I wouldn't come back if you paid me 1,000 Reichsmarks a night. I'm done taking orders from a sleaze-merchant like you."

"You little hussy!"

"You can't talk to a lady like that," snapped Michael.

"I see no lady here," Kristof said. "Monika, you'll never work in this city again." He beckoned to two men in suits. "Please show our two young friends the back door. And don't make a fuss."

One of the bouncers grabbed Monika. "Get your hands off me, you filthy ape!"

The man seemed to know when to back down and let go.

"I'll walk out of here myself. Goodbye, Kristof. What a legacy you've built here."

She strode away and Michael followed as fast as he could. The bouncer led them to a service door to the alley outside, and shut the metal door with a loud *clunk* after their exit. And they were alone again.

"I'm sorry," Michael said. "That was all my fault."

"You're right, it was." She pulled up the hem of her evening gown and traipsed through the alley to the street. They passed trash cans piled high with wasted food and emerged onto Unter den Linden. She looked so beautiful under the streetlights. Her face was lit with anger, but the sadness in her eyes was plain to see.

"But you didn't want to work that room anymore. You said that yourself."

"I say a lot of things. That was my only source of income. It was easy money, and now it's gone."

"Can I buy you a drink?"

She glared at him. "I suppose it's the least you can do. Let's get off Unter den Linden. I want to put as much distance as I can between the Adlon and me right now."

"I'm not as quick on my feet as I usually am, but I'll try."

Men stared at Monika as they passed, but she either didn't notice or ignored their attentions. Michael was proud to be here with her, and the truth was, it didn't matter where they went as long as she was there. They found a café on a side street and took a seat outside.

"We're a little overdressed," she said.

"Nothing wrong with looking good."

"How long were you dancing in the Adlon?"

"A few months." She put her head down and whispered, "I know what you're thinking—I wasn't a full-service dancer. Maybe that was the problem."

"I wasn't thinking that."

"You're a bad liar. How did you find me?"

"I ran into Miner at a party in the US Embassy last night."

"What did he tell you?"

"He told me he knew your father."

Monika seemed to take a few seconds to digest his words. "Yes, he died in a camp a few months ago. They never said how. The official cause of death was 'an accident'."

"I'm so sorry."

"That was when I started working in the hotel. The money he left ran out, and I had to pay for his funeral. It's been so hard."

"You don't have any other family?"

"An aunt who looks in on me every week or so, and some cousins, but not much." Without warning, she stood up. "You want to take me home to my apartment to talk somewhere safe? Don't get any ideas. I'm not that type of girl. If I was, I'd probably still be working in the Adlon."

"If that's what you want."

"It is."

"You can beat me with my crutches if I try anything inappropriate."

"It wouldn't be the first time I did that."

"I'd think most people telling me that were joking, but with you... I don't know."

She smiled at him. He threw down some money on the table—less for the two drinks than one beer in the hotel.

She flagged down a taxi and they got in. He reached over and took her hand and held it as they drove.

The city was alive with revelers celebrating the games, and the traffic was unusually heavy for the time of night. It was almost eleven o'clock when they pulled up outside a gray apartment building on a quiet and clean street. Several Nazi flags hung from a greengrocer's shop across the road.

"They took down the JEWS NOT WELCOME HERE sign for the games," she said as they got out. Michael paid the taxi driver with little thought of how he'd get home. That didn't matter.

She led him inside. "I'm sorry. The apartment's on the fourth floor—I didn't think."

"It's ok. We'll take one flight at a time."

He tried to hide the difficulty of taking the stairs, but he was tired and his leg hurt. He was sweating as they reached the third floor, and needed a rest.

"You're doing great." She sat down beside him on the top step of the dark stairwell. She took his hand, and he looked into her eyes. The feather touch of her lips on his was the most perfect thing he could ever have imagined. He breathed in her scent and pulled her body into his. And she stood up all too soon.

"You ok to keep going?"

"Of course I am." He hobbled the rest of the way up the stairs. She could have been taking him to the seventy-fifth floor, and he would have followed her.

The apartment was simply furnished and immaculately clean. An old framed photo of Monika with her parents stood in the middle of the coffee table in the living room.

"Have a seat on the balcony," she said, opening two long windows to the night. "I have some wine. You want some?"

"That'd be great."

"I'll be out in a minute."

He sat down on one of the two metal chairs on the small balcony overlooking the street.

"My father and I used to sit out here and have dinner on warm nights," she said as she brought the wine glasses out. "You're the first man to sit in his seat since they took him."

"I'm sorry—"

"Don't be. Thank you for coming. *I'm* sorry I didn't wait for you at the stadium yesterday."

"At least you came to the race."

"I wouldn't have missed it, but I got scared afterward. It's not easy to let people in. I'm a coward, I suppose."

"You didn't seem like a coward when you were talking to that maître d'."

"That was all lies and bluster. I'm an expert at that. You deserve better than the likes of me."

"But I want you."

"No, you don't. My life is a disaster, Michael. One calamity after another."

He said nothing; they stared together over the city. The sound of singing interrupted their silence. Several Brownshirts were on the street below, pushing each other and laughing as they roared their marching songs.

"The local thug brigade," Monika said through gritted teeth. "I knew a few of them growing up. They were the biggest idiots in school, and now they push people around and give orders to strangers."

"The scum is seeping to the top."

"I hate them."

He hesitated. "I have a question for you, but I don't mean to upset you."

"You'd do well to upset me more after the night I've had."

"Why did you want to get to Goebbels if your father's already dead? What good would that have done?"

A tear broke down her cheek. "Because his minions killed my father—the only person I loved in this horrible world."

He reached over and took her hand. She made an excuse and went inside for a moment, then came back with the bottle and sat down. "You want some more wine?"

"I haven't drunk this glass yet. You never answered my question."

Several seconds passed. "You really want to know?"

He didn't answer—just waited.

She drained her glass. "Ok, I'll tell you. I wanted to get close to Goebbels because I know he likes pretty girls. I was going to use the only thing I have at my disposal to get revenge for my father."

It took him a few seconds to figure out how to react to what she said. "You were going to kill Goebbels? Hitler's Minister for Propaganda? The Gestapo would execute you for even saying those words."

"That didn't matter to me." She poured herself more wine. "I've thought about jumping off this balcony so many times these last few months. I fell into a great abyss after my father died, depressed and angry. But more than anything, I was lonely. I had nothing else to do but retreat into myself. Most of the people I've interacted with since then have either tried to use me, or I wanted to use them. I never thought I'd live my life this way."

"You can't confide in your aunt, or the cousins you mentioned?"

"They're family, but that was one of my cousins with the Brownshirts on the street earlier. My aunt flies a swastika from her house and has a portrait of Hitler above the fireplace. It's all I can do not to rip it down when I go over there. Exacting some kind of revenge for my father is all that's keeping me alive. It's the glue that binds my life together now. The only thing."

"My mother died when I was eleven," Michael said. "I know

the anger and pain you're feeling. My father left—he couldn't take it either. And my anger doubled. My family fell apart just because of the disease my mother got. It didn't seem fair."

"It wasn't."

"But what is? You think your father wants you to pay for his life with yours? You think he wants revenge that badly?"

"You didn't know him."

"No, I didn't. I never met him and I never will, but I know he loved you, and he'd never want that for you."

"You still had a family. Your father came back."

"Yes, and I forgave him as soon as he did. I didn't think I would, but I did, and I'm glad. That was the reason we were able to move on and get our life back. My sister held on to the anger for much longer."

"I've never known anything like this." Tears rolled down her cheeks. "I feel like I'm at the bottom of a great deep hole, and all I can see is the dark all around me."

He reached across and took her in his arms. She allowed his embrace for 30 seconds or more, weeping on his shoulder.

He pulled back and spoke again. "You have to decide if you deserve a life, or not, after all the punishment you received for no good reason. All the suffering you've gone through. You don't deserve any of this. None of it."

"My father was a trade union leader. He just wanted to stand up for his workers."

"And he'd want you to live. Wouldn't he?"

"Yes."

"You throwing your life away for his is the last thing he ever would have wanted. You've got to change your perspective. This might sound ridiculous, but you've got to figure out some kind of way to love yourself."

She shook her head. "You barely know me."

"It's strange, but I feel like I've known you for years. I can't say why. It's ridiculous, really—we've only met three times.

This time last week, I didn't even know you existed. Maybe it was in a previous life."

"I feel the same," she admitted and wiped her tears from her cheeks. Her light mascara was running down in black rivulets. "Thank you. I think you're the person I needed to meet right now. Can I see you tomorrow?"

He rolled his eyes. "Are you kicking me out already?"

She shot him a sideways smile. "Well, if this is something serious, it has to be a proper courtship. We could go for a walk or something."

"Walking isn't my strong suit right now, but if that's the only way I get to see you..."

Seeing her laugh lifted his heart. She stood, leaned over him, and kissed him on the cheek. He drew in her scent once more. "Can you manage the stairs?"

"I can always roll down if I need to."

"I'll make sure you reach the street in one piece."

She walked with him, although descending the stairs was much easier than the opposite. They arrived at the street together, and she flagged down a taxi. The car pulled up and she opened the door for him.

He paused before getting in. "Thank you for an illuminating night. Call me if you have any of those bad thoughts again—no matter what time."

"You're too sweet to me." She kissed him again and he got into the cab. He peered out the back window as it drove away, watching her standing on the side of the street until the taxi turned the corner.

11

Friday, August 6

Helga was at her desk, talking on the phone. She was one of the most successful businesswomen in the city, and an ardent member of the party to boot, yet Benz and the other Nazis in the factory still came to Seamus, despite the fact that she was just as much owner as he. It seemed there were some things the brown-shirted masses just couldn't get over. Seamus was quite the opposite in his views. He still consulted her and worked alongside her, despite the fact that she was a National Socialist. She was the only family he had in this city, apart from the ones under his own roof, and she was wily and sharp as the point of a bayonet. The suspicions they'd harbored in the past toward one another had given way to their shared goal of maintaining her late father's business. They almost never spoke of anything other than business or his family, and she knew Maureen, Michael, and the other three children as well as any dedicated aunt.

She took the glasses from her face as he entered her office. Seamus took a seat without waiting for her to offer it. They spoke about various client accounts and the problem with a supplier before she said something he wasn't expecting: "Business is good."

"Let's keep it that way."

She never criticized him over his reticence in accepting the government contracts that were the foundation of the thriving business they'd built. She could have, as it was her idea, but she never did.

"I think it's high time we think about expanding," she said.

"We're at capacity now. You want to open another facility?"

"We should think bigger. The working capital is there to produce much more than bullets and shells."

Seamus felt a burning sensation in his chest. He'd known this was coming for a while. The government's rearmament program was gearing up day by day, and showed no signs of abating. The opportunities for munitions dealers were boundless. War—or at least the preparation for it—had propelled German industry into a boom time. The fact that the workers were still living at subsistence wages wasn't the government's, or most business owners', concern.

"What are you thinking?" he asked.

"Airplanes."

Seamus laughed while his cousin retained her stoic gaze. "You can't be serious? What do we know about producing war planes?"

"Not a lot, yet, but I've engaged with some contacts in the Reich Chancellery and I'm confident we could get a low interest loan. And with the subsidies and tax breaks offered to produce armaments—"

"We've only been in munitions for a year."

"Now is the time. Word is, the government is going to spend upward of 5 billion Reichsmarks on rearmament next year, more than 2 billion of that on the Luftwaffe. We can't miss out on that gold rush."

Helga put down her glasses and leaned forward with the same look in her eye she'd had the previous year when she launched them down the road to producing bullets and shells for the burgeoning Nazi military.

"What's the risk?" was the best Seamus could come up with as an argument. The reality was that apart from his conscience roaring at him from within, there was no good reason not to pursue this.

"I'll get the numbers together and we can make the decision together over the next few weeks. I know you've had a lot on your mind lately."

Seamus glanced over at the picture of his children on Helga's desk. The one of her with Michael in his racing singlet with the swastika on the chest was front and center. This was exactly what Hayden would want—for him to get even more information and to get even deeper into the industrial hierarchy.

"Send on the figures when you have them. We'll make the best decision for the company."

"That's all I ask."

He stood up and walked back to his office, visions of warplanes he'd produce strafing civilians on the ground already forming in his mind.

Half an hour later, the phone rang on his desk. The sound was like an electric shock through his body, and he reached for it to dull the pain.

"Seamus?" Hayden asked.

"Bill."

"Time waits for no man, my friend. Do you have 20 minutes for me this afternoon?"

"For you? Of course."

"I'll be in your office in about fifteen."

His old army buddy hung up before Seamus could react

and was true to his word. Fifteen minutes later, he strolled in wearing gray slacks and a white shirt.

"You want to see the place?" Seamus asked.

"I haven't toured somewhere like this since the local chocolate factory in third grade."

"I can't say we produce anything as precious as chocolate to an eight-year-old." Seamus threw the file he was holding on his desk.

"Bullets are better than candy to Hitler and his acolytes," Hayden answered and shut the office door behind them.

The workers still straightened their backs and kept silent as Seamus walked around the factory—all except Benz and the other members of the Trustee Council. They carried on chatting and laughing.

Hayden spoke to a few of the workers in his almost-perfect German. They smiled and asked him questions about America.

They were out of earshot when Seamus asked him, "Do you want to meet my cousin?"

"What side of the—"

"She's a member of the Party. Loves to wear her pin around the factory. I'm sure she has it on today."

"Maybe another time."

"You speak good German," Seamus said in English. He didn't speak his first language much these days, even with his children.

"My parents were both off-the-boat Germans."

"My father was too. Mother was from Ireland."

"Hence the name—I get it. Can we go for a walk? I feel like some fresh air."

Seamus nodded and went to the main doors. The area around the factory seemed the safest place on the overcast and dull day. Two men outside on a break stubbed out their half-smoked cigarettes when they saw Seamus, and hurried back inside.

"So, Bill. I'm guessing you didn't come here to research my genealogy."

"Astute as ever."

"What are you *really* doing here?"

"In Germany, or in your parking lot?"

"Either. Both."

"You left the military soon after the war, didn't you?"

"I couldn't wait to get out. I'd seen enough by that stage."

"I stayed in for a few years and then joined the FBI. I settled down long enough to get married and have a son, but I wasn't good at it."

"It's a learned skill."

They reached the corner of the lot and stood still. "I was sent over here to gather information about the Nazis, and figure out if Hitler means what he writes about going to war, or else what he says to the British and the French about not having any territorial ambitions."

"Like what he wrote in *Mein Kampf*? Or the speech about Germany never breaking the peace in Europe he offered the Allies after remilitarizing the Rhineland in March?"

"Says one thing, does another. You ever meet him?"

"No. You?"

"I'd like to, but no." He reached into his pocket for a pack of cigarettes. A minute later, both men were smoking. "The powers that be sent me over to evaluate the situation on the ground."

"Are they interested in how the Jews are being treated? The laws subjugating them?"

"I could tell you they were, but I won't lie to you. They just want the Germans to stay quiet, and keep the peace. No one wants war. Not after what we went through."

"They don't talk about the Jews or the Roma people or the political opponents of the Nazis?"

"I wouldn't say they don't talk about it, but I wouldn't say the marginalized minorities in German society are their primary concern."

"Or any concern."

"You're getting it now. Why? Were you hoping the US government was going to come over and save the Jews? They're not too popular stateside either, I'm afraid."

"My wife has Jewish blood. She only found out back in '33. They kicked her out of the Reich Chamber of Culture for it, and now she'll never work in Germany again."

"I'm sorry to hear that." Hayden paused for a few beats as if he were building up to something. "The reason I'm here is that you're an arms manufacturer. No one knows about the military buildup like you."

"Our contracts are for bullets, shells, and helmets."

"And what better way to gauge Hitler's intentions than to keep track of those three things? For a man who says he wants peace, he seems to be very interested in stepping up military spending."

"How can I help?" Seamus asked.

"I won't ask for much. Just a list of your orders, and whatever you hear from your peers—if you know anyone building tanks, ships, or planes. I'm not looking for blueprints."

"But if I had them, you wouldn't throw them back in my face."

"Hardly."

"It's funny you should ask about producing planes. Just today my partner suggested we diversify our business into flying machines."

Hayden smiled and patted his old friend on the shoulder. "I knew I had the right man. That could be a good decision for Ritter Metalworks."

"I can get a list of my orders over to you in a few days."

"It's best if we don't deliver them through official channels.

I'll come over to your house when you're ready and pick them up."

"Whatever you think. I'd better get back to work."

"Oh, and Seamus—if any of your fellow captains of industry have the same political inclinations as you, send them my way. But be careful. Don't ask anyone unless you're 100 percent sure."

"I think I might have someone in mind."

They turned to walk back toward the factory. "A word of advice," Hayden said. "If I was living here with my family, I'd think about stashing some money away. Just in case."

"In case what?"

"You never know."

He reached into his pocket and pulled out a pen and a notepad. He jotted something down and tore off the sheet. "Go see this man. Tell him I sent you."

Seamus held up the piece of paper. "Thanks."

"Thank you. I'll be in touch. Expect to see me at your house in a few days."

"I'll get Lisa to cook up something special."

"Sounds delightful."

Hayden strolled back to his car. The sun peeked out from behind the clouds as Seamus stepped back inside the factory.

Friday, August 6

A special, extra meeting of the Subversives was called at the last minute, with only those who'd volunteered to help Maureen in her endeavor in attendance.

"You're planning to meet up with the camp guards tomorrow night?" Herman was amazed.

"Are you sure about this?" asked Gilda. "It sounds dangerous."

"You're right. She shouldn't be meeting up with those men," said Thomas.

"Your jealousy is wasted," Maureen said with a half-smile. "I'd rather kiss a skunk than one of those guards."

"I'm not jealous of those pigs. I'm worried for your safety. What if they recognize your face afterward?"

"Once the operation's over, they'll never see me again."

"I'll come with you," Thomas said.

"No, you won't."

The look on his face was like that of a child whose favorite toy had been snatched from their grip. She rested her hand on his forearm to soften the blow. "How much do you think they'll tell me if I stroll in to the bar with you on my arm?"

He sat back in his seat and folded his arms over his chest.

"She's right, son," Herman said. "Maureen needs to seem available."

"You know what's even more effective than one young pretty girl? Two young pretty girls," suggested Gilda. "Is there someone who could come with you? That might be safer."

Maureen relented. "Yes, I think I'd be more comfortable with some backup. I'll ask Karen from college. She's beautiful and wants to be an actress. Those guards will be falling over themselves to talk to her."

"Is she up to it?" Thomas asked. "And can we trust her?"

"I trust her a lot more than I trust my own sister."

"Fiona?" asked Gilda in surprise.

"She's has broken with the rest of the family about Hitler and the Nazis. A few weeks ago she had an argument with my father about a poster of the Führer she wanted to put on the wall in her room."

"A familiar story these days." Herr Schultz sighed.

"Sometimes I think her devotion to the Nazi Party is outgrowing her loyalty to the family."

"But she knows about your stepmother's Jewish lineage, doesn't she?" Herman asked.

"Yes."

"What does she say about that?"

"That our stepmother isn't a real Jew, and that she has enough Aryan blood in her to counter the bad, but she never says that in front of Lisa herself. Her League of German Girls troop is attending the Nazi rally in Nuremberg this year, and she wants to go too. We're all worried about her."

"The poor child," Herr Schultz said. "She's been here since she was what age—ten, eleven? What chance does a youthful impressionable mind have against the onslaught of propaganda young people are subjected to these days?"

Leon Gellert, a Jewish composer barred by the Nazis, spoke. "Perhaps if you could find her a Jewish friend, she'd see they want the same things she does. The Nazis derive their power from dehumanizing people. If you could reverse that, you'd be some way along to redeeming your sister's heart."

"It's not too late for her," Herman said. "Or for anyone."

"I hope you're right. I'm starting to miss the little girl I used to know."

"In the meantime, we have more pressing matters to attend to," Gilda said.

"You don't have much time," Herr Schultz said. "What if your friend can't come along?"

"I'll make do myself."

Her boyfriend looked like he was about to explode at the notion of her going alone.

She snapped, "They're police, Thomas. I'll be careful."

"I'll be waiting outside while you're in with them," he said.

They spent the next few minutes going over the minutiae of the dangers inherent in her meeting these policemen in a public place. The others sat in silence as Thomas protested everything she said.

Herman was the one who deliberately changed the subject. "Once she meets the police and finds out the information, then what? Getting thirteen human beings out of the camp is a logistical nightmare. Eleven children? Is it even possible?"

"Not in one go," Leon said. "And once you get them out of Marzahn—if you get them out—where to? You can't just drop them back to their apartment and wish them luck. They'd be back in the camp in hours and you'd be off to a KZ yourselves."

"I can get a truck," Herman said. "My cousin runs a haulage company. I could ask him for one, no questions asked."

"I saw a truck go into the camp when I was there," Maureen said.

"Who was it?" Herman asked.

"It said 'Marzahn Construction Supply' on the side."

"That's our way in," Herman said.

"I made a sketch of the logo."

"I'll take a trip out to Marzahn tomorrow," Leon said. "We need to get the lettering exactly right. I have a good eye for these things. I'll take care of it all."

"Excellent," Thomas said.

"They delivered some lumber and barrels of what I can only assume were nails and rivets," Maureen continued.

"How big were the barrels?" Gilda asked.

"Big enough to fit children inside."

"What about the others?" Thomas asked.

"We get them the tools they need to cut through the fence, and pick them up outside," Herr Schultz said.

"What about the police guarding the place? You think they're just going to lie down and let us take thirteen people out of there?" Thomas asked.

"That's where I come in," Maureen said. "We'll have a party with the guards on the last night of the games. They'll be so drunk, they won't notice if we walk Willi and his family out the front gate."

"And once they're out?" Leon asked.

"They could be at the Polish border in less than five hours," said Herman.

"Only to Poland? What if they get deported back to Germany?" Maureen worried. "They'll be straight back to where they started, or worse—to a concentration camp."

"Sure, they'd be better off in Denmark or Sweden. But there's only so much we can do. Getting visas for thirteen people in ten days would be impossible for anyone, let alone a Roma couple and their eleven children. They'll have to take their chances once they arrive," Gilda said.

"One question's been on my mind," Herman said. "Why this family? Why are you doing this? Who is Willi to you?"

"That's the big mystery," Thomas said.

Maureen smiled and opened one of the beers on the table. "You know what? I don't even know his full name. It's ridiculous. But you know what my father does for a living."

The silence around the table was answer enough.

"He makes the bullets and artillery shells that Hitler might use one day to invade the USSR or Poland, or to take back the Sudetenland in Czechoslovakia. He made the decision to protect his workers and the legacy of his dead uncle, but he also wanted to get rich and give his family the life he's always wanted to. I have to live with his decision every day. Maybe saving Willi, his parents, and his ten siblings might ease the guilt that hits me every morning when I open my eyes in the luxurious home my father inherited. I need this chance to atone."

12

Saturday, August 7

Michael spent a few minutes stretching his hamstring in the backyard's morning rays. The injury wasn't as severe as it first seemed, and he could walk without the crutches now. It would be a few weeks until he'd be able to run again, but that didn't seem like the worst penance right now. For the first time in as long as he could remember, running wasn't at the forefront of his mind. Monika's face appeared before him. He held the image as long as he could before it faded like smoke in the breeze. He hadn't heard from her since he left her apartment on Thursday night. She didn't have a phone, but had his number. It was up to her to contact him, and he was content with that. It enforced discipline on him, and what was the point in hounding her? How long would he leave it before he wrote her a letter, or even called over to see her? He hadn't decided yet, but perhaps a week? Maybe he wouldn't need to.

Leaving the crutches behind, he walked into the house.

Thomas was at the dining room table with Maureen. "So Karen won't do it?"

"Karen won't do what?" Michael asked.

They looked up at him like he'd caught them with their hands in the cookie jar. "Just a project for university," Maureen said. "Nothing for you to concern yourself with. What are you doing today?"

"Right now, I'm planning on having a beer in the backyard and considering my future."

"It's not even lunchtime!" his sister said.

"But according to our father, it's never too early to consider one's future. What about you, Maureen? What are you planning to do with yours?"

She looked distracted, but he didn't relent and waited for an answer.

She sighed. "I'll get my degree and become a surgeon."

"In Germany?"

"This is where I'm studying, and where Thomas lives." She pointed, and he smiled as she continued. "Why? Are you thinking about going back?"

He shrugged. "Father thinks I should apply to college in America. It's too late for the fall semester, but maybe after Christmas."

As soon as he said it, the pesky image of Monika's beautiful face appeared in front of his eyes again. He tried to see past it to a future in America, running for the flag of a free country, and not the Nazi swastika. "Or else I could stay here and work for Father."

"Would you want to do that? Work in munitions?"

He bristled. "Where do you think all our money comes from? You don't mind spending it. Join me for a beer, Thomas?"

"It's a bit early for me."

"What about you, Miss Holier-Than-Thou?"

"Same, but thanks for the offer. You enjoy it."

"More for me to savor." He shuffled into the kitchen. He dug his fingers into his hamstring, trying to massage away the pain before opening the refrigerator and reaching for a bottle of cold beer. They'd never had one of these cold contraptions in Aunt Maeve's house. He wondered how his girl cousins were and felt a pang of guilt as he realized he hadn't written to them in months. It was something for him to do this afternoon—they'd love to hear about his experience in the games.

The phone rang as he closed the refrigerator door. He didn't pay it any mind and started to walk back to his chair in the sunny backyard the best he could.

Maureen's voice interrupted his progress. "Michael, it's for you. A girl. Monika?"

"Ok," he said, trying to hide his inner tumult. The smile on his sister's face caused him to question the effectiveness of his efforts.

"Monika?" he asked as he picked up the receiver. "Where are you calling from?"

"The Adlon. I know, I know... I shouldn't have bothered going back, but it was easy money."

"How did the bridge rebuilding efforts go?"

"Let's just say that it'd take a greater engineering feat than building the Eiffel Tower to get my place back on the dance floor here."

"Time to move on to greener pastures?"

"Wherever they might be. I'm eager to find out."

"You're not too far away from my house."

"That's what I was going to ask about. Can I come over and have lunch? I don't want to seem like the type who invites themselves over, even though that's exactly what I'm doing."

"No, I mean, yes. Come over. I was just about to have a beer in the backyard. My sister and her boyfriend are here. The rest of them are out for the day in Wannsee, but yes, please, they'd love to meet you."

"You're sure it's no trouble?"

"When are you coming over?"

She laughed and asked for the address. Michael hung up the phone and punched the air.

"What are you so happy about?" Maureen asked.

"My friend is coming over for lunch."

"The girl? Figures," she said.

A thought occurred to him, and he stopped dead by the table and turned to his sister. "My new friend, Monika, has suffered a lot because of the Nazis. Her father died in a concentration camp a few months ago. I think it would mean a lot to her if we opened up to her about what we think about the regime."

"If you're sure we can trust her..."

"Oh, I'm positive."

"I'll talk to her after lunch," Maureen said. "I know how lonely it can be to be the only sane person in a sea of Nazi supporters."

"Thanks," he said and carried on outside.

Time drew out like a blade, but the doorbell rang after the longest 28 minutes he could remember. Trying to look as casual as possible, he strolled to the door. She was alone, holding her bike, resplendent in a white summer dress pocked with tiny blue flowers.

"I hope I'm not disturbing you," she said with a half smile.

"Disturbing what? Sitting in the yard alone? Come in."

Thomas and his sister stood up as they entered the dining room.

"This is Monika Horn."

She greeted them both with polite handshakes and smiles.

"Welcome," Maureen said. "Michael spent the last 20 minutes preparing lunch for you both."

She smiled at him. "Did you?"

He shrugged, a little embarrassed. "I threw a few things together. Nothing fancy."

But she seemed impressed by the bread and sliced meats and beer he laid out for her in the garden. She gazed around as they sat down to eat.

"Your house is incredible."

"A lot better than where we lived before we came here. I used to share a room with my three siblings in Newark, New Jersey."

"When your father was away... What was the phrase you used? 'Riding the rails'?"

"For two years. Maureen found it hard to forgive him. You know how it is."

"I never had anything to forgive my father for. It wasn't his fault he was taken away."

"I didn't mean it like—"

She brushed a stray lock of auburn hair from her face. "I know what you meant. I've been thinking about what you said to me the other night. I replayed the conversation in my mind 100 times, if I'm honest. It's been a slow few days, what with my losing my only means of supporting myself." She smiled. "I've had a lot of time to think."

"About what comes next?"

"Yes, but also what you said about my father, and what he'd want. I know now he would want me to live. So what do I do now, if I'm not going to murder Goebbels and swing for it?"

"Indeed. What does the future hold for us now?"

"Are you thinking about going back to America?"

"My father was talking about sending me to college there."

"Go," she said. "I'd get out of here in a heartbeat if I had anywhere to go. You got any room in your suitcase? I'll stow away with you?"

She laughed as she said it, but Michael couldn't contemplate anything more wonderful.

"College is an option. I should be able to get on the running team somewhere."

"With your talent? You'd walk onto any team. They'd be lucky to have you."

They talked about her father and growing up in Berlin in the '20s. He told her about training and his mother. Time seemed to disappear when he was with her. The only way to judge it was the empty beer bottles on the table in front of them. The count was four each when Maureen came out.

"You two have been out here for almost three hours! Do you mind if I join you for a little?"

"Of course not," Monika said. "I'd love that."

His sister seemed nervous as she pulled up a chair. They made small talk for a few minutes about Maureen's studies and her boyfriend, before she got to what she wanted to say. "My brother tells me you're no friend of the Nazis."

The smile faded from Monika's face. "I'm trying to deal with how I feel about Hitler and the rest of his murderers. The things happening in this country these days make my blood boil. I used to try to ignore it, but I'm not sure I can anymore."

"I'm so sorry about your father."

"I had all these dreams about killing a prominent Nazi as revenge for what they did to him. My life in return for revenge for my father's. But I realized that's not what he ever would have wanted. It took me a while to figure that out. I think I just needed a little help to see it."

The look she gave Michael almost melted his heart. He reached over and took her hand, and she curled her fingers around his.

"You don't have any other family?" Maureen asked.

"None that aren't hardcore Nazi sympathizers. I go over and Hitler's on the wall, glaring down at me with those beady eyes. They rail on about the Jewish threat and the conspiracy that lost the war—the whole barrel of lies. It's hard to take. I just wish I had something to cling to, you know. I was so focused on my insane scheme these last few months. Now that I've realized how crazy I was to even contemplate it, what do I do now? But I feel like I need to do something. Not talk about how awful the powers that be are, but to do something. Anything good to make this better, even in the tiniest way."

Maureen sat in silence for a long two seconds before sitting forward. "Are you doing anything tonight?"

MONIKA WAS the same size as Maureen and was able to fit into a dress she gave her.

"You look beautiful," Maureen said. "Those guards don't stand a chance."

"It's your dress that is beautiful. Thank you for letting me wear it."

"You're welcome. Let's be careful and we should be fine."

Michael insisted on coming with them to Marzahn. It had been impossible to leave him out of the plan. At first he'd been as horrified as Thomas, and when Thomas turned up to drive them in his car, the two young men complained the whole way.

It took a while to find Walter's Bar among the quiet, residential streets of the eastern suburb. When they saw it, Thomas drove past and parked 100 yards down the road on the opposite side.

"I'll be here watching. If I see any kind of commotion, I'll come running."

"And I'll come hobbling," said Michael.

Monika laughed. "Try not to worry. It's not the first time either of us have met boys in a bar."

"You had to say that?"

Maureen put her hand on her brother's arm. "Stop worrying. Everything is going to be fine."

The bar's wooden façade was adorned with both Olympic and Nazi flags, just like the renamed Via Triumphalis in the center city. It was just after eight o'clock. The guards had been here since about six.

"Perfect," Maureen said as they sauntered inside.

The bar was wooden, the varnish chipped and cracking. A large mirror hung on the wall behind it, and a lanky bartender in a flat cap served drinks. Smoke and stale beer lingered in the air like a mist. Loud jazz music played from the record player set up at the back—another sign of the loosening of restrictions during the games. At least a dozen men at the bar turned around to stare as she and Monika walked in. Seconds later, she heard his voice.

"Hello!" Moritz called out. "You made it. And who's this?" In full uniform, he pushed his way from the other end of the bar and was with them in seconds.

Monika held out her hand for him to kiss. He was more than happy to oblige. "Now, where are all these brave policemen I've heard so much about?"

The four other guards, also in full uniform, were at the end of the bar. None were immune to Monika's charms as she ambled over.

The young man introduced them and the girls settled at the bar.

"Now, who's going to buy us a drink?" Monika asked.

All five men scrambled to reach into their pockets. A policeman named Robert won the race, and soon the girls were drinking frothy beer from steins with traditional metal lids on top.

It took several minutes for the guards to get over the fact that the girls came, and then they seemed frozen. Monika was the one to get things moving once more.

"So, my friend told me about the wonderful job you're doing keeping the gypsies off the streets during the games."

"How long have you known each other?"

Monika spouted out, "We were born in the same hospital on the same day. We have the same birthday. Would you believe it? Destined to be best friends!"

"It was written in the stars," Maureen added.

"Two beautiful girls in the same hospital on the same day!" Moritz marveled.

"Our parents are best friends, so we grew up together."

"More like sisters."

"Do any of your brave men want to take me out dancing?" Monika asked.

A small area in front of the record player seemed designated a dance floor, and several patrons were using it.

"I will," Robert said and reached over for her hand before any other man could take it.

The other guards gave Moritz space to sit beside Maureen. It seemed he'd laid claim to her before they arrived.

"Do you like your job?" she asked as he stared at her.

His dull eyes lit up. "Yes. My father was on the force before I was—"

"No, I mean guarding the people in the camp."

"Of course." He reached into his pocket for a pack of cigarettes, offering her one, but she refused. He took a puff and continued. "I like to do what I'm ordered."

"It sounds scary, though. Have any of the people tried to escape?"

"Some. They didn't get more than a few yards past the fence."

"How did you catch them?"

"We're there to do a job. The dogs are handy, too."

A whoop from the dance floor caused them both to turn their heads. Robert was swinging Monika around.

"She knows how to have fun," Maureen said. "Tell me what

happened when you caught the escapees. I love exciting stories. Were you there?"

"Right on the spot. I saw them try to sneak through a hole in the fence. Someone dozed off and those rats tried to take advantage with a fence cutter. We showed them who was boss afterward," he said with an ugly grin.

She shuddered. "Could it happen again? I don't like the thought of those people being out and wandering the streets."

"No. The fence is fixed now. The only way out is the front gate, and they can't get through without permission. None of those vermin are escaping while we're watching."

He stubbed out his cigarette and glanced at Monika on the dance floor again. She was laughing and dancing with several of the men. "Is she always like this?"

"She doesn't know any other way to be. She loves to have fun. Maybe we should have a proper party. We could visit you at the camp."

He looked like he'd tasted something sour. "Why on earth would you come to the camp? Those people carry disease."

"But you must be so bored, being there all night without company! We girls like to do our bit for the Reich. Would we be let in through the gate? Does anyone visit you?"

"The only visitors are trucks with the building supplies for the barracks. No one else needs to come in, and we wouldn't let them if they tried."

"Can't you make an exception for us girls?"

"Oh, my little temptress..."

Before he could say more, she dragged him onto the dance floor. He wrapped his arms around her and slobbered across her cheek. It was hard to hide both her revulsion for him and the fact that she couldn't dance nearly as well as Monika, but Moritz didn't seem to notice—or care—about either.

After two more Tommy Dorsey songs, she excused herself

to the bathroom, locked herself in the stall and sat on the toilet with the seat down.

I have to get him to agree to the party.

Reinvigorated, she steeled herself for what she knew was to come. This wasn't the first time she'd had to endure unwanted male attention. It wasn't even the fiftieth or hundredth time, but never before had so much depended on how she handled a desperate man. Sometimes she wondered what drove men to the lengths they seemed prepared to go to be with a woman. Was it their nature, or a sense of entitlement? Did one feed the other? She went to the mirror. Another lady about ten years older than her stood alone, washing her hands. Maureen thought to ask her what she thought before realizing she couldn't trust anyone here. *Who knows who she's with?*

Moritz was waiting where she left him. His eyes were clouding over and his speech was slowing. He handed her a new beer, though the last one was still sitting on the bar, only half drunk.

"Your friend knows how to have a good time."

Monika was dancing with three men, pretending to rope them in like a cowgirl bringing down steers.

"She's a character, but unfortunately, we have to leave soon."

His face dropped. "Are you sure you have to go?"

He reached out to her. Fighting her instincts, she let his hands fall on her forearms. Nothing about it felt right.

"We do. I promised her parents I'd have her home by midnight."

"Where do you live? I could take you."

"You have a car?"

"No, but I could walk you."

"My father's picking us up, and I think it'd be best if you didn't meet him tonight. He's old-fashioned."

"I understand."

"Can we meet again soon? What do you think about my idea of us coming to you for a party?"

"I'm not so sure—"

"How about on the last night of the games? You men could use cheering up."

He grinned, running his eyes over her. "We'd rather be drinking that night, that's for sure."

"You're right. I don't think you should be alone—not while the rest of the city is celebrating. We'll come with enough whiskey and schnapps for everyone!"

He was nodding now, like a stupid dog eyeing up a plate of sausages. "Ok. You come."

She forced herself to kiss him on the cheek and left him standing by the bar in a drunken stupor. Monika seemed surprised they were going, but didn't argue.

Thomas and Michael were parked in the same place as they hurried up the street. Thomas started the car after they climbed into the back.

"Are you both all right?"

"Fine," Maureen said. "No problem at all." She wasn't about to tell them about the party yet—particularly before discussing it with Monika.

"Did you get anything useful out of them?"

"A marriage proposal," Monika said.

In a release of tension, both girls nearly cried with laughter, but Michael clearly didn't find Monika's answer quite as funny as they did, and Thomas was grim-faced as he pulled out to drive them home.

13

Monday, August 10

The Olympics might have been over for Michael Ritter, but the competition continued nonetheless, and Berlin was still in the viselike grip of Olympic fever. For the duration of the games, the trees lining Kurfürstendamm were fitted with loudspeakers so people could follow the action at the Olympiastadion.

Seamus thought of Willi in the newsstand as the Nazi-approved commentator called the day's events. It must have been as if the trees were taunting him, reminding him through the day of how little anyone cared of his family's fate. The tinny voice from the loudspeakers was a constant reminder of the side of Berlin the Nazis wanted to show the world, while the camp at Marzahn, and those elsewhere, were the opposite.

Seamus flicked open the newspaper on his lap as the train picked up speed. Lisa and Hannah were peering out the window. The little girl waved to several people on the platform, who returned the gesture with bright smiling faces.

"I didn't even realize Helene Mayer already finished her

event," he said, but his wife and stepdaughter weren't listening. He closed his eyes, leaning his head back against the seat.

Helene was once a star of the German sports world. A fencing prodigy, she won the first of many consecutive German championships in 1925 at the tender age of fourteen. In 1928 she won gold at the Amsterdam Olympics, and became a bona fide star in her homeland. Her charisma won over the hearts of millions, and the fans roared as she entered the arena. And in her white fencing outfit, with her blond hair done up in fashionable plaits, she looked the part. Helene was the pride of the nation and received a special award from President Paul von Hindenburg, but everything changed for her on January 30, 1933.

Within three months of Hitler becoming chancellor, her hometown fencing club in Offenbach struck her name from their rolls. Helene's great sin wasn't anything she did, but who she was. According to the ideology of the new regime, she was deemed a "half-Jew." She learned of the decision while in California, where she had received a scholarship. Realizing the gravity of the situation, Helene decided to stay in America, teaching fencing and German. But the day's politics caught her in its web.

Jews were excluded from sports clubs in the Reich and were not eligible for the Olympics. The Americans threatened to boycott the games, so Hitler decided to play ball. Helene Mayer would be the compromise Jewish athlete. She returned to Germany, more out of homesickness than any obligation to compete, and decided to accept the invitation to the games. Including Helene in the German team took the wind out of the sails of the movement to boycott the games, and so the Americans and all the rest of the international squads made the journey to the Olympics. Hitler won again.

The picture in the paper was of Helene with the silver medal she earned, giving the Hitler salute at the awards ceremony. Who knows what might have occurred if she'd declined the offer to compete? *Perhaps the games would never have happened at all*, Seamus thought. The train had left Berlin Central Station, and Lisa and Hannah were settling back in their seats for the 8-hour journey. Seamus handed his wife the paper. She looked at the story and handed it back.

"Why did she offer the salute?"

"To conform, I suppose. She just wanted to compete. She didn't care about politics or her Jewish heritage, even if the authorities did."

"Sounds familiar." Lisa reached into her bag for a pack of cards. She dealt them on the table between the three of them, and they began what Seamus imagined would be the first of many games of Quartet between there and the Swiss border.

They waited until the little girl was asleep in the cot that folded out from the wall of their private cabin to talk about the situation on their minds.

"When do you expect the Gestapo to board the train?" she asked.

"Not until the border. If we stick to the plan and keep calm, nothing will happen. As far as Hannah thinks, we're going to Basel for a couple of days' vacation—she won't be able to give the game away."

"What if they find—"

"They won't. We have to believe that."

"We haven't had the chance to talk like this in a while," she said. "What do we do if Michael decides to go back to America?"

"Whatever we decide. What would you like to do?"

"I'm torn. It's a strange thought to move to a country I've never even been to."

"People do it all the time. My mother arrived from Ireland not knowing anyone. My father found her crying on the docks after her ship was diverted because of a storm."

Lisa sat next to him, making sure Hannah was asleep before planting her lips on his. "You found me too. Your damsel in distress."

"You didn't need me."

"No, but I wanted you."

The sun was setting over the countryside of southern Germany, painting the idyllic green landscapes orange and red.

Seamus lowered his voice, even though his wife was inches away from him. "I've found another business contact for Hayden. He's based in Hamburg, but he's going to be in Berlin for the games. Turns out he's a big sports fan. He wants to meet Michael."

"Bring him to the house—I'll make dinner. Are you sure you can trust him?"

"I met him at the annual Industrial Chamber of Commerce dinner back in '33. We've kept in touch by letter since, and we see each other every year at the event."

"How well do you know him?"

"Well enough to know he's different than the rest of the fat cats at that event. He's no friend of the Nazis. He's as desperate about the situation in the Reich as we are."

Seamus looked out at the darkening landscape, thinking about his wife's question. How well did he know Roland Eidinger? He'd met the man at the Kaiserhof Hotel when Goebbels came begging the richest men in Germany for the money to keep the Nazi Party afloat. It was so difficult to know who was trustworthy—instincts were all he had to rely on. His own daughter, Fiona... He loved her with all his heart, but it was hard to trust her.

The train came to a screeching halt as the sign for Weil am Rhein—the last stop before Switzerland—came into view. Seamus tried to control the fear that seeing the sign for the small town on the German side of the Swiss border engendered in him. The look in Lisa's eyes told him she was battling the same demons. Her hands were sweaty in his.

"It's ok. They won't find a thing."

She nodded.

The sound of boots reverberated through the carriage as the border police boarded the train. *What's the penalty for smuggling money in the Reich these days? Whatever the Nazi judge sees fit to hand down?*

A face appeared at the door to their cabin and the policeman knocked on the glass. He was in his forties, with a thick mustache. Seamus had the same thought he always did when greeted by experienced policemen: *How did he manage the jump from being a regular servant of the peace to being a Nazi pawn?*

"Papers, please," he said.

Seamus handed him the three passports. He eyed each. Nothing in there indicated Lisa was half Jewish, or whatever the Nazis deemed her to be.

"Thank you, Officer," Lisa said with a charming grin as he handed her back the passport.

"You're welcome," he said. "Where is your baggage?"

Seamus stood up and reached for the briefcase and leather bag stowed above the cot where Hannah was still sleeping. The policeman noticed her and smiled before taking the baggage and placing it down on the seat. He dug into the case, removing clothes and toiletries, and laid them out in an untidy pile. Seamus didn't dare look at his wife and held his breath.

The man moved on to the briefcase. "Open it." Seamus did as he was told and revealed the papers inside.

"What's your reason for visiting Switzerland?"

"Business. I'm in armaments production. I'm meeting a supplier."

The policeman looked through the papers and closed the briefcase again. "I won't disturb the child. Enjoy your trip."

And he was gone. They waited until the train moved over the border to exhale. The train arrived in Basel with a loud whistle that woke Hannah up.

"Oh, my big girl!" Lisa helped her down from the cot. "You did so well."

The bleary-eyed little girl had no idea. Seamus reached under her mattress for the stacks of banknotes they'd stashed there. Lisa kept watch as he placed them back into their bag. Safe once more, he threw it up over his shoulder. Lisa was smiling as she carried her still-half-asleep daughter off the train. A taxi outside the station took them to the hotel, and they settled down for a night's sleep.

They went to the bank the following day. The teller was a young girl around Maureen's age. Seamus still had the piece of paper Bill Hayden gave him in his pocket, though he knew the words his old buddy had written by heart.

"Welcome to Credit Suisse."

"I'm here to see Ingo Varner."

Varner was a small man with black hair and eyes to match. He greeted them like old friends.

"Any friend of Bill Hayden's is a friend of mine," he said as he led them to his office.

He accepted the 15,000 Reichsmarks they gave him to deposit with the glee of a crocodile taking down an antelope at a watering hole. Hannah stayed quiet as they opened the joint account.

"You have equal access to the money," Varner said. "If one of you comes alone, the other does not need to countersign."

"That's how we want it," Seamus said, looking at his wife. "One more thing. Could we arrange for a safe-deposit box?"

"Of course."

The banker led them down a hallway into the depths of the bank. He opened a door into a room with safe-deposit boxes, one on top of another in the walls.

"Yes, this one's free." He took one out. "What would you like to put in?"

Lisa took the necklace Uncle Helmut left Seamus from around her neck. "It's for our daughter on her wedding day, passed down from one generation to the next."

"No safer place for it than here," Varner said.

She handed it to Seamus. He held it up, marveling at the massive diamond at the center of the pendant. "I'm not breaking my promise," he said to his dead uncle. "Just keeping it safe."

The box rattled as he placed it inside. Varner closed it up and gave each of them a key. "We can drill it if necessary, but I'd advise you don't lose those."

"We won't," Seamus said.

They said goodbye to Varner and left the bank. They walked through the medieval streets of Basel until they reached the Rhine. The Reich stretched out in the distance beyond the city.

"How does it feel to leave Germany behind?"

"Just fine," his wife answered in English.

Tuesday, August 11

Maureen stepped off the cream-colored tram car and into the hustle and bustle of Kurfürstendamm. The famous street was always busy, but seemed to have developed into the city's heart during the games. She almost had to push her way through the thick crowds. It was a fine day, and the cafés and bars that lined the avenue were packed to the point where people were lining up outside, hoping that someone would be foolish enough to give up their seat on the terrace. A large crowd gathered underneath one of the loudspeakers set up to cover the events from the stadium. Maureen joined them for a few seconds. The final of the women's 100-meter relay was just about to begin, and the people were in a jovial mood. Germany was a heavy favorite to take home yet another gold and extend their lead at the top of the medals table. The men's version of the relay had taken place the day before, where Germany came second. Michael would have won a silver medal but for his injury. She was proud of the way he reacted to the race. He was happy for his teammates, but didn't shed any tears. He knew his time would come. It was only four years to 1940, and barring injury, what could stop him then?

Many of the listeners had beers their hands. A hush fell over the throng as the runners lined up. The commentator wondered aloud if the German women might even break the world record. The race began, and the German sprinter took the lead. The crowd cheered along, and the commentator's words were momentarily lost in the racket. The home team was still leading going into the third leg when the commentator cried out as if he'd been shot. The German athlete had dropped the baton, and the US team raced past. It was all over less than fifteen seconds later. The people on the street looked around, not knowing what to say or do. Some called out that the Americans had cheated.

Maureen walked on, wondering what it would be like to spend four years training for an event in which everyone expected you to win, and then drop the baton. The crowd of people would get over the race in minutes, but what about the athlete herself?

The newsstand came into view. A young man she assumed was Willi stood behind the counter, chatting to the man in front of her for several seconds about the games, marveling at the story of the women's 100-meter relay, agreeing that the Americans had cheated. She admired his ability to do that. She would have spit in people's faces if her family was locked up in that camp. The man in front of her left, and she took a copy of the *Völkischer Beobachter* and placed it on the counter. The newspaper seller looked ill. His cheeks were sunken, and he had red streaks through the whites of his eyes.

"Are you Willi?"

"Yes," he said with a gaunt smile. "Who's asking?"

"Can we talk?" she asked under her breath. "About Marzahn?"

The smile faded. "Give me a minute." He pulled down the awning and came out the back. "I can close up for ten minutes or so. Who are you?"

"I'm Maureen, Seamus Ritter's daughter."

Relief flooded his thin face. "I was hoping someone would come. Follow me."

He led her down a side street to the back of one of the restaurants. The rancid smell of rotting trash filled the air. No tourists would be coming down here.

"Where's your father?" he asked.

"Who else knows you spoke to my father? Have you told any of your friends in the camp? Any of the other families?"

"Not a soul."

"Good. Please never mention his name to anyone. Meanwhile, I'm in charge. I have a group of people determined to get you out of the country. Is your family prepared for a difficult journey?"

"I think they'd take a trip to hell with Lucifer himself rather than stay in the camp. Where are you thinking?"

"You might have to settle for Poland."

"My sister lives there, but she's moving to Sweden soon. My father doesn't want to settle in Poland. He says the Nazis will be there soon."

"That's up to you. Send your sister a letter and tell her to expect visitors. We're going to come for you on the last night of the games."

His starved eyes blurred with puzzlement. "In five days' time?"

"Can you be ready?"

"The sooner the better. The children are getting thinner by the day. We've all got skin diseases, and the smell of raw sewage is stuck to us. How are you going to get us out?"

"You know the guard, Moritz?"

"Moritz Müller? He beat my friend black and blue last week for the crime of talking back. The swine enjoyed it. I could see it in his eyes."

Maureen took a few seconds to digest what she heard. "He and the other guards will be getting drunk that night. We're going to supply the booze and the girls. Around nine or so, a van from the Marzahn Construction Supply will arrive with a late delivery..." She outlined the plan as he listened for five minutes or so, only stopping her to ask questions.

When she finished speaking, he said, "I'd better get back to the newsstand before someone sees us together. Tell your father I'm grateful, and that his name will never pass my lips."

"If we don't meet again, good luck in your new life," said Maureen.

He turned away, but after a few steps he came back to her again. "Thank you for helping us."

She gazed into his hollow eyes, bright now with hope. "What's your last name, Willi? I don't think my father even knows."

"Behrens. The Behrens family is in your hands."

She watched him walk down the alley and fade into the crowd on Kurfürstendamm.

∼

Wednesday, August 12

Many of the foreign dignitaries in town for the games were staying at the Eden Hotel. Located on the corner of Budapester Strasse and Nürnberger Strasse, it had long been one of the most luxurious hotels in Berlin. It was also the one the Nazis put people up in when they wanted to impress them. It was also where Roland Eidinger, the shipping magnate Seamus had become friends with, was lodging for the duration of the games.

The heat of the day had faded, but Seamus still felt a drip of sweat on his neck. He adjusted the collar of his shirt as he stopped on the edge of the terrace, searching the tables for his friend. The formal five o'clock tea on the rooftop deck was a major social event for the chattering classes. Waiters in white tuxedoes buzzed from table to table, serving triangle-shaped sandwiches and kaleidoscopic cocktails in glasses stuffed with fruit. Lively dance music pulsed from the far end of the enclosed area, and Seamus smiled and shook his head at the patrons playing on the mini-golf course beside the tables. Eidinger held up a hand, and Seamus slalomed through the tables set with pristine white cloths. His friend was seated with a couple, and all three stood to greet him.

"Seamus, I'm so glad you're here," Roland said in English. "This is Arnold Baxter of the Chicago Baxters, and his lovely wife, Lady Philomena Guinness of the Irish brewing family."

Arnold was a portly man with a blond mustache in his sixties. His wife was much younger, closer to Seamus's age, and wore a white summer dress with a matching hat.

They took their seats. "My mother was Irish."

"Hence the name, I suppose," Lady Philomena said in an English accent. "I still visit Ireland from time to time, but I've lived abroad for years."

"You're based in America?"

"In Surrey," Arnold said with a strange faux English accent. "I gave up my American citizenship a few years ago."

"Seamus is an old friend in the metalworks business," Roland said in his thick Hamburg accent. He was a fit man in his fifties. He'd inherited a small shipping concern from his father and turned it into a business empire. It was hard to know, as no one kept lists, but he might have been one of the richest men in the Reich.

The quartet spoke about the games for a few minutes until Roland told his friends about Michael and the 100 meters. Seamus was prepared for the conversation and went through his son's training methods and his experience in the Olympiastadion. Baxter and his wife sat in fascinated silence as he spoke.

"He couldn't compete with Jesse Owens?" Baxter asked.

"Did you see the race? I don't see how anyone could have."

"I heard his trainer told Jesse to imagine he was running over hot coals," Roland said. "His feet hardly touched the ground the whole race."

"You must be proud as punch," Lady Guinness said.

"I am. We're looking forward to 1940 in Tokyo."

They ordered cocktails and spoke for another hour or so until Baxter and his wife announced they had dinner plans and took their leave. Seamus shook the man's hand and kissed his wife on the knuckles before taking his seat at the table once more. He looked around. No Nazis here, and no one seemed to be listening in. It still wasn't worth taking a chance.

"Can we speak somewhere a little more private?"

He didn't need to be asked twice. "We can go to my room."

"Maybe somewhere outside the hotel? The zoological gardens are ten minutes away."

Roland held up his hand to ask the waiter for the bill. After a short tussle, Seamus agreed to let his friend pay for the drinks, and they left together.

Roland wasn't in the mood to walk, so the two men took a

carriage to the gardens. Seamus gave the driver a generous tip, and then they were alone. They made small talk until they were inside the park, and the only other people around were couples or people out walking their dogs.

"How did Michael feel about running for the swastika?" Roland asked.

"Much the same as most of the other athletes, I'd imagine. He just wanted to compete."

"We thought things would get better, didn't we? But the Nazis are more popular than ever. It's hard to believe what a joke they were just four years ago."

"How's business?"

"Booming, but at what cost? The country's falling to pieces. My grandchildren are all in the Hitler Youth. I'm wondering if it's all worthwhile. Are you thinking about moving back to America?"

They turned the corner onto a silent stretch of garden with colorful flowers on each side. Seamus waited to begin again.

"I know what'll happen if I do—my business will become a bastion of Nazi supporters. My cousin—"

"You've told me about Helga before, but the time may come when you need to prioritize your family over your promise to your dead uncle, and even your workers. I knew Helmut for years. How could anyone who died in '32, like he did, have predicted what would happen between then and now? I think he'd understand."

"What about my Jewish workers and the foreigners? You think they'll get jobs somewhere else?"

"Maybe it's time they thought about getting out of the Reich too."

"It's not that easy. They don't have the money, and the authorities are imposing a 90 percent flight tax on their assets."

"You can't save the world, Seamus."

"No, but I don't want to leave anyone behind. Gert Bernheim, my factory manager, is Jewish and one of my best friends. I couldn't live with myself if something happened to him."

"And what about your family? What about Lisa?"

"Those horrific laws they passed about the Jews last year haven't affected her so far."

Roland stopped walking and put his hand on his friend's shoulder. "So far. Listen to yourself, Seamus. What if the Nazis pass new laws? What do you think they have in store for the Jews in this country?"

"Lisa isn't classified as a full Jew. She's a *Mischling*."

"And who's to say that won't change?"

No one else spoke to him like this, and Roland's words weighed a ton.

"What do people say to you about the Nazis? You think it's going to get worse?"

"I don't have a crystal ball, my friend. I don't know what's going to happen in 1940 or 1950 or even tomorrow, but it seems to me that things are going to get worse before they get better—for the minorities in society who the Nazis bully, anyway. For us? The rich? Things will stay good, and maybe get even better if Hitler doesn't drag us into some useless war. Like it or not, Seamus, you've joined the elite of German society. Things don't get worse for us unless the country collapses. I'm not worried about our bank accounts. It's our children's minds and the country they'll grow up in that concerns me."

"I wonder what Baxter and his wife think about the Reich, and our dear leader?"

"They can't see what all the fuss is about. They see a vibrant, beautiful city, and a hotel with a mini-golf course on the roof terrace. What does the treatment of Jews, or others the Nazis deem as unacceptable, mean to the likes of them? People are concerned about their day-to-day lives. They'll go home and tell their friends what a wonderful place Germany is."

A young couple strolled by holding hands, and the men waited until they passed before resuming again.

"You haven't sold out, have you, Seamus?"

"What do you mean?"

"I know how hard life was for you in America. You're an important man here. A rich man. Are you afraid you'll lose all that if you go back?"

"Have you ever been poor, one day of your life?"

"Never," Roland said. "And I see the effect that has on my children. My son Erich is twenty-two and expects everything to be given to him. It's something I fight against every day."

Seamus walked on. Thoughts of the camp in Ohio, of digging ditches and sleeping in a tent with three strangers, returned to him for the first time in as long as he could remember.

"I've been so poor that I had to leave my family to feed them, and let me assure you, this life is better. We want for nothing here. Back in America, I didn't have two cents to scrape together. I owe Helmut so much; I can't just betray him. What about you, anyway? Are you thinking about leaving?"

"Maybe. My daughter's kids are teenagers now, and I'll be damned if they don't love Hitler more than me. I've been looking at relocating the business to Rotterdam."

"You speak Dutch?"

"I speak English. So do they."

"You still run shipping out of Rostock?"

"Of course. To Malmo and Trelleborg in Sweden, and Gedser in Denmark, just across the sea."

"Have you ever done anything to soothe your conscience about living in the Reich? About the tacit support we offer the Nazis by paying our taxes and not protesting?"

"Protesters end up in KZ's. I'm not that brave."

"But do you ever do anything?"

Roland looked around to make sure no one was listening—

the so-called "German look" over one's shoulder that so many practiced in the Reich these days. "What are you getting at?"

"Something's come up. *Someone,* more like."

"Who?"

"An old war buddy of mine, working for the American Embassy."

"A diplomat?"

"That's his official title, but his work doesn't seem too diplomatic." Roland's face tightened and he turned away. He walked on a few feet, taking a blue hydrangea in his hand.

Seamus looked around to double-check no one was listening and kept on. "He wants me to help him keep a close eye on the Nazis."

"I don't think—"

"He asked me for copies of my orders for the Wehrmacht. Nothing too dangerous. He also inquired if I knew anyone who could help."

"And you came to me," Roland said. He turned back to face Seamus, and the two men walked on together. "Even if I wanted to assist your endeavor, what makes you think I could?"

"You told me about your work for the government, and I know you invested in that shipyard in Hamburg. All my contact wants is to know the scope of the Nazis' rearmament. If Hitler is so adamant on racing toward war, don't you think the world is a safer place if it knows how fast?"

Roland pursed his lips, taking a few seconds to answer. "I don't know. The Nazis are ruthless thugs."

"You can deliver the documents to me, and I'll bring them straight to my man. We'll keep the loop so small that no one would ever notice."

"He just wants lists of purchase orders and the like?"

"And to know the general sentiment. If you hear anything of interest, just tell me and I'll pass it on."

"I just hope we don't live to regret this."

"I think we're more likely to regret doing nothing, and sucking from the Nazi teat, than trying to do the right thing."

Roland smiled and clapped his friend on the shoulder. "Why did I ever agree to meet you?"

"Because of my charming personality."

The two friends walked through the gardens and stopped at a bar on the other side to get a drink. They watched one of the small television screens the government had set up to show the events at the stadium, for those who couldn't make it there to see them live.

14

Michael's heart leaped as he answered the door and he kissed Monika on the cheek before leading her inside. She looked stunning in a red dress and matching hat. The whole family was waiting in the living room, except Fiona, who was yet to arrive home from her League meeting. Lisa stepped forward and took the girl's hand.

"So good to meet you." She kissed her on the cheek. "Michael hasn't stopped talking about you these last few days. I feel like I know you already."

A tinge of embarrassment pinched his insides as Monika glanced at him with a smile. "I've been talking about him too," she said, and the tension within him turned to joy.

"Then it is high time we met." His father shook her hand with a bright smile on his face.

They took a seat outside and had a glass of wine while Lisa finished preparing the roast lamb with fresh vegetables. Michael sat in silence for much of the time. Monika didn't need him or anyone else to speak for her, and the fact that she had already met Maureen made it all the easier. She talked about growing up in the city and asked his father questions about America and his business. He told her the story of how they came to Germany, and even though she'd heard it all before, she sat there rapt, sipping her wine as she listened.

"How do you know each other?" his father asked, pointing to Maureen and their guest.

"Monika called over for lunch last weekend while you were in Wannsee. And we all went out that night with Thomas."

"It was quite the occasion," Monika added. "Your son told me about the delicate matter of the house at the lake. How was it?"

"We don't know what to do. We aired it out, and Lisa agreed to stay there for one night at least. I suppose we'll sell it and buy something else down there."

Lisa called them in and they took their places at the dining room table.

Fiona arrived, red-faced from running home from her League of German Girls meeting, and ran upstairs to change. At least now she knew better than to wear her uniform to dinner. Conversation during the meal was as easy as it had been outside. Lisa and his father seemed as taken with Monika as Michael was. Even with all that was going on, Michael's mind drifted to what was to happen in two days' time. His leg was getting better, and the plan for Sunday night was coming together, but certain details still needed to be ironed out.

Once they cleared the table and the dishes were done, Maureen called Michael and Monika out into the backyard to talk. Their nightly conferences in Monika's apartment had become a regular event these last few days. After making sure that Fiona or Michael's parents weren't listening in, they gathered at the shed at the end of the garden as the sun faded out and night began to take hold.

"That beard you're growing is coming along," Maureen said.

"It should hide my face a little. That and the hat I'll wear."

"The problems of fame, eh? Thomas is growing one too."

The time to air the doubts dogging him was now. "Are you sure you want to do this?" he asked Monika.

"You don't think I'm up to it?" she asked with venom.

"It's not that..."

"I want to be a part of this, and you need me."

"She was incredible in the pub last week," Maureen said. "You should have seen her. Those men would have followed her off a cliff."

"The more people involved, the more risk of the Gestapo dragging us off to a KZ," he said.

"Let's just stick to the plan. If we can't get them out, we'll back down," Maureen said.

Michael doubted the veracity of her comments, as he knew neither she nor Monika were in favor of turning back.

"What if these policemen remember your faces?"

"There won't be any connection between us and the escape, and even if they do look, how are they going to find us?" Maureen asked. "We gave them fake names. Are they going to search the city for someone who looks like her? Monika and I will fade in the background of a city of millions."

"Well, then, would it be safer to bring even more girls along? Ladies of the night, even?" Michael asked.

"Then the conspiracy gets wider. Do you think some lady we hired for the night would keep it quiet? I see where you're coming from, brother, but trust is everything here. We can't even trust our own family. It's not just Fiona—our father is too anxious about money to lift a finger for the resistance. It's down to us."

INSIDE THE HOUSE, the phone rang. Seamus picked it up.

"Hello, old friend," Bill Hayden said. "You free for a stroll?"

"I will be in about five minutes."

"I'll be at your house in ten."

Seamus plucked the envelope Hayden wanted from the cabinet and waited outside. True to his word, his old war buddy drove up precisely ten minutes after calling. Seamus got in the passenger seat. They rode for a few minutes before stopping on the side of a residential street lined with mansions. Seamus handed his friend the envelope.

"I hope you know how much a risk I'm taking, giving this to you."

"No risk at all. You know you can trust me with your life. I'm not about to run to the Gestapo. You think they're watching your house?"

"I don't see why they would be."

"Then all this is one old war buddy sitting in a car with another."

They got out and began to stroll along the deserted sidewalk, going nowhere.

"What's in it?" Bill asked.

"A copy of our orders for the year to date. Numbers, allocations, our suppliers, and who we're selling them to."

"Who you're selling them to?"

"The different branches of the military. The SS, the army, the navy."

Hayden shook his head. "The naval buildup has me more worried than anything else. Agreeing to let the Nazis produce a percentage of Britain's fleet by weight was the worst thing they could have done. Now they're producing small submarines by the dozens."

"We've sent a lot of ammunition to the naval yards these past few months. I might have some more information about that soon. A friend in shipping, who does a lot of work with the navy, agreed to participate in our venture. He should have something for us in a week or two."

"Excellent. Leaders don't build submarines to keep the peace on the streets—they're weapons of war."

"I presume you'll want more reports like this going forward."

"As many as you can. What do you know about the other manufacturers?"

"Not much more than you, I'd imagine. The big ones are churning out ships and planes—Farben and Krupp, and my old friend Otto Milch."

"Ah, yes, of the venerable Milchs. I met him a few weeks ago at an event in the city. I mentioned your name, and suddenly he looked like someone slipped dirt in his drink."

"We've had some issues in the past."

"I thought as much from his reaction. He's a rich man now. Rearmament is one way to turn an economy around."

"So is forcing young people to engage in labor and erasing Jews and other undesirables from the workforce."

Bill placed the envelope into his jacket pocket and took out a silver cigarette case. He lit both their cigarettes and they walked on.

"Yeah, you wonder when the whole house of cards Hitler has constructed is going to come crashing down. You ever think this is all a part of his plan?"

"What, exactly?"

"Leverage the economy, remove the non-Germans from the workforce, and then when the bankers won't extend any more debt, plunder the east to pay them off?"

"Makes sense. Kings have been doing the same thing since before the ancient Egyptians. If you can't create something, just take what everyone else has."

"You don't think I'll face any sanctions if I decide to move back to the States with Lisa and the family?"

"It's not impossible." Bill exhaled. "It'll be worse if Hitler starts using those bullets you make. I could put in a good word for you—more reports like these would help your cause."

"You're not trying to blackmail me, are you, Bill?"

"No. You're a patriot. I know you'll do your utmost to support the free world in its ongoing battle against the scourge of fascism."

"What if I got into a bind? Could you help me out?"

"You got a body buried in your backyard or something?"

Seamus tried to laugh off the notion of having a body in the backyard, but found himself unable. "No, but you never know what's likely to happen these days. What if the Gestapo catch wind of what we're doing?"

"I'll do what I can, but honestly, those butchers don't abide by any laws." He reached into his pocket for a business card. "I'll tell you what, if you ever need fingerprints on a candlestick at three in the morning, you call me. The embassy arranged a nice little two-bed apartment for me in Mitte. I'll be around if you need me. Address is on the back."

"Thanks." Seamus said and pocketed the card.

"But you know the way this works—you get what you give."

"I'm well aware that friendship only goes so far."

"You're not the only one under pressure. My bosses in Washington demand results."

They came to a halt outside a house that looked more like an embassy than a private residence.

"I'll dig around and see if I can find anything useful to you."

"I knew I had the right man."

They turned and began to amble back toward the parked car.

"How did you get into espionage?" Seamus asked.

Bill smiled. "Someone saw a need I could fill."

"Is that what I'm doing? Filling a need?"

"That, and helping keep an eye on the most dangerous regime in Europe. No one wants another war."

They arrived back at the car and drove off. They pulled up at Seamus's house a few minutes later.

"Whatever you need," Hayden said through the open window and drove away.

Seamus wondered if he'd tell this story about how he first got into international espionage in years to come.

15

Michael huddled beside the radio, listening to the announcer brag that 100,000 SS and SA men were lining the Via Triumphalis to salute the Führer as he traveled to the closing ceremony of the 1936 Olympic Games. The rest of the family and Monika heard the commentator liken his journey almost to that of a God ascending back to heaven. He stated that foreign dignitaries, such as Arnold Baxter and his wife Lady Philomena Guinness, were waiting in the stadium with captains of industry, like Otto Milch and Roland Eidinger.

"You didn't get an invite?" Lisa mocked her husband.

"Maybe I need to learn to brown nose a little more—like Roland."

Hannah and Conor grew bored with the live broadcast and wandered off, and Fiona was out marching with her little Nazi friends. The rest of them stayed seated as the radio coverage continued.

"The crowd erupts as Hitler enters the Olympiastadion!" the commentator shouted.

Over the cheers, the Ritter family also heard the shouts of "Sieg heil!" The Führer was not scheduled to have an official role in the closing ceremony, but still commanded everyone's attention.

The announcer said, "Now that the Führer has been seated, the last event of the Games of the XI Olympiad will now begin! Horses and riders are trotting out for the equestrian finals."

"You know any of the German riders?" Maureen asked Michael.

He shook his head. Listening to the games was a mere distraction for him. He couldn't get Monika out of his mind— and the danger he had dragged her into, thanks to his sister.

Once the German team sealed the final gold medal of the games, and his father and Lisa left the room, they began to talk about what was swimming through his mind.

"I have a bad feeling about this."

Monika reached and took his hand. "Everything's in place —the trucks, the booze for the party. We all just have to do our jobs."

"You think everything is going to fall into place and the policemen won't notice thirteen people sneaking out? It's not getting them out of the country I'm worried about—it's the camp."

"We have to try," Maureen said. "The whole city is in the stadium in west Berlin, while a few miles away, hundreds of innocent people are languishing behind razor wire in that horrible place."

"Some things in life are too difficult, too dangerous to affect."

"I watched a dozen men die in a van hooked up to an exhaust pipe last summer. I swore to myself that day I wouldn't sit back and have that happen again. We can't save all those

people, but one family? Those children? That would be enough
—for now, anyway."

"Just be careful," he said to Monika. "If anything happened
to you, I'd die myself."

She took him in her arms. "No one's going to know. The
only people they'll see will be us girls, and we won't have any
connection to the escape. This is going to work." She hugged
him tightly for a moment. "When are we leaving?"

"Any minute now," Maureen said. "I'd like to be at the camp
as soon as darkness falls."

Michael took Monika's face between his hands and kissed
her on the lips, and then the women went upstairs to get ready.

A few minutes later they returned, ready for what was to
come. Monika looked even more stunning than ever. His sister
was at her best also.

"Please be careful, and look after each other. I'm counting
on you," he said.

Thomas arrived in his father's car and came inside. He
spoke to Lisa and Michael's father, his skin pasty white and his
hands shaking.

"I like the new look." Lisa pointed to the beard the young
man had grown for the occasion.

"Thanks. I thought I'd try out something new."

"Just like Michael. Enjoy your night out." Lisa walked them
to the door.

They got into the car to put their plan underway. Night was
drawing in, and the light of the lamps and taverns sprayed gold
on the streets. Every bar in the city was packed to the point
where people were spilling out onto the sidewalks. The sound
of firecrackers filled the air, and everywhere people had smiles
on their faces and drinks in their hands.

"The grand illusion of the Olympic Games is coming to an
end," Maureen said. "The Nazis will show their true selves
again in days."

Monika was in the back seat, exquisite in her red dress. Since it was a warm evening, they were able to show their arms. As Monika said, the more skin, the more men go crazy.

"You know the plan?"

"Yes, Maureen, of course," Thomas said.

"Monika?"

"I know it," she said with a quaking voice. "And I want to thank you for letting me help. This means more to me than I can say."

"Let's just make sure no one gets hurt...or draws the attention of the Gestapo. You can thank me by being careful."

THOMAS DROPPED the women off at the tram to Marzahn with enough whiskey and schnapps to put an elephant in the Emergency Room.

"I'll pick you up when it's all over," Michael said.

"Good luck," Thomas said.

Maureen kissed him, and he drove away. The car disappeared as the tram arrived in a silent shimmer.

The girls stepped onboard, hoping to avoid the drunken rabble of SA men at the back singing the "Horst Wessel Song." One of the braver—and possibly drunker—members of the bunch approached them with a smile below his mustache. He was about their age.

"Are you off to a party?" he asked. No doubt he noticed the booze they were carrying.

The other men were still singing, and instead of engaging him in conversation, Monika joined the song. Somehow, she knew all the words to the Nazi anthem and belted them out in an impressive voice, just long enough that they reached their stop without having to talk to the Brownshirts. They jumped off the tram, waving to the SA man as it moved off.

"You ok with those bags?" Monika asked.

Maureen nodded. "The camp's just a couple of blocks away."

They moved in silence. The stench soon hit them, and Maureen felt cold, even though it was August.

"You weren't lying about the smell," Monika said.

They crested a hill, and the camp came into view below them. A few blocks away, a rocket flew into the air and exploded in a cascade of color, with firecrackers following in its wake. Two bonfires were burning inside the camp, and she could make out a dozen or so figures around each. Otherwise, all was quiet. Most of the Roma people seemed to be asleep.

"A fine place to celebrate the end of the games," Monika said. "Where are the guards?"

"By the front gate, probably. Follow me."

Maureen made sure to take care walking down the dirt track in her high heels. Her heart was beating so hard, she was sure they'd hear it as she approached.

Seven or eight guards were sitting around a campfire, their faces illuminated as they stared into it.

Monika was the one to call out to them. "Hello, gentlemen. Look who's here!" She held up the bags, which *clinked* in the air, as if to signify the party was about to begin.

Several guards cheered. All were on their feet. Moritz appeared from the dark.

"You made it! I didn't think I'd ever see you again."

"I told you we'd come, didn't I?"

Maureen forced herself to kiss him on the cheek, although it felt like a betrayal. Could Thomas see her? She wondered when he and Michael were coming, but then forced the thought from her mind. It had no place in this moment.

"Does anybody have a phonograph? I want to dance," Monika said.

The men swarmed around her as she passed out bottles of liquor. Few waited for the cups at the bottom of the bag.

"Where we go, the party follows!" Maureen said.

"Come, take a seat by the fire," Moritz said.

The young policeman offered her a stool, and she sat down. She was just opening the first bottle when a harsh voice sounded behind them.

"What's going on here?"

"It's Sergeant Peters. He's the officer on duty," Moritz whispered. "Leave him to me."

He stood up and walked over to the older man. "We met these girls last week in the bar. They decided to come and join us tonight to celebrate the last day of the games."

Monika stood up and went to the officer. "Drink?"

Peters took the bottle from her hand. "You shouldn't be here."

"It's the last day of the Olympics," she said. "We didn't think it was right that you men were all alone."

Peters was about thirty, with a handsome, angular face. He took a lock of Monika's hair between his fingers. "Maybe we could make an exception for one night. But what about the gap in the wire? We can't have those rats sneaking out as we entertain these beautiful ladies."

"Why don't we set up the party there?" Maureen asked. "They can't get out the front gate, can they? Is the opening in the wire the only vulnerable place?"

"Yes."

"Well, they'll hardly be able to sneak out if we're right there, will they?"

"She's right," Moritz said, the fire dancing in his eyes as he spoke. "We can carry the stools down and set up there."

The hole in the fence was on the right-hand side, about thirty yards long.

"Why is it taking so long to build, anyway?" Monika asked.

"Disagreements between the powers that be, and we were using the gap to move lumber in," Peters said. "It's all sorted now, and it'll be finished by Tuesday."

"So let's go," Moritz said.

None of the other men raised any objection, and Peters nodded to give the go-ahead. One unlucky policeman was told he had to stay behind to man the gate. He cut a lonely figure as the others left.

The men carried the firewood and stools for everyone. Within a few minutes, they were all sitting by the gap in the wire with a new fire blazing. No one mentioned the hundreds of innocent people held against their will just a few yards away.

They sat in a circle around the fire—the two women and eight men. Soon, the three other guards patrolling the fence came over for a drink.

"He's so cute," Maureen said and reached out to pat the dog one of the guards had on a tight leash.

Moritz grabbed her hand and pulled it back. "I wouldn't. She doesn't like strangers."

"Or people in general!" the man holding the leash said. He tied the dog to a tree and sat down as more fireworks from the town burst in the night sky.

Maureen almost felt sorry for the men.

"Now, who here has ever played Truth?" Monika asked. The men all looked at each other, but none spoke. "None of you? We used to play this all the time when we were younger."

"Every weekend," Maureen added.

"I'll go first. I'll take truth. Ask me a question and I have to answer it. If I choose not to, I have to have a drink."

"Does your father know you're here?" one of the men across the fire asked.

Monika drank some from her cup. The men laughed.

The game continued for another hour or so. The young guard from the gate joined them about an hour later, and by that time, no one was sober enough to care that he'd left his post—including Peters.

The darkness had fallen in earnest when Maureen saw the truck's headlights approaching the camp. The policemen turned.

"Who is that?" Peters slurred. "Haas, get back to the gate. Deal with it." He put a hand on Monika's leg.

The truck slowed to a halt and Haas staggered away toward the front of the camp.

"I think it's my turn," Maureen said, with the intention of speaking anything but the truth. She did her best to not look back at the truck at the gate, but it was hard. She knew who was in the truck—Thomas and her brother, risking their lives for her crazy plan.

THOMAS ROLLED down the window and flicked his cigarette into the night as the guard approached. Michael sat beside him in the front cabin. Both were dressed in overalls, with flat caps pulled down as far as they'd go over their eyes. The fireworks began again in the night sky as the policeman started to speak.

"What are you doing here?"

"Yeah, sorry, friend," Thomas said. "This one nearly slipped through the net. I was meant to bring down the lumber and nails in the back on Friday, but I messed up. This stuff needs to be here by tomorrow morning, or else my boss is going to skin me alive."

The guard was young—not much older than Thomas—and blind drunk. Alone at the gate, he looked longingly over toward the glow of a campfire at the side of the camp.

"I wasn't told anything about this."

"You want to take a look in the back? Let's go." He pushed

the door open and jumped down before the young policeman had a chance to say anything. Michael joined them.

"Yeah, I'm sorry to spring this on you, but if my boss gets here tomorrow morning and this delivery isn't here, I'm done." They pulled up the tarpaulin at the back of the truck to reveal the lumber and barrels of nails inside, the official stamp of Marzahn Construction Supply on each.

"Listen, this is my job we're talking about here. If there was anything I could do to make this easier for you..." Thomas handed the guard 50 Reichsmarks.

The young man put the bill in his pocket without looking at it. "I think this is all in order. But you go in and come right out, all right?"

"You won't even know we came. We want to get back to the bar."

"He dragged me out when I was four beers deep!" Michael said and pointed to Thomas.

"I hate that," the guard replied.

"Thanks for keeping these animals penned in where they belong."

The guard seemed to appreciate Michael's praise and nodded to them. The two men got back in the truck and the young policeman opened the gate.

Another man in uniform appeared, swaying on his feet, and the pair got out again. The guard introduced himself as Sergeant Peters, and he seemed to be in charge. He took a few seconds to inspect the truck, but he believed them—just as the first man did. Why wouldn't they when Leon had painted the sides to bear the same logo as the Marzahn Construction Supply company?

Peters's breath reeked of whiskey. Michael peeked over at the bonfire Peters had walked over from and thought of Monika and Maureen. The faster they got out of here, the better.

"The other guard realized the gravity of the situation."

Thomas presented Peters with a similar amount of money. "I have to get inside the camp tonight."

Peters pocketed the banknote. "This happens one time, or I'll tell your boss myself."

"You have my word," Thomas said.

The first guard stumbled as he turned and fell against the side of the truck. Michael's stomach dropped as he saw the still-wet lettering left a white patch on his sleeve.

"We'll let you get back to your party now," he said.

Thomas's eyes widened as he noticed the paint on the guard's uniform, but he kept quiet. The guards shuffled away, oblivious. But surely it wouldn't be long until someone noticed?

Neither dared speak as Thomas started the engine once more. Peters strode back toward the campfire as the first man went to the gate. He lifted it and the truck inched through. Thomas had to pretend he knew where he was going.

"Picture the map Maureen sketched," Michael whispered. "Take a left at the end of the caravans and go all the way down."

They drove past the campfire where his girlfriend and sister were sitting with the guards. Two smoldering fires in the camp were the only sign of life outside the cabins. The Roma people were inside. It was as if they knew better than to come out.

The truck rumbled through the darkness of the camp.

"The barracks, and the barrels in front!"

"Keep an eye out," Michael answered.

The end of the fence came into view, and Thomas brought the truck to a gentle stop. They climbed down onto the soft ground and began unloading the nails first. With the back gate lowered, they rolled the barrels onto the dirt before moving them onto hand carts. Michael knew at least three or four separate sets of eyes were on them at any one time, and the two men worked in silence.

"Quickly now," he whispered as he rolled the last one down the slope at the back of the truck.

They set them in a line by the edge of the half-built barracks and then returned for the lumber. After stacking it, they strolled around the corner to the used barrels they were to take away. Michael tried not to think of the children inside them. It was better to imagine they were just there to take the faulty nails away.

"Get the handcarts," Michael said, and Thomas came back with them.

They loaded the first barrel and Thomas walked it back to the truck. "How's your leg?" he asked.

"A little sore, but I can walk."

"You're being careful with the barrels?"

"As much as possible."

The two men placed the next barrel on the handcart and they all loaded it into the truck together.

Ten minutes later, the five barrels were loaded. Michael climbed into the back of the truck, where he could faintly hear the children breathing inside the barrels. He leaned over until his mouth was a few inches away from the nearest barrel— there was whimpering from inside.

"My name is Michael," he whispered. "We're going to get you out of here, but you have to be quiet. The quietest you've ever been. That goes for all of you!"

"Ok," came the muffled voice from inside.

"Time to go," Thomas said.

Michael nodded and left the children. He didn't dare think of how terrified they must have been. He had his own demons to fight.

He reached into his pocket for a handkerchief to wipe the sweat off his hands. The two men got back into the truck, and Thomas started the engine.

~

MAUREEN TRIED NOT TO WATCH. Several of the men wondered why a delivery truck was coming in at this time on a Sunday.

"What? Is it almost midnight?" one man asked across the fire.

"I dealt with it," Peters said. "Some idiot forgot to come on Friday. I told Haas to search the truck on the way out, anyway." Monika was inches from him, and he turned to her with a lecherous smile. "And you, my dear, were telling us about the first time you ever kissed a boy. Please go on."

Monika began again. The lights of the truck flashed on once more—ten minutes had passed since they drove in. Maureen closed her eyes as the vehicle approached the front gate. The idea to run over and distract the guard came to her, but it was too late. She'd never beat the truck there, even as slowly as it was moving. All she could do was hope.

The men around her were laughing at Monika's story, and Moritz had his hand on her leg. She looked at him and smiled. *Can he feel how cold I am?*

Her eyes were drawn to the truck at the gate. It was impossible not to look.

"What's wrong?" Moritz asked.

"Nothing. I think I'm a little drunk," she said.

The young policeman looked down at her cup. "But you've barely touched a drop."

"It doesn't take me much," she said with a smile.

The truck was still stuck at the gate. *How long has it been? Thirty seconds? A minute? How long do these things take?*

Monika was on her feet, acting out her storytelling, and one of the guards tried to grab her.

"Keep your hands to yourself," Peters said, and the other man sat down. Monika seemed relieved and continued.

~

"HERE WE GO," Michael whispered as they approached the gate. The guard stepped out, illuminated by the funnel of light from the truck's headlights. He held an arm up to indicate the barrier was down again. Michael wondered if they could breach it with so little head start.

Thomas pressed down on the brake and the truck came to a halt.

The man's face appeared at the window. "I need to check things out before you leave."

"It's just a routine drop off," Thomas answered with a smile. "And we need to get back to the depot."

"I have my orders," the man slurred.

They hadn't counted on this, but they had little choice. It was up to the children in the back now. Michael tried to gulp back the tension inside him and opened the door to see the guard on his haunches, shining a flashlight under the truck.

"Ah, you can't be too careful," Michael said.

The guard didn't respond and got back to his feet. Thomas was with them now too, looking like he would be sick. A thousand thoughts darted through Michael's mind. Should he run? Get in the truck and blast through the gate? Admit to what they'd done?

The policeman walked past the smudged logo on the side of the truck. The remnants of the paint were still on his sleeve. Somehow, he hadn't noticed. "Raise the tarpaulin on the back," he ordered.

"What a night, eh?" Michael said as they did as they were told. "I can't wait to get back to the bar and celebrate! What are you doing after this?"

"Having a few drinks after you leave with two local girls— they seem like they're up for anything." A crooked smile came over his face.

The guard climbed into the truck. The children in the barrels must have known exactly what was going on, and what this meant. Their lives were in their own hands now. They were aged ten, eight, seven, six, and Klaus was only five. Michael stepped into the back beside the guard, who was shining his flashlight around.

"What was that noise?" the guard asked.

One of the children in the barrels was crying.

"From the party over yonder, I think," Thomas said, pointing toward the campfire.

"So, tell me more about these girls," Michael said. "Are they lookers?"

The guard turned to face him, smiling again. "Oh, yeah," he said, barely able to stand up straight. The children were silent. One more noise and they were done, no matter how drunk the policeman was.

"I think I have something in the front they'll like," Michael said. "A surprise to smooth the way with the ladies."

"Oh, yeah?"

"You can have it."

"But what's in the barrels? That noise. I should check them."

Michael put his shaking hand on the closest one. "The noise was from the party—where you should be. These are nailed shut. It's going to take us ten minutes to get each one open to find nothing. Come on, let me show you what I have."

The guard peered at him through slitted eyes. "Something to impress the girls?"

The policeman climbed out of the truck and Michael led him to the passenger side. A small bottle of perfume he'd intended to give Monika afterward lay on the seat wrapped up with a red bow. "I was going to give this to my girl, but you can have it."

"Thanks." The guard took it eagerly.

Thomas, already back in the driver's seat, started the engine.

"It's time we got back," Michael said. "Can you get the gate?"

He walked around the front of the vehicle and lifted the barrier, and Thomas eased through. Michael struggled to keep the tears back as they reached the road.

"Oh, my God."

A bright grin spread across Thomas's face and he clapped Michael on the back. "I think we did it! Our part, anyway."

"Don't speak too soon. We've a long way to go yet."

The car was a few blocks away, and Thomas stopped the truck to let his friend out. "We should be back in an hour or so. Go back for the girls alone if we get delayed."

"Got it," Michael answered and waved him off.

THOMAS DROVE ON ALONE, block after block. Every second seemed like an hour.

"This is it," he said aloud, "on the right."

He drove down the deserted street and pulled into an empty lot where a truck waited. He pulled in beside it. Herman waved to him.

"Come on."

He hopped out and Herman followed him around the back of the truck. Thomas climbed in and pried open the first barrel with a hammer. He heard the whimper before he saw the shock of hair.

"Hello?" Thomas said, with Herman beside him. "Who are you?"

"Joseph," came the voice from the barrel. "I'm seven."

The boy was shaking, but otherwise fine. "You're safe. Your parents will be with you soon."

Thomas picked him up while Herman started on the other barrels. The little girls had tears rolling down their cheeks.

"Eight-year-old Maria and six-year-old Elsa, I presume?" Herman asked.

The girls nodded between sobs. Ten-year-old Uwe tried to keep a brave face as he got out, but little Klaus was a mess of dirt and tears. He ran to Maria to throw his arms around her.

"You all did so well," Herman said, "but the journey is only beginning. I'm going to take you all the way to the border to your sister, who's waiting in Poland."

"Where are our parents?" Maria asked.

"They're coming," Herman answered. "Along with the rest of the family."

Thomas nodded, but could only hope that was true.

WILLI CREPT out of the caravan, with his father just behind him. The men stayed low to the ground as they inched toward the barracks. The sound of laughter and the glow of the campfire by the gap in the wire 200 yards away were constant reminders of the dangers inherent in what they were doing. It took the duo 10 minutes to get to the barrels, when they could have walked it in less than one in the daytime. Seamus and his friends were as good as their word—the top on the first barrel was loose. Willi reached in and came back brandishing wire cutters. He could see his father smiling in the half-light, but neither said a thing. Willi held the two-foot-long wire cutters in both hands, hoping the guards wouldn't see a metallic glint in the night.

The others were ready as they returned.

"Are we going now?" Willi's mother asked. The older children were huddled around her.

"Yes," his father said, looking at his watch. "It's 12:35. The guards should be nice and drunk now."

Willi nodded and took one final look around the inside of the cramped caravan, hoping it was his final view.

Willi's father took the wire cutters and led the seven remaining members of his family out of the caravan. Willi was last out the door, watching his fourteen-year-old twin sisters. The other caravans were the worry now. No one else knew, and if someone noticed them, they'd want to come along too. As much as it hurt to leave the others behind in this stinking pit, Willi knew they were pushing it already with just his family. Any more people would ensure their passage not just back here, but to a concentration camp.

They all knew where they were going—to the corner. A double line of barbedwire awaited them, but it would be no match for the fence cutters. Willi's father motioned for them to stop after only moving a few yards. He quietly moved to Willi at the back of the convoy.

"You stay here with the twins." One of the girls made a whining sound to protest being left behind, but their father cut her off. "Stop! We're not leaving you. It's just safer this way. Wait five minutes and follow. You know where you're going?"

"With my eyes closed," Willi answered.

His father cupped his face with his massive hand and turned to creep back to the rest of the family.

"No talking," Willi hissed to his sisters and motioned that they should sit.

The others crept into the darkness and disappeared around the corner of a line of caravans. Deep sadness overtook Willi as he sat in the cold dirt. A process of mourning began in his heart for all those he would leave behind tonight, and for the city of his birth that he had thought he'd die in. He'd never left Berlin before, and now he was to live in Poland—and probably then Sweden, as his father had talked about. He fantasized about taking everyone and forming a community of Roma in some bright, colorful place in a country he'd never thought about until a few days ago. A tear fled down his cheek. It was so ridiculous. They weren't even free yet and he was already looking back on this moment as if it had already happened.

They waited five minutes and rose to their haunches. The bonfire at the gap in the wire was still burning, and the conversation and laughter were getting louder. He scanned the fence line for flashlights or the dog, but saw neither. The ruse seemed to be working.

"Come on," he whispered, taking the lead. The people in the caravans were asleep. No one seemed to care about the end of the Olympics here.

Abruptly, a door swung open a few feet in front of them, and Willi stopped dead. He whirled around to his sisters, raising an urgent finger to his lips. They were in the open, and the nearest cover was perhaps 10 feet away. "Stay still," he whispered.

The fence and his family were only 100 yards away. A figure emerged from the caravan and peered toward them. They were exposed.

"Willi?" It was his friend, Ivan, still bearing the bruises of the beating Moritz gave him. He was the eldest of five children, and he had the power to stop the escape. Willi stood up.

"You getting out?" Ivan asked.

Willi nodded. "I'm sorry."

"The others are asleep."

Tears welled in Willi's eyes. He knew he couldn't bring more. Certainly not Ivan, his four siblings, and their parents. And they'd suffer if he escaped alone. His friend sat down on the step. "You're leaving me behind?"

He glanced over at the campfire by the gap in the fence. The sound of drunken laughter wafted through the air. Ivan dropped his head into his hands. Willi went to him, and put a hand on his shoulder.

"I can't do it. We can't bring any more."

"Go," Ivan said, not looking at him.

Willi gestured to the girls.

"Good luck," Ivan said as his voice cracked.

"Thank you," Willi whispered.

It took them three minutes to traverse the distance to the corner fence, where their father was waiting alone.

"Where are the others?" his sister asked.

"On the other side," their father whispered, pointing into the bushes beyond the wire.

The girls climbed through the gap their father had cut in the wire. Their mother appeared and brought them into the opaqueness of the bushes.

"Your turn, my son." His father patted him on the shoulder.

Willi's heart swelled, but felt broken at the same time. He stepped through the wire to where the others were waiting, then went through the bushes and up the hill to another wire fence. Their father still had the clippers and used them to cut a hole. They climbed through one by one as Willi watched and listened for any sign of the guards. He ducked through the fence last.

They scurried through the empty lot to the cars by the road —just where Maureen Ritter said they'd be. The doors opened and a man and a woman stepped out. They shepherded the family into the two cars. Willi got in with his mother and the twins.

"My name is Gilda. We have no time to waste," the woman said from the driver's seat. "If anyone stops us, we're going home after a party."

"Thank you." Willi's mother hugged her from the passenger seat.

"Let's wait to celebrate until we get to Poland!"

She started the car and followed the other vehicle out onto the road. Willi thought of Bruno Kurth and how, in a strange way, he owed his freedom to him.

"Thank you," he whispered.

∾

THE GUARD from the front gate returned a few minutes after the truck departed with a small gift box tied up in a bow. He attempted to give it to Monika while Peters was in the bush taking a pee, but the sergeant snatched it from him upon his return and presented it to her himself.

Maureen waited for the best part of an hour past the appointed time. She didn't want to be here once the guards discovered the new gap in the wire, but giving the family enough time to get out was paramount. Peters's hand on Monika's leg was like a metal clamp. Moritz was a little more subtle, but she knew what he was thinking. His eyes were growing cloudier and less distinct as the night wore on. His words ran into one another, and he was telling the same stories repeatedly. Maureen's entire body was stiff as steel and cold as marble. She could tell Monika was the same. Her act was a convincing one, but her eyes didn't lie.

"It's almost time for us to go home," Maureen said aloud to a chorus of disapproval.

"What? You're leaving?" Moritz asked.

She didn't want to hurt him. "My brother's coming to pick us up in a few minutes. We don't have any choice. This isn't the end—just time to go for now. We can meet again. How about in the same bar as last time?"

Giving him some hope seemed like the easiest way to get out of there.

"Time to leave," Monika said.

"No. No way," Peters said, gripping onto her like a vise.

Moritz seemed like a disappointed child, but Peters was more like a leopard defending its fresh kill.

"Your brother's coming to get you?" Peters asked. "Why

don't you go up and check if he's on the road, and then come back for Monika?"

Maureen didn't say anything, but waited for an indication from her friend.

"Yeah, you come back for me."

"Can I walk you up?" Moritz asked.

"I don't think that's a good idea. My brother hates me fraternizing with boys, and you've been drinking. It wouldn't create a good impression—not if we're to have a future together."

"When will I see you again?"

"How about outside the same bar as last time?"

"Tomorrow night?"

"Wednesday?"

A smile spread across his face. "I can be there at eight."

"It's a date, then."

She let him peck her on the lips, though it felt wrong in 100 different ways.

"Until Wednesday," he said.

Maureen stood up and nodded. "I'll be back in a few minutes," she said to Monika. The men stood up to say goodbye and shook her hand. She lied to them also—telling them she'd see them again.

A dirt path led up the hill to a bridge over the train tracks, and the road where Michael was waiting. She started up the trail when she heard a voice behind her.

"Wait," Moritz said. "I don't even know your last name."

"It's Furman," Maureen said. "Gisela Furman."

"Good night, Fräulein Furman."

Maureen waved and kept on. The pathway weaved up the hill to a cleared, flattened area where the bridge extended over the train tracks. Fireworks burst over her head, perhaps a half mile away. Firecrackers followed in her wake like gunshots in the night.

Michael was sitting in Thomas's car with the engine

running. A bright smile painted his face. It faded as he noticed his girl wasn't with her.

"Where's Monika?" he asked as he got out.

"I have to go back for her. How did everything go?"

"We did it!" Michael said. "They're gone."

She hugged him, her own fireworks of joy exploding inside her.

"I just need to go back for Monika."

"I'll go down with you."

"No," Maureen said. "Don't follow me."

She had decided not to tell him about Peters and his lecherous looks and busy hands. Once they had Monika, none of that would ever matter again.

She set off back down the hill. About 10 yards from the bonfire, she saw Peters in the brush on top of Monika, holding her down. Monika screamed and he slapped her with an open palm. His belt buckle *clinked* as he undid it. She used her free hand to hit him, but he leaned on it again and pulled his pants down a few inches before reaching up inside her dress.

Maureen was running now, but out of nowhere, Michael powered past her. He caught the policeman with a kick in the face, and he tumbled into the dirt. More fireworks thundered as Peters rolled over and reached for the holster around his waist.

Maureen picked up a large rock, but the gun exploded before she reached him. Blood spilled from her brother's torso. Maureen heard herself scream and saw the policeman's eyes. He tried to level the gun at her, but was too slow. She brought the rock down on his head and his body went still.

Monika was crying, leaning over Michael. Maureen ran to them. "Oh no!" she said.

Michael moved his hands over his wound. It was on the left side of his chest, six inches below his heart.

"We have to go," Monika said. "Get him back to the car! Can

you move?" she asked Michael, but he seemed unable to answer.

Maureen looked back at Peters and knew her life hinged on this moment. His eyes were open, his forehead covered in crimson blood.

More firecrackers sounded.

"The others might not realize it was a gunshot," Monika said. "We have to get him out of here now!"

"No hospital," Michael mumbled.

The two ladies raised him to his feet, and the trio stumbled up the trail to the bridge.

"How did this happen?" Maureen asked.

"I left alone, but that animal followed me up the trail and pulled me into the bush."

Michael grew heavier with each step, his legs almost dragging on the ground.

"Hang on, Michael," Maureen said through her tears. His body seemed to weaken with every step they took. Somehow, they struggled up the stairs and reached the car.

"You're a doctor, aren't you?" Monika asked.

"I'm just a medical student."

His wound was oozing crimson. "He's going to bleed to death. Do something!"

They laid him down on the back seat. Maureen found an old shirt under the seat and pressed it against the hole in his chest.

"We need to get out of here. Now!" Monika said. "Get in the back with him."

Maureen did as she was told and Monika got behind the wheel. She sped down the street and around the corner.

"We've got to get him to a hospital," Maureen said.

"No," Michael whispered. "Everyone will go to KZ's."

"He's losing a lot of blood!" Maureen said. "We can't wait."

"Where do I drive?"

Maureen slowed her breath, trying to form rational thoughts. Bringing Michael to the hospital would almost certainly mean tying Monika, and possibly her, to the death of a police officer.

"What if we just drop him off at the hospital and leave?" Monika asked. "No one saw him at the camp."

"But then they'll find me through him and the whole house of cards collapses. We'll face the executioner for killing Peters, and the rest of my friends will end up in a KZ."

"You're a medical student. You must know someone!" Monika shouted. "We can't just let him die."

"You think I'm going to let that happen? Just let me think!" Michael's face grew pale, and Maureen stroked his cheek with her hand. "Where are we?"

"Driving west on Landsberger Allee, toward your house. I didn't know where else to make for."

"Head to Mitte. I might have a way out of this." She turned her attention to her brother. "How are you? Can you hold on for me?"

He nodded his head, biting his lip to stave off the pain. Five minutes later, they were on a quiet street. Maureen directed her the rest of the way.

"Whose house is this?" Monika asked as they pulled into the driveway outside a red-brick mansion.

"My friend, Karen Weber's. Her father is a surgeon. Her mother's a vet. It's either this or we find the nearest hospital and take our chances."

"Agreed."

"Wait here." Maureen let her brother's head rest on the back seat.

She ran to the front door, breath thundering in and out of her lungs. The house was dark. Of course—it was almost two in the morning. She rang the doorbell and used the knocker. Wary of waking the neighbors, she resisted the temptation to scream. No one answered, and Maureen picked up a stone and threw it at Karen's window. A few seconds later, her friend's weary face appeared.

"Maureen? What on earth?"

"Wake your father! It's an emergency. Michael's been shot. We can't go to the hospital. Hurry!"

Karen disappeared, but the light went on in her room. A few seconds later she opened the door in her nightdress. Maureen was already at the car, and Karen ran out. Michael groaned as they lifted him off the back seat and brought him inside. Karen's father stood at the bottom of the stairs.

"What is this about?" he asked. "If he's injured, he needs to go to the hospital."

"We can't bring him there. Help us, please!" Maureen said.

His Hippocratic instincts seemed to trump his questions about why they were there, and he ran to them.

"Get him into the dining room," Dr. Weber said. "I don't see how I can do anything—"

"Of course, you can," Maureen said. "Please don't let my brother die. A man tried to rape his girlfriend. He shot Michael. I saw it all happen with my own eyes."

"What else do I need to know?"

"That's all I can tell you."

Dr. Weber took a hard look at Maureen as they laid her brother down on the table.

"I can't be a party to anything illegal."

Maureen clasped her hands together. "I'm begging you. The man tried to force himself on Monika. If we bring him to the hospital, we'll be the next to die." Dr. Weber didn't move. "You know me—we've met a dozen times or more. You know what kind of person I am. I need your help."

The surgeon nodded and snapped into action. "All right. First thing we have to do is stop the bleeding. Karen, run and get as many kitchen towels as you can carry, and bring the gauze in my drawer."

His daughter returned a few seconds later. "I want everyone to wash their hands thoroughly. What's your name?"

"Monika."

"Monika, hold this towel on the wound. Put all your weight on it. We're trying to stop the bleeding."

All three ran to the kitchen to wash their hands. Karen's mother was by the table when they returned, her mouth open. Maureen explained the situation to her.

"We have a patient in need of emergency surgery, most likely. Can you help?" her husband asked.

"Yes. Move him out to my office. We can put him on the table there."

"You don't think there's any chance of infection where you treat the animals?" Maureen asked.

"No more than here," she answered.

They propped Michael up and brought him out to the surgery Karen's mother had at the side of the house. She asked the same questions her husband had and received the same answers from Maureen. Michael's skin was a sickly pallid tone now.

"What's his blood type?"

"A," Maureen replied. "Same as mine."

"Good," Dr. Weber said. "We're going to need you to give him some."

"I can do that," Karen said. She soon found a needle and a bag. Maureen sat back as it filled with dark red blood.

Monika kept applying pressure to the wound until Karen's mother asked her to step back. The two doctors looked at the wound and nodded at one another.

"Significant internal bleeding. We're going to need to operate," Dr. Weber said. His wife agreed.

"Do you have any painkillers?" Maureen asked.

"Yes. They work on horses, so they'll work on him."

"Will he be all right?" Monika asked as tears ran down her face.

"We'll try our best," Dr. Weber said.

Maureen detached the now-full bag of blood from her arm and held some gauze on the wound.

"I think its best if you both wait outside," Karen's mother said.

"Can I use your telephone?" Maureen asked.

"It's by the front door."

Karen stayed to help. Maureen and Monika walked out into the half-light of the house.

The phone rang for a while before her father picked up.

"Are you ok?" he asked with a tired voice.

"I'm fine, and so is Monika, but it's Michael," she said. "He's ill. Come to my college friend's house."

"Your college friend? How ill?" Her father's clipped language was necessary—he didn't know who might be listening in.

"Just come. You know where."

Maureen hung up the phone and sat beside Monika.

"I'm so sorry."

"You've nothing to apologize for," Maureen responded.

SEAMUS ALMOST HAD to fight his wife to let him leave without her, but it was safer that way. Something was going on—he knew it. The less her involvement, the better. He promised to call her when he got to Karen's house, and as soon as he knew what was going on. Nightmares clogged up his consciousness as he drove the 20 minutes to the house.

Maureen was crying like a child as she opened the door. "Michael's been shot."

"What? How? Where is he?"

"They're still working on him. We came here because we couldn't go to the hospital. They've been inside almost an hour now. Please let them be, Father," she said. "I know you want to see him, but not like this. Dr. Weber is one of the finest surgeons in the city, and we can trust him. I know we can."

"You couldn't go to the hospital? Who shot my son?"

"A policeman tried to rape me. Michael stopped it," Monika said, "but the man went for his gun."

"How did this happen? Where?"

"Outside the camp at Marzahn."

"At Marzahn? What were you doing there?"

Maureen spoke. "We organized a team to break Willi and his family out."

"You broke Willi out?" Seamus felt like his insides were in a grinder. "How?"

Maureen told him how she and Monika went to the camp to distract the guards, while Michael and Thomas got the children out in the truck.

Seamus put his hands on his head. He didn't know what to feel amid the swirl of fear, anger, and confusion inside him. Maureen took him to the dining room table a few feet away—still speckled with her brother's blood—and forced him to sit.

She told him how she masterminded the rescue and organized a crew with Michael, Monika, Thomas, and several other friends to extricate Willi's family from the camp and transport them to safety. Shock permeated every part of him.

Maureen put her arms around him. "I'm so scared," she said. "Michael should never have been the one to get hurt."

He fought back his emotions, wanting to be strong for his daughter. The urge to roar at her for dragging Michael into this was difficult to ignore.

"Oh, my son." He dropped his face into his hands.

Monika approached them in tears and told Seamus the full

story of how she tried to walk after Maureen, and how Peters followed her. She apologized again, but they both told her she had nothing to be sorry for.

"You think that guard is dead?" Seamus asked.

Maureen nodded.

A wave of guilt threatened to overwhelm Seamus. This was all his fault—he should never have involved Maureen. Of course she would step in. He knew the person his daughter was. *Why did I go to her? This is all on my shoulders.* It seemed the ghost of Ernst Milch was laughing at them once again. He let his head fall to his hands, but felt his daughter's touch on his shoulder.

"None of this is your fault. It's mine."

He didn't engage with her—this wasn't the time. But her words were like drops of icy water on the fire raging inside him.

"What happened to Willi's family?" he asked.

"They got away," Monika said. "They'll be at the border soon and crossing over into Poland."

Her words were met with somber silence. The triumph of what they achieved was obliterated.

An hour more of agony passed before the door to the office opened and Dr. Weber walked out. They all stood. The apron over his pajamas was stained red.

"That's one strong young man," he said. "We managed to stop the bleeding and repair the damage to his intestines. He was lucky—very lucky. The bullet missed his vital organs, and didn't hit any bones, either. We still might have lost him except that he's sturdy as a mountain."

Relief cascaded into Seamus. His entire body loosened and he could breathe again. "Can I see him?"

"Yes, but he's unconscious and going to need bed rest. He won't be able to go anywhere for at least a week."

"Oh, thank you!" Maureen hugged the doctor. Seamus shook his bloody hand and said the same.

"I'm sorry, but he can't stay here," Dr. Weber said. His eyes were dull, and his eyelids drooped. "But you can't move him after that. It might kill him."

They pushed through the door. Michael was on the table, his eyes closed, with a clean blanket over him. Karen and her mother were covered in his blood.

"Oh, Michael," Seamus said, unable to hold back the tears. He put a hand on his forehead, comforted by the warmth he felt. "What did they do to you?"

Maureen embraced her friend, then her mother. Monika stood in the background, staring at her stricken boyfriend's face.

"When do we need to move him?" Seamus asked.

"In order to avoid the attention of the Gestapo, we're going to ask you do so tonight," Dr. Weber said.

"I understand."

"We have about three hours of darkness left. I think it would be best if you used it."

"Can we have a few minutes to decide what to do?" Seamus asked.

"Of course." Karen and her parents left.

All three stood in silence. Maureen ran her hand through her hair. "I'm so sorry for getting you involved in all this, Father. I know you want to keep your head down and steer clear of the resistance. I'll never endanger the family like this again. I'm sure my friends will help me get away. It's just... I didn't know who else to call."

A single tear ran down her cheek and she was like a little girl again—just for that single moment.

"You called the right person." He put his hands on her shoulder. "I'll help you. Do you really think I've been doing nothing all this time? You won't need anyone else. I'm going to make sure you and Michael and Monika get away. I give you my word on that."

It seemed to take a few seconds for her to digest what he told her. "Thank you," she said and embraced him.

"Monika, you were with Peters all night?"

"Yes."

"They'll have found him by now and will be sending out descriptions of you, and posting your face all over the city."

"What about me?" Maureen asked.

Seamus gulped back a lump in his throat. "The same. They'll be looking for you too—to get to her, if nothing else."

"I'm not leaving Michael while he's like this," Maureen said.

"Me neither. I'm not running away."

"We need to worry about Michael for now, and where we're going to take him," Seamus said.

"We've got less than three hours to get him out of here," his daughter added.

"Let me think," Seamus said. A thousand thoughts jumbled together in the morass of his mind. He took a few seconds to sift through them. "Ok," he said. "First things first. Monika, ask the doctors for cleaning products and scrub every drop of blood from the car and this house. We need them sparkling. Maureen, can you help her?"

"Yes, but where are we going to take him? We can't bring him home. I can't even go there."

"I think I have an idea. Just leave it with me for a few minutes."

"Come on," Monika said, and they pushed through the door, leaving Seamus alone with his son. He put his ear to Michael's face to listen to the soft hum of his breath. "I'm so sorry, but I'm going to get you out of here."

Their options seemed few. Monika's empty apartment might be swarming with police soon. Whatever was to happen had to be decided now—it was up to him. His subsequent decisions would determine whether his son died or his daughter was executed for defending her friend. The familiarity of the moment wasn't lost on him.

Seamus reached into his wallet and drew out the card Hayden gave him. What other choice did he have?

"I don't know where else to take you," he said aloud.

Karen's mother, Dr. Ilse Weber, came through the door. She was in a fresh dressing gown, her hands scrubbed clean. "Have you decided where you're going to take him yet?"

"Can you keep an eye on him while I use your telephone?"

The doctor nodded and Seamus left. His daughter walked by with sponges and detergent in hand. He went to the phone and picked up the receiver. It took a few seconds for the operator to connect him, but a tired voice came on the other end.

"Bill? I'm sorry to wake you."

"Seamus? What time is it?"

"About four in the morning. I need a favor."

"You need some fingerprints on a candlestick?"

"No, just someone I can trust."

The line was quiet for a few agonizing seconds before he spoke again. "Ok. What is it?"

"Can I come over?"

"Now?"

"It has to be."

Hayden's laughter echoed down the line. "I said that candlestick thing as a joke, you know?" The line fell silent again. Seamus knew Hayden had to be the next one to speak. "Ok, come on over. You know where it is?"

"I have the address you gave me. I'll be there soon."

"Ok."

Seamus hung up.

The three of them spent the next 20 minutes cleaning. When Seamus was happy the car wasn't an invitation to every policeman in the city, they went back inside. Karen and her parents were with Michael. He was still unconscious, but wrapped in a thick white sheet and dressed in some of the doctor's pajamas. Maureen drove around to the back of the house, where the animals came in for surgery, and they all lifted the prostrate figure of his son out to the car.

"Be careful. Those sutures are fresh," Dr. Weber said as they laid Michael on the back seat. His eyes were clamped shut, but his breathing was steady. Maureen sat next to him with his head on her lap. Monika got in the front.

Seamus thanked Karen and her parents individually. He fought the instinct to offer them something for their services.

"If you ever need anything from me, don't hesitate." He put one foot in the car and turned back to them. "Can I come to you if he suffers any complications?"

"Yes, but discretion is paramount," Dr. Weber said.

"In everything we do these days." Seamus got in and set off.

"What about your car?" Maureen asked as they pulled away.

"I'll come and get it in a few hours."

Berlin was still cloaked in darkness. The silence on the streets was punctuated only by a few random partygoers on their way back to their beds. Seamus was glad of the cover of night as they parked outside Hayden's apartment block. The building was well tended, and the street was dotted with restaurants and upscale bars.

"Stay put. I'll be back in a few seconds."

Hayden appeared at the door in a full suit. Seamus didn't ask why.

"Who's in the car?"

"My son's been shot."

"What?"

Seamus explained what happened and where they'd come from.

"And you want to bring him here? To recuperate?" Hayden asked, appalled.

"Where else can I? And not just him, either."

"The other two? They can't hide out here!"

"They've nowhere else to go. Only until he recovers, and then I'll get them out of the country."

"With every policeman in the city looking for them? They don't take kindly to losing their own, rapist or not."

"I'll worry about that later. Right now, I need somewhere my son can recover in safety."

"I'm no doctor."

"Maureen will look after him."

Hayden took a long five seconds to think. "Ok, bring him in, but you owe me for this."

"Thank you." Seamus hurried back to the car. The street was deserted as they extracted Michael, and Maureen took along a bag Dr. Weber gave her. Hayden helped them up the steps, and he and Seamus took the young man to the elevator. The sun was beginning to peek up over the horizon. The apartment was on the fifth floor and offered a beautiful view as the city woke from its slumber.

The furnishings were new, and the floors and surfaces were clean.

"Bring him into the spare room," Hayden said.

Michael groaned a little as they set him down on the bed. Monika drew the curtains.

"He'll need to rest here for a week or so."

"With these two? It's going to be a tight squeeze," Hayden said. "Come on."

They sat at the dining room table as the sun painted the rooftops and spirals of Berlin with splashes of gold.

"I can't say I was expecting this when I went to bed four hours ago," Hayden said.

"Thank you," Maureen said.

"I need the full truth—everything. If I'm an accessory to something, I need to know what."

"Don't you have diplomatic immunity?" Seamus asked.

"You think the Nazis care about that? The Olympics are over, Seamus. They'll unleash the hounds now."

"Tell him," Seamus said.

Maureen started, then seemed to trip on her tongue.

"You can trust me. You're going to have to."

Seamus let her tell the story.

Hayden shook his head as she finished. "I knew you were the rebellious type, but breaking out a family of thirteen gypsies does surprise me. How much danger is Michael in?"

"We have to watch him for the next 48 hours or so," Maureen said. "I'll give him any blood he might need. The doctors provided me with a basic medical kit."

"We can take shifts," Monika said.

"I didn't think I'd be getting roommates," Hayden said. "Seamus, can we talk?"

The two men got up and went to the front door. "I have to step aside if the police come."

"I know, but I don't think it'll come to that."

"What are you going to say if they visit you?"

"That Maureen and her brother are on vacation for a few weeks."

"Who's the girl?"

"We can trust her."

"Ok. I'll do this. But one thing—you owe me. I needed someone on the inside, and you're mine now. They can leave Berlin, but you're not going anywhere until I say so, got it?"

"Of course."

They walked back to the table, but the girls were in the bedroom tending to Michael. "I guess we're all going to get to know each other pretty well over the next week or so," Bill said.

Seamus nodded. The light of the morning sun flooded the apartment, and somewhere in the distance, he heard the soft lilt of birdsong.

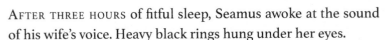

AFTER THREE HOURS of fitful sleep, Seamus awoke at the sound
of his wife's voice. Heavy black rings hung under her eyes.

"I got Roland on the phone before he checked out of the
Eden. I told him to meet you in the alley opposite the factory in
an hour."

"Thank you, my love." Seamus kissed her, then got up and
forced some food down.

He arrived at the rendezvous 15 minutes early. Roland
pulled up in a taxi. Seamus waited in the shade of the alley as
his friend approached. He explained the story from the night
before, just as he'd heard it.

"Are you joking? They broke out thirteen people? And
killed a guard?"

"I need your help. I have to smuggle them out of the
country."

He closed his eyes. "You know how serious this all is?"

"That's why I need your help. If we get them straight to
Rostock, could you put them on a cargo ship?"

The sour stink of trash filled their nostrils, but neither man
moved.

"It's not implausible. Why not Poland, like the others?"

"I don't want to risk getting across the border, and I don't
like the thought of sending them to a country Hitler clearly has
designs on. The Behrens family won't be there long."

"I don't know..."

"What's more important to you? Being a rich industrialist or
living in a free country where your children won't have to grow
up with swastikas on their biceps? This is another chance to do
something good."

Roland walked on a few feet and kicked an empty trash can
lying on its side. Seamus gave him a few seconds before asking
him again.

"Just make sure none of this comes back to me." Roland turned to face his friend.

"I will." Seamus shook his hand. "Michael is too ill to move right now. It'll be a week or so."

"Please give him my best regards."

"Thank you."

"What about the others who helped with the escape? The other boy who drove the truck?"

"Thomas is fine and the family is safe. The authorities may want to suppress the story, and who really knew who was in that camp other than the guards? Maybe they didn't tell anyone about the escape. My kids would have gotten away with it if it wasn't for what that animal tried to do to Monika."

"I'll talk to my man in Rostock, but I'll skimp on the details of where they're coming from."

The conspiracy was growing wider.

"Thank you, my friend. I'll come see you to finalize the details."

"Let me know."

Seamus shook his hand and watched him walk away. The taxi was still waiting around the corner, and Roland was gone in seconds. The meeting had lasted less than five minutes, but Seamus knew it was the most important one he'd ever had.

16

Wednesday, August 19

S eamus pushed open the front door, dropped his hat and briefcase in a heap by the coat stand, and carried on inside. Lisa was at the dining room table alone. The black rims under her eyes took nothing away from her beauty, and he embraced her as she came to him. She drew away in less than a second.

"How is Michael?"

"Bill said he's doing better. He's awake and seems to have beaten the fever. Maureen knew what pills to give him, and she and Monika stayed up in shifts the past few nights."

"Is he going to be ok?"

"Hayden said the first 48 hours are critical, and Michael's made it through them. I don't know much else." He shrugged. "I just wish I was with him."

Lisa seemed like she didn't know whether to be pleased with the news or not. "When can we see him?" she asked.

"Hard to say." He reached into his jacket pocket. "I saw this on my way home. They're going up all over the city."

He handed his wife a folded-up poster, and she opened it. Her face dropped as she saw the artist's renderings of Maureen's and Monika's faces. Managing to regain a stoic expression, she handed it back. "It's only a matter of time before they come here looking for her."

Seamus ripped it to shreds and threw it into the wastepaper can in the corner of the room, which was otherwise filled with Hannah's childish drawings.

Seamus buried his head in Lisa's lap. "Be careful. The children," she said.

He raised himself up as he heard sound from the living room. Fiona marched up to him with Hannah in tow. Conor was in the backyard, practicing his soccer skills.

"When are Michael and Maureen coming back? Who is this friend of theirs they're visiting?"

"A college friend of your sister's, and you know Michael— he's always interested in the chance to meet a pretty girl," Lisa answered.

"They'll be back in a week or two," Seamus added.

"But why didn't they say goodbye?"

"It was a last-minute decision. Maureen's still off for another few weeks, and Michael's leg was well enough that he could go. It was spontaneous."

"Can I write them a letter?" Hannah asked.

"Of course, my darling," Seamus answered. "I'll see that it gets to them.

"I thought Michael was with Monika now," Fiona said.

"I think she's meeting them in Paris, isn't she, Lisa?"

"He did mention something about that."

Seamus hated lying to his children. It was strange to be wary of your own daughter and who she might tell. Hitler had designed his information system to perfection. Germany was now a country where children informed on their families and shook their heads in shame as their parents were led off to concentration camps to atone. He couldn't trust Fiona with the truth any more than a butcher's dog with a meaty bone.

He reached out and put a hand on her shoulder, wanting to draw her in to hug him, but she shrugged him off. Apparently unconvinced by his story, she shot daggers from her eyes before retreating to the living room with Hannah.

Seamus felt helpless as he opened the liquor cabinet for a drink.

THEY CAME AFTER DINNER. The knock on the door seemed so loud as to warn the neighbors what was going on. It was more of a thundering. The doorbell was ignored. They wanted to send a message, even before Seamus had the chance to open the door.

Two men in suits stood there with stern faces. One looked in his late fifties, the other man perhaps ten years younger.

"I'm Inspektor Koch," the older man said. "This is Inspektor Bauer. Is your daughter, Maureen, here?"

"No, she's not."

"Can we come in?"

"Of course," he answered, knowing he had no choice.

Lisa herded the children to their rooms before joining the men at the dining room table.

"Where is she?" Bauer asked.

"What's this in connection with?"

The younger man took the same poster Seamus had shown his wife a few hours before from his pocket and pushed it across the table to them. "These two are wanted for questioning in connection with the murder of a member of the police last Sunday night. Someone identified this woman as being your daughter."

He pointed at the drawing across from Monika's likeness.

The artist had done an impeccable job. An icicle of fear ran down Seamus's spine as he realized that anyone would recognize her from it. Her time at the university was over.

Lisa picked up the poster and held it a few inches from her face. "This isn't Maureen, and I can assure you—"

Koch cut her off. "I ask again: where is she?"

"In Paris visiting a friend."

"When did she leave?"

"Sunday afternoon."

"You're sure of that?"

"They left at about... Three in the afternoon, wasn't it, dear?" Seamus asked.

His wife nodded.

"Who is this friend? What's their address there?"

"I'm really not sure. Do you know, Lisa?"

"She said she'd write with an address once she arrived."

Lisa's stare didn't waver. The men jotted down some notes on pads of paper they withdrew from their pockets.

"You mentioned 'they left,'" Bauer said.

"Yes, her brother Michael went too."

"Do you know who this other woman is?" Koch asked.

"I don't," Seamus said. "And that's not Maureen either."

Lisa asked a few questions pertaining to the crime itself, no doubt to deflect the attentions of the two detectives. Bauer discussed the heroic policeman killed on the trail to the road from the camp at Marzahn, but never mentioned the escape. There'd been nothing about it in the newspapers either. Peters' death had made the front page, but it seemed the Behrens family's escape was unworthy of mention. It made sense. Who wanted to draw attention to the fact that such a place existed? Nothing about the concentration camps was ever reported. Everything the public knew about them was hearsay. To most people, they were little more than a rumor.

"Your daughter is a person of interest in the murder of a

Berlin policeman," Koch said. "There are few matters we take more seriously."

"I'll have her contact you as soon as she returns, but due to the fact that she wasn't in the city at the time, there's no way she could have committed this crime."

"Let us know as soon as you hear from her," Bauer said.

"You're lying," Koch said in a flat tone.

It wasn't hard to act indignantly, and Seamus did so. "What are you accusing me of, Inspektor? My daughter is innocent of this crime."

"You think you can cover this up? That your little girl and her friend can get away with luring Sergeant Peters away from his post before battering him to death? The man had a wife and two children at home."

"I don't know anything about the crime or the victim," Seamus said. "And I'd be most grateful if you left my house now."

The policemen got up. The skin on Koch's face was tight as a snare drum, and his jawbones were jutting out from beneath.

"Thank you for your visit," Lisa said. "We'll be sure to inform you once we hear from Maureen or her brother."

Seamus stood back a few yards from the door as his wife saw the two men out, wondering if Maureen would ever set foot in this house again.

Wednesday, August 28

Michael was sitting on the edge of the bed as Maureen came in. The suit he wore was a little too big, but would do for now. He had lost weight, but the color had returned to his face these last few days, and he could move around the apartment independently. Maureen set about cleaning up the bedding on the floor she'd slept on these last ten nights. But sleep had been a rare luxury during their time here. It came mainly in the afternoon when Monika sat with Michael. Their host was rarely home and stayed the night elsewhere for half of their time in his apartment.

Her father was right that this apartment was safe. No one had come for them. Their only reliable source of news and the only other person they'd seen during their time here, Bill Hayden, told them that the police were scouring the city for them and showed the posters to prove it. When Maureen saw the artist's renderings of her and Monika's faces in the newspaper, she realized that the life she knew was over, and her dreams of being a doctor—in Germany, at least—had died with Peters in Marzahn.

"How are you feeling?" she asked.

"Like I'd be a millionaire if I had a pfennig for every time you or Monika asked me that."

He stood up from the bed as Maureen folded the blanket. She moved to let him walk across to the window, observing his movement as he went.

"Where's Monika?"

"In the bath. Are you up to this? It's going to be hard."

"I'm a lot stronger than I was yesterday, and like an ox compared to last week. I can make it."

Maureen placed the blanket on the bed and joined him at the window. It seemed like so long since they'd been out. The late afternoon sun was bathing the city.

"No one saw you, Michael. Are you sure you have to come?"

"What if some Gestapo agent pulls me into a darkened room with one lightbulb hanging from the ceiling? Father told them I went away with you. If they think I have information on where you are, they'll skin me alive."

"And this has nothing to do with the fact that Monika has to leave?"

He looked at her for a few seconds. "I've had enough of this place, and I don't want to let her go. What about Thomas?"

"I don't know," she said. "It's not fair to ask him to run."

"But will you?"

"Bill will be back any minute. I'll start dinner."

The American arrived 20 minutes later, just in time for the meal Maureen and Michael prepared. No one spoke much as they ate. They were almost finished when Hayden broke the silence.

"I spoke to your father this afternoon. We go tonight. Are you ready, Michael?"

"To leave this country? More than you know." He threw down his fork, his plate clean.

"Can I go back to my apartment first? Just to get some photographs?" Monika asked.

"I'll bet there's a car parked across the street from your apartment building right now with two grumpy, foul-smelling Gestapo men existing on coffee and cigarettes. You going back would be like all their Christmases come at once," Hayden said.

Monika didn't argue, just plunged her fork into the one remaining slice of potato on her plate. "When are we leaving?" she asked. "It's not like we have anything to pack!"

All three were dressed in clothes Hayden bought them. The clothes they wore the night of the escape were long since incinerated.

"There are plenty of nice stores in Copenhagen, and with the money your father's going to send you off with, you'll be able to afford whatever you want." Hayden lit up a cigarette. "We go at midnight. Enjoy your last evening in Berlin for a while."

"For a while?" Maureen asked.

"You father thinks you can come back once the heat dies down. Maybe in a year or two."

"What do you think?" Monika asked.

"I think the Gestapo might forget about you if someone else catches their eye, but I don't like your chances of running for mayor of Berlin anytime soon. It might be time to take the boat back to America."

"They don't have any real evidence," Michael said. "It's all circumstantial. No witnesses. The girls just went to a party."

"And I was the last person to see Peters alive," Monika said. "It's more than enough for the Nazi courts. They need a scapegoat, so we have no choice."

"I won't miss the Nazis," Michael said. "I can't believe I ran with that swastika on my arm."

"Next time you won't have to," Hayden said.

"If I ever run again."

"We'll all be there in Tokyo in four years, cheering for you." Monika said, her hand on his.

He managed a smile. "That seems like a speck on a cloudy horizon right now."

They spent their last night in Berlin in Hayden's living room. No one wanted to drink initially, but the American diplomat forced them to have one last beer with him to celebrate. They agreed as soon as he asked. There wasn't much he could have asked that they wouldn't have agreed to.

Maureen's father pulled up outside right on time, with Thomas in the passenger seat. She went down to the front door alone and got into the car with as little fuss as possible. Her father drove for a few blocks before he stopped to let her boyfriend get out and climb into the back of the car beside her. Then they set off for the port of Rostock.

Thomas held her hand as they left Berlin behind. He promised her again and again that he'd follow her wherever she went.

She let him speak, unsure of the veracity of his words. The time to talk would come at the dock.

Leaving behind the city and her dreams of becoming a

doctor didn't hit her as she thought it would. Saying goodbye to Berlin and the Nazis wasn't something to be mourned. It was something to remember and learn from. As much as she thought about America, the picture of those men Dr. Walz murdered outside the hospital in Babelsberg came into her mind more often, and she realized that this wasn't an end at all. It was merely a new chapter to a story, of which the end was uncertain. Two things were sure, however—the things she'd seen and done here had changed her forever. And her time as a subversive wasn't over.

Hayden beat them to the port somehow, and he, Michael, and Monika were standing by the American diplomat's car as they arrived.

Maureen's father hugged Michael as they got out. It was hard to remember either of them closer to tears.

"Lisa was so sorry she couldn't come to say goodbye."

"We'll see her in Basel next week," Michael said. "And Conor, Hannah, and Fiona too."

"I wonder how Fiona will react to this," Maureen said.

"I'll deal with her," her father answered.

Eidinger's man, Pohl, was waiting at the last warehouse and brought them in. The port was quiet, lit only by electric lamps.

The steel container was tall enough to stand up in and long enough that they could all lie down end to end. It was fitted with benches riveted to the sides and airholes punched in the steel. Gedser was a short trip across the North Sea, less than two hours away.

"You'll be in Denmark for breakfast," her father said. "Just keep quiet in there."

"I'll give you folks a chance to say your goodbyes," Hayden said.

Each took a moment to thank him.

"It was a pleasure. Stay safe, and maybe I'll see you in the Adlon for lunch sometime."

"No, I'm not welcome there," Monika said. The diplomat tilted his head with a smile. "It's a long story."

"I look forward to hearing it sometime."

He hugged her and Maureen before shaking Michael's hand, then he disappeared into the darkness.

"Ship's leaving in two hours. We need to get loaded up before the other dockers arrive," Pohl said. "I left a lamp in there for you."

Maureen's father reached into his pocket for a money clip. "Plenty there to get you to Copenhagen and then down to Basel in a few days. Remember, send a blank postcard and I'll bring everyone down to the Hotel les Trois Rois on the Saturday after I get it. We'll see you there. All three of you." He turned to Monika. Michael was standing with his arms around her.

"What are we going to do once we get to Switzerland?" Michael asked.

"What do you want to do?"

"I want to continue what I started here," Maureen answered.

Thomas took her hand and drew her aside. The others finished their goodbyes and sat in the shipping container.

"I'll be down to see you with your father, and I'll stay."

She held him to her and kissed him. A tear ran down her cheek. "I'll have to drop out of university, and I can't come back here for a long time. Maybe never."

"Then I'll drop out too. I hear wherever you're going to be is a wonderful place."

"What about your degree, and your mother? You can't just leave her."

His face dropped. He stood back and ran a hand through his hair.

"You don't want me to come?"

"Of course, I do," she said, wiping the wet from her cheeks.

"Leaving you was never my choice, but things have changed now."

"Not for me."

Pohl called out to them. It was time.

"I have no idea where I'll be next week or next year. Your mother needs you now, and I can't ask you to drop out for me."

"My education is my decision, but you never know... Maybe this'll all blow over and you can come back soon."

"I'm a fugitive from the law, Thomas. I killed a man."

"Who shot your brother and tried to rape your friend."

"None of that matters to the Gestapo. But I'll be waiting, if you decide to drop out, and once your mother can let you go."

He smiled and nodded, seeming to accept the magnitude of what it would take for them to be together again. He took hold of her hand, but let his fingers fall from hers as she strode back toward the shipping container.

Thomas helped Pohl and the other men load it onto a flatbed truck.

"Time to get in," the dockworker said. "I need to get it on the ship so no one asks any questions."

Michael hugged his father one last time before he and Monika climbed inside. They sat, holding hands. Maureen hugged her father.

"I'm so sorry. I should never have come to you," he whispered and grasped her harder.

"Then those thirteen people would still be in that camp," she said. "I'll be in touch and see you soon."

She drew back. His face was contorted with grief, but still the tears did not come. He nodded once and stepped back.

Thomas held her in his arms.

"I'll write soon," she said.

Maureen took his face in her hands and kissed him one last time before she got into the shipping container. Pohl closed the door behind them and almost all the light was extinguished.

"Thank you," Monika said to Michael.

"For forcing you into exile?"

"For giving me something to live for." She turned to Maureen. "You think Thomas will come?"

"I hope so." Maureen settled back for the journey ahead.

EPILOGUE

Thursday, September 3

The phone call came before five, just as he was about to leave his office. Seamus knew who it was before the person on the other end spoke.

"Come see me. I'm in the Euro Café on the corner of Wichmannstrasse and Keithstrasse."

"I know the place."

"I'll see you in fifteen." The line went dead.

Hayden was sitting alone and threw down a few Reichsmarks to cover the bill as he saw Seamus approaching. "Let's go to your car."

They made small talk about the weather and Seamus's day at work. Once they were in the car, the real conversation began.

"Have you heard from Maureen and Michael?"

"A postcard arrived in the mail today. I haven't seen it. Lisa called me in the office earlier to let me know."

Bill's relief seemed genuine. "Best postcard you ever got, huh?"

"Tell me about it."

"Have you noticed any unusual police presence since they left? Anyone watching you?"

"Apart from the two Gestapo men parked outside my house for the last five days, you mean?"

"Do they follow you to work?"

"No, and Lisa said they left this afternoon."

Hayden pushed out a breath. "We'll wait."

"For what?"

"For you to be my eyes and ears. Your country needs you."

Seamus shifted in his seat. A light rain began falling on the windshield.

"Don't think about following the kids—you're too important here. I told Maureen who I was when she was staying with me, and we talked. I need you to become one of the group she was a member of, and find out everything the resistance is planning. On the other side of things, you and Helga are going to pursue her ideas to expand the business, and you're going to get to know every rich industrialist bigwig in this city. I want you to know what they're thinking before they know themselves. We're partners now."

He held out his hand. Seamus shook it with little enthusiasm.

"Don't worry," Bill continued. "I won't put you in the line of fire, but the State Department doesn't appreciate your role in rearming the Wehrmacht. This'll smooth it all out." He smiled and clapped his old friend on the shoulder. "I'll be in touch."

He stepped into the rain and jogged up the street. Seamus felt like he'd just been mugged. He sat in the car for several minutes before he started the engine.

As Lisa said, the Gestapo men were gone when he arrived home. It was a relief to feel in some way normal again—whatever that was.

The house felt empty without his older children. Fiona still stomped around in her League of German Girls uniform, and

Conor and Hannah still played and shouted and sang. The living room swelled with the chatter of the wireless almost all day long, but somehow their home seemed quiet now. Maureen's closet was full of her clothes, and her dresser was still a mess of the makeup the Nazis didn't want her to wear. Newspaper clippings of Michael's numerous achievements still hung in frames on his walls, and all over the house. The singlet he wore for the 100-meter final just a month before hung in his wardrobe, Nazi swastika and all. They all felt the lack of them in the house, especially Maureen's passion and Michael's determination. His laugh and her smile.

Fiona didn't believe a word he or Lisa told them anymore. She wasn't stupid. She'd seen the pictures of Maureen and Monika in the newspaper. Seamus rode out her inquiries into her sister's whereabouts as if he were on a raft adrift on a raging fourteen-year-old sea. He felt for her—no doubt she missed her siblings as much as he did. The hard truth was he couldn't trust that anything he told her wouldn't be relayed to her troop leaders, and then to the Gestapo.

The letter and postcard lay on the table. Lisa took his hand as he picked it up. The postcard was of Basel, the striking red medieval buildings set over the wondrous blue of the Rhine River.

"What do we do about Fiona?" he asked.

Lisa took the blank postcard from him and held it in her hand. "It doesn't seem as if her afternoon with Gert and Lil has altered her allegiances."

"They've agreed to see her again. It's going to take more than just a few hours."

"We can't bring her to see her siblings in Basel."

"We'd have the Gestapo camped on our doorstep—not just across the street." Seamus put his hands over his face.

"What choice do we have?" Lisa asked.

"None that I can see. Is there somewhere else we can send her this weekend?"

"Her troop is having a camping trip in the Spandauer Forest. I wasn't going to send her, but we can't bring her to Switzerland."

"And so her indoctrination continues."

"I don't see any other way."

"I'll tell her about the camping trip first. That might soften the blow a little."

"Soften? You mean she'll be happier to miss out on seeing Michael and Maureen because at least she gets to go away with her friends?"

"It's a relative term."

Lisa put her hand on his and then held up the letter. "This arrived too, postmarked from Poland."

It was addressed to him, and he took a knife from the table to slice it open. He read aloud to his wife.

HERR RITTER,

I HOPE THIS LETTER FINDS YOU AND YOUR FAMILY WELL. WE ALL REGRETTED WE COULDN'T SAY GOODBYE. THE JOURNEY WAS EASY, AND SOON WE'LL BE TRAVELING NORTH TO SWEDEN, WHERE WE HOPE TO SETTLE.

MY FIVE-YEAR-OLD BROTHER ASKED ME YESTERDAY WHY WE'RE HERE. I TOLD HIM WHY. AND FOR THAT, I'LL BE GRATEFUL FOR THE REST OF MY DAYS. EVEN IF WE NEVER MEET AGAIN, MY FAMILY—AND MY OWN CHILDREN, SOMEDAY—WILL KNOW YOUR NAMES. FOR YOU ARE THE ONES WHO GAVE US EVERYTHING.

I HOPE WITH ALL MY HEART THAT I'LL BE ABLE TO REPAY YOU AND YOUR FAMILY'S IMMENSE KINDNESS TO US SOMEDAY.

YOUR FRIEND ALWAYS,

WB

A swell of pride brought tears to his eyes. "Do you think I can ever be half the person Maureen already is?"

Lisa smiled and hugged him.

He stood up from the table and took his wife's hand. They walked to the garden, where Fiona, Conor, and Hannah were playing.

"Don't tell her yet," Lisa said to him. "Let's enjoy this for a while first."

They sat on the patio together. He took her hand in his and kissed it. And though he knew the battles ahead, nothing could check the exultation within him at that moment. Lisa reached over and kissed him on the mouth. She whispered something to him in a voice so low that it escaped him. He thought to ask again, but there was no need. The smile on her face said enough.

THE END

ACKNOWLEDGMENTS

I'm incredibly grateful to my regular crew, my sister, Orla, my brother Brian, my mother, and especially to my brother Conor who is a great writer in his own right. Thanks to my fantastic editors. Massive thanks to my beta readers, Vickie Martin, Carol McDuell, Cindy Bonner, AJ Ventresca, Maria Reed, Michelle Schulten, Kevin Hall, Cynthia Sand, Frank Callahan, Richard Schwarz, and so many others I don't have space to mention here. Thanks to my fabulous new friends in Italy, and as always, thanks to my beautiful wife, Jill and our three crazy little boys, Robbie, Sam and Jack. The kids make my job a lot harder but all the more worthwhile.

A NOTE TO THE READER

I hope you enjoyed my book. Head over to www.eoindempseybooks.com to sign up for my readers' club. It's free and always will be. If you want to get in touch with me send an email to eoin@eoindempseybooks.com. I love hearing from readers so don't be a stranger!

Reviews are life-blood to authors these days. If you enjoyed the book and can spare a minute please leave a review on Amazon and/or Goodreads. My loyal and committed readers have put me where I am today. Their honest reviews have brought my books to the attention of other readers. I'd be eternally grateful if you could leave a review. It can be short as you like.

ALSO BY EOIN DEMPSEY

Stand Alone Titles

Finding Rebecca

The Bogside Boys

White Rose, Black Forest

Toward the Midnight Sun

The Longest Echo

The Hidden Soldier

The Lion's Den Series

1. The Lion's Den

2. A New Dawn

3. The Golden Age

4. The Grand Illusion

ABOUT THE AUTHOR

Eoin (Owen) was born and raised in Ireland. His books have been translated into fourteen languages and also optioned for film and radio broadcast. He lives in Philadelphia with his wonderful wife and three crazy sons.

You can connect with him at eoindempseybooks.com or on Facebook at https://www.facebook.com/eoindempseybooks/ or by email at eoin@eoindempseybooks.com.